NEVER AGAIN

Never Again

By

Katherine Adams

CFI
Springville, Utah

The views expressed within this work are the sole responsibility of the author and do not necessarily reflect the position of Cedar Fort, Inc., or any other entity.

This is a work of fiction. The characters, names, incidents, places, and dialogue are products of the author's imagination, and are not to be construed as real.

ISBN 13: 978-1-59955-174-6

Published by CFI, an imprint of Cedar Fort, Inc., 2373 W. 700 S., Springville, UT 84663
Distributed by Cedar Fort, Inc., www.cedarfort.com

LIBRARY OF CONGRESS CATALOGING-IN-PUBLICATION DATA
Adams, Katherine.
Never again / Katherine Adams.
p. cm.
ISBN 978-1-59955-174-6 (acid-free paper)
1. Abused wives—Fiction. 2. Men—Sexual behavior—Fiction. 3. Pornography—Fiction. I. Title.

PS35601.D376N48 2008
813'.54--dc22

2008024816

Cover design by Nicole Williams
Cover design © 2008 by Lyle Mortimer
Edited and typeset by Christy M. Bigelow and Natalie A. Hepworth

Printed in the United States of America

10 9 8 7 6 5 4 3 2 1

Printed on acid-free paper

To my husband who has always believed in me,
to my children who have put up with my monopolizing the computer, and last of all
to my parents who encouraged me to write.

ACKNOWLEDGMENTS

A special thanks to my friend, Carolyn, who gave me good advice. I also appreciate Linda Prince, Christy, and Natalie for all their support.

Chapter One

In one brief moment everything changed. The instant Megan recognized the familiar handwriting on the crisp, white envelope, all the pain that she had so carefully protected herself from came rushing back. The entire stack of mail fluttered down in a disjointed, surreal motion and landed on the tiled entry. Megan shuddered and her hands began to shake uncontrollably. Fortunately, she had enough presence of mind to kick the front door shut before she staggered to the couch. As she rested her head back, she felt both dizzy and nauseated. Frustration and anger began to sizzle inside of her. She couldn't decide whom she was the most irritated with: herself or him.

Megan closed her eyes and prayed for strength. Too many times before she had allowed him to affect her. This time it was going to be different. Finding an inner reserve, she rose serenely from the couch and returned to the pile of scattered mail.

The desire to burn or shred his letter was intense. Instead, she tore the envelope open and began to read. He was in therapy now and starting to build a new life. With all her heart, she wished him well. She of all people had seen his brilliant potential, recognized his tremendous talent, and understood his terrible weakness. Hoping more than believing that therapy would change him, Megan finished reading the letter. He ended by apologizing for all the years of pain he had put her through.

Megan stood motionless for a few seconds before she neatly refolded his letter and slid it back into the torn envelope. She decided she had forgiven him as much as she could right now. The rest of her forgiveness would have to come with time.

In a quiet, somber mood, Megan collected the remaining mail, consisting of the usual bills, advertisements, and credit card applications. She walked listlessly into the kitchen, set the mail on the table, and began to fix dinner. The empty loneliness of her life suddenly seemed to have grown and flourished. She tried not to think about anything as she grilled her cheese sandwich and opened a can of string beans. Cooking had become a chore. Nights alone in her condominium were always the hardest. During the day, her employment absorbed her time and her energy. Recently, the firm had been demanding that she put in long hours on evenings and weekends. Being overworked had become a pleasure. Briefs and research occupied Megan's mind, not allowing her thoughts to wander and relive the past.

Unfortunately, Scott's letter had touched sensitive wounds and torn open pathways that Megan had learned to keep blocked. Freed from their usual restraint, Megan's thoughts skimmed erratically like a scratched CD, skipping and repeating portions in a disconnected sequence. One scene stuck and replayed in a slow, distorted haze. She remembered sitting there in Scott's car, gripping the seat belt and refusing to go in. They had been parked there so long that Megan's fingers had begun to ache from curling around the strap.

The specialty store in the strip mall made Megan feel queasy. She shrank back in her seat and looked away from the window displaying black leather skirts that were too short, tank tops that were too tight, and silver studded belts and chains that were too heavy. Scott was shouting at her, using words that tore at her self-esteem and broke her sensitive spirit. Suddenly he softened, and his fingers smoothed her hair. His voice pleaded convincingly. "Just go in with me and look around. It can't hurt to go in, can it?"

Megan shifted restlessly and her grip on the lap harness

relaxed slightly.

"If you don't want to buy anything, that's okay. I only want you to be happy." He paused and began rubbing the tense muscles in her neck. "I'm sorry. I didn't mean to loose my temper. It's been a hard day and I felt like it would be fun to buy you something pretty. Why won't you let me?"

Megan glanced once more at the fashions displayed in the shop windows. "Scott, it's not my kind of store. I've never worn anything like that." Megan's shoulders drooped and her head lowered.

"Then how do you know you wouldn't like it?"

"I don't feel comfortable with clothes like that."

"There's nothing wrong with putting a little class in your life. Listen, honey, your clothes are drab and boring. I just want you to look cute and attractive. Will you do that for me?" He leaned his head toward her and touched his lips softly to her cheek. "Please, come in with me. I really want to buy you something."

Megan raised her eyes to his, wavering and uncertain.

"Come on." He slid out of the car and went around to open her door. Without asking her anything more, Scott unbuckled her seat belt, took her hands, and gently helped her out of the car.

Megan stood hesitantly. "I don't think—" she began.

"No, don't think. Just come and be with me. It'll be fun."

Inside the store things only got worse. The oppressive atmosphere preyed upon Megan, withering her soul with its darkness. Hadn't he said they didn't need to be in here long? She glanced up at Scott, hoping that he wouldn't demand this of her and that they could leave. Scott wasn't even looking at her. Instead, his dark brown eyes were focused on the sales clerk with a humiliating intensity. Flashing a brilliant smile, he asked the attractive young woman where he could find a leather skirt like hers in a size six.

The clerk lifted one shoulder coquettishly and twirled around, modeling the microscopic leather that passed for a skirt. "Do you really like it?"

He grinned appreciatively, "I love it."

"Really?"

Absolutely." Scott's voice throbbed with innuendo. Megan stood paralyzed while Scott followed the clerk to one side of the sale's room. Their laughter and noisy flirtation carried back clearly to Megan, despite the hideous music that permeated the store. Unwillingly but unable to stop herself, Megan watched Scott tip his head rakishly to one side and then slither his hand down the girl's bare arm. If Megan stayed another moment, she'd throw up. Blinded by tears, she groped for the door. She was drowning in pain and needed air.

Leaning against the car for support, Megan tried to breathe normally. Fearing that Scott would be angry if he saw her tears, she quickly wiped them away. She blinked her eyes rapidly and wondered what she was going to do. Lately, Megan felt so fragile and paper thin that she was terrified she'd break into a thousand confetti-sized pieces. She didn't know what to do. Life wasn't supposed to be like this.

"Megan, are you okay?" He was standing beside her, taking her hand and helping her back into the car.

Megan stiffened. A spark of anger flared and hot words came flooding out of her mouth. "How can you flirt with other women like that?"

Scott gave her a disdainful roll of his eyes. He deliberately made Megan wait for an answer while he walked around the car and dropped with an irritated slump into his seat. "I wasn't flirting with her. You always get the wrong idea and make a big deal out of something that doesn't mean anything." Scott jerked his arm up in an angry gesture that made Megan shrink back in her seat. He appeared to be immune to her response. "You just don't get it, do you? Every time I try to do something nice for someone, you get all jealous and upset. The girl looked like she was having a rough day, and all I did was try to cheer the poor thing up."

Megan looked at him, wanting to believe. It was so much easier to believe.

The smell of blackened bread burned away the past, leaving a smoky aftertaste in Megan's mouth and throat. She realized she'd burnt her dinner. Flipping the offending sandwich out onto the counter and removing the pan from the heat, Megan felt like giving up and letting her stinging eyes weep forever. Instead, she held her breath and glanced dejectedly at the mangled mess on the counter top. Cheese that looked like tar dripped from the black slices of bread. Her dinner had become hideously distasteful, but it was not nearly as distasteful as her life had become.

Tossing her head in angry defiance, Megan decided that it was time for a change. After switching off the stove, she marched determinedly out of the kitchen and into her office. She yanked open a desk drawer, snatched up a 3x5 index card, and wrote quickly. Now all she needed to do was find out where the institute building was. They would have a bulletin board where she could post her sign.

A sense of satisfaction lifted Megan's spirits as she returned to her blackened dinner. She pulled off the worst edges of her toasted cheese sandwich and took a bite. Immediately she knew that starvation was the better course.

As Amber scanned the bulletin board, she concluded that the worst part about having a roommate get married was finding a replacement. Since the number of LDS women in Boston wasn't exactly astronomical, the task was rather daunting.

Amber's blue eyes widened as she stared in disbelief at the 3x5 card. She read it again just to make sure she wasn't hallucinating. "Single Adult Woman looking for an LDS roommate." It was followed by a phone number. "Yes!" Amber silently cheered and then instantly halted in her jubilation. It was never this easy. There had to be some big, huge glitch, like the woman would leave piles of greasy dishes in the sink, or she would play her music so loud that the walls would vibrate. Or worse still, she would be a whiner and complain all the time. Amber could see it now. The whole apartment would be thick with the yellow smog of her depression.

Cautiously Amber unpinned the ad and stared suspiciously at it. If only this stiff piece of paper could talk. "The person who placed me up here is the sweetest, most wonderful woman," or

"Danger, do not touch! I was stuck up here by the most inconsiderate human being imaginable." Amber chuckled at her insane fantasy and concluded that she should at least check it out. Her lease was almost up, and so were her financial reserves. If she couldn't find another roommate, she'd have to relocate to a less expensive place. It wasn't hard to visualize the squalor of the new apartment she'd be forced to rent.

Amber flipped open her cell phone and punched in the number written on the card.

The voice that answered didn't sound like a slob. In fact, the tone was a cool alto that radiated confident professionalism. Slightly reassured, Amber invited the woman to come and take a look at her apartment.

"I'm sorry, but I already have a condominium that I am leasing." The voice paused and then continued, "I was looking for someone to share my condo."

"I see," Amber was doing some quick calculating. "That might be possible. My lease is up at the end of the month."

"It would probably be a good idea to meet and get to know each other." The other woman sounded competent and reasonable.

"Where exactly is your condo located?" Amber asked apprehensively. She knew nothing about this person, where she lived, or who she was.

"I'm in Cambridge on Chestnut Street."

The location was good. About two and half miles from Longfellow Park and the institute building. Amber sighed, still feeling uncertain since there were so many unknowns.

"Why don't you come by on Saturday morning around ten? You can check out the area, and we'll see what happens," the woman suggested.

Amber took a deep breath and agreed. As she wrote the name and address she thought, "Surely, it couldn't hurt to meet the lady." Amber was surprised that she already considered this unknown woman to be a lady. There was something classy about the way the woman conducted herself over the phone. Maybe she was older and more mature. Well, no matter whether she was old or young, Amber would know by this weekend if moving in with her was a possibility.

Saturday morning produced several surprises for Amber. The condominium was situated at the nicer, more exclusive end of Chestnut Street where older brick buildings had been elegantly restored and renovated. The prestigious location made Amber wish she'd asked how much rent would be. Whatever the dollar amount, Amber already knew that it was beyond her resources. This was a waste of time.

Despite her misgivings, Amber pressed the bell and asked to be buzzed in. She climbed the stairs, thinking that someday, in another lifetime, she'd live in a place like this. The walls were freshly painted, highlighting the carved wood of the moldings and cornices. Megan Spencer's door was engraved and varnished to such an extent that Amber almost considered it a work of art.

As the spectacular door opened, Amber was bombarded with her second shock of the day. Megan Spencer was an incredibly beautiful woman in her late twenties. Standing serenely in the open doorway, Megan looked like a princess from a fairy tale. She could have been Snow White, with her creamy, clear complexion and her shimmering black hair. Her eyes were perfect for the part as well. They were a light cloudy grey with flecks of crystal blue floating in them.

Amber decided that Megan must be very good with her makeup, because nobody looked this fabulous without cosmetics. Her third surprise of the morning came as Amber realized Megan's cheeks were scrubbed clean and the only trace of makeup detectable was a thin coat of mascara.

Amber gulped down a swallow and made an effort to pay attention to what Megan was saying.

"Why don't you come in?"

Amber plucked nervously on the fabric of her coat sleeve. She felt grimy and dumpy in her jeans, sweatshirt, and old baggy jacket. As she stepped onto the marble tile, she thought of ways to diplomatically excuse herself. This would never work.

"Would you like to sit down?"

Amber sat eyeing Megan's dress slacks and silky blouse with admiration. She stiffened her shoulders and without preamble confessed, "I'm noisy and sometimes my friends from institute hang out at my apartment. They're noisy too."

In a serene voice, Megan said, "I'd like that."

Amber stared with such a look of astonishment on her face that Megan started to laugh. The laughter changed Megan. Everything about her sophisticated, professional appearance softened, and her perfectly defined edges were blurred. Amber found herself smiling and then joining in the amusement.

"Am I so formidable?" Megan cheerfully asked.

"Yes!" came Amber's honest reply. "You seem so perfect."

"Appearances can be deceiving," Megan repeated the old cliché while inside her heart was pierced by the years of practice that had gone into her carefully constructed image. Was nothing genuine about her anymore? Had she become such a master of illusion that reality permanently escaped her?

"You aren't attending the single's ward or institute, are you?"

Megan shook her head.

"I didn't think so. I would have remembered you."

Megan stood and gracefully motioned toward several open doorways. "Let me show you the condo and you can see what you think." Before Amber had a chance to protest, Megan continued on. "There are two bedrooms and a small office. This would be your room."

Amber meekly trailed behind Megan and wondered how to explain that she could never afford the rent. She lost her train of thought as she stared at the beautifully proportioned room. Unlike her apartment, the window of this room looked down into a tiny cobbled courtyard. There were metal chairs and pots that would hold flowers in the spring. Best of all there was no brick apartment two feet from the window pane. As Amber turned her eyes back to the interior, she visualized the wonderful possibilities of decorating this bedroom. Instantly, she blocked this line of creative expression; she would never be able to afford to live here.

"It's lovely," Amber attempted to end this unbelievable dream, "but the rent will be too much."

Megan nodded. "Whatever rent you're paying now would be acceptable."

"But you don't even know what I'm paying," Amber sputtered feeling the magnitude of the differences lying between them. "It's a pittance compared to what this place should rent for," Amber warned, waving her hand around the newly carpeted and expensively renovated room. With a jerk of her head, which sent her long, brown hair swaying, Amber finished with, "Besides I'm not sure we'd get along. I'm casual, laid back. And you're . . ." Amber searched for the right words, "the epitome of class."

Megan smiled. Once again it was amazing to Amber how an expression could transform Megan's face into something softer and more approachable.

"Thank you, but I think I prefer casual and laid back. There is an artificiality that comes with sophistication. My job requires it, but at home I like to relax."

Amber was still not satisfied. She took one last peek at the lovely little courtyard and tried not to think about the view that her current apartment offered. Red brick was not inspiring.

"I do have one other question before we settle on the rent," Megan said as she leaned back against the bare wall. "Are you clean? I have a difficult time with clutter and mess."

"I'm addicted to the job chart," Amber mumbled while her mind focused on enjoying her last view of the cobbled area. She determinedly pivoted and faced Megan. "Every Saturday morning the job chart is my highest priority. Actually, I had to clean before I came this morning."

"I like that."

"Before we agree to anything, I think you should get to know me better. You could come to my apartment tonight and see the kind of friends I hang out with. We're all getting together to play games or watch a movie." Amber attempted to read Megan's expression. "You're welcome to come. I mean, if you don't already have plans." Amber twisted a strand of her hair around her finger and nervously looked down at the carpet. The sound of Megan's voice soothed some of the tension Amber was feeling.

"That sounds like fun. If you'd write down your address and the directions of how to get there, I'll try to make it. What time do you plan to start the party?"

"At seven."

"Could I bring something?" Megan offered politely.

"We all bring our favorite munchie." Amber looked directly at Megan. "Most of the people who are coming tonight attend the singles ward. It meets at nine o'clock in the institute building by Longfellow Park."

Megan pushed off the wall and straightened up. "Shall we go back into the living room and sit down?"

As they walked back into the front room, Amber was puzzled by several different things she had noticed. The apartment appeared to be pristinely new. It obviously hadn't been lived in for any length of time. Megan also did not have the New England accent. In addition to these observations, there was also the fact that Amber had never seen Megan Spencer at any of the singles activities. Amber sat on the edge of the couch and gave into her curiosity, "How long have you been living here?"

"Not long," was Megan's cryptic reply.

Amber tried again. "Where are you from?"

"The Salt Lake area."

"What made you come out East?"

"I was recruited by a headhunter."

Amber choked and her eyes went wide.

"When a big company needs a new employee, they sometimes hire someone to search out the right person for the job. I was wooed away from my last company. Besides, I was ready for a change."

"What do you do?"

"I'm an attorney, and I specialize in corporate employee/employer disputes."

"An attorney," Amber repeated cheerfully. "You should fit right in with our group. My roommate Tressa is a paralegal and her soon-to-be husband is in law school. What law firm do you work for?"

"Schaffer, Cronin, and Schaffer."

"You've got to be kidding!" Amber gushed.

"No. Why?"

"That's where Tressa, my roommate, works." Amber flipped a thick length of her brown hair behind her shoulder. "I don't know if Tressa will be at the party tonight. At the moment, she's pretty busy with all the wedding plans." Amber wiggled her foot and began twisting her hair again. "I guess I should warn you. All of my roommates get married."

For half a second, Megan looked uneasy. She ran a hand through her shoulder-length hair, smoothing it away from her face, and proclaimed, "I don't think you need to worry. I'm not the marrying kind."

Amber tilted her head to one side and thoughtfully regarded Megan before saying, "Well, that would be great with me. I've decided that I'm never going to be anything more than a friend to every guy I meet. I've learned to accept it. That's why having a roommate for more than a few months is appealing. It's a real pain to find someone good to live with."

Amber was looking at Megan as if she expected her to agree so that they could complain and console one another. Megan thought of several things she could say, but all of them were too revealing. She had no intention of discussing her past with anyone, not now or ever. Finally Megan settled on a safe, non-committal statement of fact. "I'm older. I haven't had roommates for a while."

Something about Megan's cautiously nonchalant response aroused Amber's curiosity. In a pattern that Amber had cultivated over the years, she simply waited. There was a story here. This Amber knew for sure, but she was content to be patient, make friends, and wait for the story to unfold.

"Do you need a place to park your car?" Megan inquired

hesitantly. The condo only had a tiny parking area off the alley behind the main building. Unfortunately the lot didn't even have enough spaces for every condominium. Megan had been lucky to lease a slot for her car.

"I don't have a car. I ride the bus or the T everywhere."

"But what if you want to go home to your family?" Megan looked puzzled. "What do you do then?"

"My brother comes to get me. Right now he's living part of the time in Amherst and part of the time in Wooster."

"Where?" Megan asked.

"In Worcester. We pronounce it Wooster. It's about forty-five minutes west of Boston," Amber smiled. "You'll find that we New Englanders say a lot of things differently than you Westerners. Anyhow, there shouldn't be any parking problem." Amber picked up her baggy jacket, which she had set beside her on the couch and said, "I should get going. Saturday is my only free day, and I have a ton of things to do." Amber rose and moved in the direction of the front door.

"Why don't you let me take you home? Then I'll know how to find your apartment," Megan suggested, walking toward the coat closet.

Amber was agreeable. It would save her from waiting for the bus. "Sure, that would be great."

Chapter Two

By the time the sun set on Saturday afternoon, Megan had decided at least ten times not to go to the party. Conversely she had decided nine times to go. She could formulate a million reasons why attending Amber's party was a bad idea. She was too old and the people in the group could be as young as eighteen. Besides, she had two books checked out from the law library that she should be reviewing. On top of that, tomorrow was Sunday, and she hadn't had a chance to go to the grocery store.

At this ridiculous point, Megan threw her head back and laughed bitterly. How ironic that she would never shop on Sunday, yet she hadn't been to church for a month. Her first Sunday in Boston, she'd been so busy unpacking her car and getting settled in her condo that she hadn't bothered to find her new ward. On the second Sunday, her work had scheduled a formal luncheon. Attendance had been mandatory. The third Sunday found Megan debating with herself over whether she should attend a family ward or the singles ward. It had not been difficult to let the day slide by. And last Sunday, she had sat on the couch remembering all the years of going to church and pretending that everything was fine while inside she felt old and ugly. The women at church flowed into the building in beautiful skirts and dresses, smiling at everyone. They were like fresh cut flowers, vibrant and colorful, while she was a dried-up, thorny weed. Shrugging with self loathing, Megan had gone back to bed.

She would go to church tomorrow, Megan promised herself. But she didn't know the time or place the family ward met. Was this how people became less active? The thought was terrifying. In her heart, she cried, "I have a testimony!"

It would be so easy to go off somewhere that was peaceful and tranquil like a small house in the country where there were grassy green meadows and trees. Megan shook her head and grumbled out loud, "Yeah right. I'd go insane. Now I'm so lonely that I'm offering to take in an unknown roommate. After one week at a quiet cottage in the country, I'd be so depressed that I'd have to move out."

Returning her attention to the present, Megan glanced at herself in the mirror once more. Jeans and a sweater; she looked okay. She might as well go to Amber's party since she had no friends, no ward, no nothing here in Boston. It was time to start the new life she had promised herself. A tiny voice in her head whispered that now was the time to open up and develop friendships once again. Megan refused to consider these thoughts. As she tossed her leather jacket over her shoulders, she felt insecure and uncomfortable. Despite her best efforts to maintain her aloof manner, a small crack was forming in her deliberately constructed facade. Megan was tired of being alone.

The party was worse and better than Megan had anticipated. It was worse because she had been out of the dating scene for so long that she didn't feel at ease around all the young men. Yet it was better because Megan felt a wonderful spirit of camaraderie among the men and women. The welcoming attitude of the group was like some magical elixir for her aching soul. She sat savoring the taste while struggling to maintain her protective, aloof posture. It was a difficult paradox, since Megan had vowed never again to risk the emotional pain of involvement. And yet she was starved for any kind of connection with warm, loving people.

Megan left the party with ambivalent feelings and an invitation to come to the singles ward. She knew she would attend church tomorrow, because she missed feeling the Savior's spirit and partaking of the sacrament. Her insecurity lay more with the members of the ward. She did not dare let them get too close. She would not allow it. A picture of Amber's innocent, smiling face flashed into her mind, and Megan couldn't help but wonder what she had done.

Megan sat in her prestigious office at Schaffer, Cronin, and Schaffer and marveled at the far-reaching effects of attending the singles ward the day before. The welcoming arms of the members had immediately invaded her life. Everyone took it for granted that she was exactly like them: happy, vital, and alive. She'd been dead for years now, but no one seemed to notice.

Tressa, who was Amber's current roommate, lost no time in visiting Megan at the law firm. She had stuck her head in the open doorway and asked if Megan minded being introduced to the best paralegals the firm had. After pulling two older women into the office, Tressa grinned and cheerfully exclaimed, "I know you're one of the full-time attorneys and we're simply the lowly paralegals, but since you don't even work on the same floor or in the same department as we do, I thought you would like to meet these two ladies. They know the firm inside and out."

The tall, thin lady snorted, causing Megan to regard her with amused interest. She noticed that the woman had lovely olive tones, dark black hair, and a starched no-nonsense manner which perfectly matched her tall, slim body and her ultra-short hair.

"This is Esther Stein," Tressa gestured toward the woman who had snorted. "And this is Jane Mallory."

Jane was soft and round in a huggable way. The light brown curls around her face bounced as she bobbed her head and smiled warmly. Her plump arm was extended. Megan rose and shook Jane's hand.

"I'm Megan Spencer."

"We've heard such nice things about you," Jane enthused sincerely. "We both work on the third floor."

Esther stood back, her eyes occupied with intricately evaluating everything from the size and design of the office to Megan Spencer's formidable appearance. Tressa and Jane did not seem to be aware of Esther's cautious reserve, while Megan was deeply conscious of it.

Tressa was radiant with her own personal happiness. Megan had noticed this quality about her yesterday at church when they had met. The girl was in love with the tall, dark-haired man who had never been far from her side. They had both shared the same starry-eyed expression. Megan was surprised that Tressa had even remembered her, let alone taken the time to introduce her friends.

"It's nice to meet you both," Megan said, reverting back to her elegant facade.

"You do employee/employer disputes," Jane chirped, tilting her head like a chubby little bird without any neck. "We hear the firm lured you away from your company out West."

Megan smiled. The curvature of her lips was perfectly formulated to fit the situation. "Yes, they did."

"I bet it was for the Silverton Supermarket case. I'm sure you'll be great!" Jane did not seem to understand social correctness. There was a sweet innocence that permeated the air around her like a fragrant lilac bush in full bloom.

With a start, Megan realized that the plump little woman was genuine. Megan felt her defenses crack a little as she thanked Jane.

"It's so difficult when you're new to the area. If you'd like, you could have lunch with the three of us," Jane enthusiastically invited.

"I brought my lunch."

Jane's grin broadened. "We all bring our lunch. We like to walk in the Commons if the weather isn't too nasty."

For the first time, Esther spoke. Her voice was cool and matter-of-fact, but Megan knew she was being tested. "It may be beneath your dignity to have lunch with us."

An irritated nerve twitched on the side of Megan's throat,

but otherwise she appeared to be unmoved. Her perfect smile was fixed resiliently on her lips and her eyes did not betray her. "I'd love to walk in the Commons with all of you." It was the last thing Megan wanted, but the urge to prove Esther Stein wrong was extremely powerful.

"Great!" Jane cried, oblivious to all the swirling undercurrents.

Tressa cast one troubled look at Esther and Megan and discretely looked down at her watch. "Shall we meet in the lobby a few minutes after noon?" Tressa glanced first at Esther, who nodded glumly, and then at Megan, who was still cultivating that calm, serene manner. Anyone who was paying close attention could see Tressa's thoughts clearly reflected in her eyes. She was thinking, "Interesting, interesting."

Two hours later as they walked in the Boston Commons, Megan noticed that the sun highlighted little sparkles in the snow and made them glitter. She instantly decided that getting outside to enjoy the fresh air and nature was worth any amount of small talk she would be forced to endure. Actually, she wasn't being expected to engage in that much conversation. Tressa and Jane had moved ahead and only little phrases of their discussion floated back to Esther and Megan.

"No bridesmaids!" Jane was exclaiming.

"No, I'm going for simplicity."

Megan let her mind drift and enjoyed the pleasure of the cool wind rippling through her hair. She forgot to control her facial features. A soft serenity smoothed out the artificial stiffness of her expression. Concluding that there was a healing power in nature, Megan allowed the beauty of the winter scene to wash over her. Work was stressful. Life was chaotic. Walks like this were therapeutic.

Megan was wrenched away from her private thoughts by Esther Stein's acute observation. "It's therapeutic."

Wondering if she had spoken aloud, Megan almost stumbled and stared before mumbling some kind of agreement.

"And no, you didn't speak out loud," Esther briskly informed Megan. "It's wasn't a very difficult deduction. You've been walking along like a zombie, and your face slowly relaxed into a more natural state."

Megan stopped walking and began to search for something to say. Esther chuckled, "Besides, Tressa and Jane sat on a bench way over there." Esther pointed at the other two ladies who were chatting and eating their lunches.

A mixture of surprise and fear caused Megan to speak without considering her words. "Am I that open?"

"In this case, yes. But on the whole, I doubt it." Esther turned abruptly away and sat on a nearby bench. Megan followed, thinking that Esther Stein was an unusual person. No conversation flowed between them. They sat silently eating their lunch. Strangely enough, it was a comfortable, companionable quiet.

The lengthy silence finally penetrated Megan's nerves. Quickly she asked the first thing that came into her mind. "Have you lived in Boston your whole life?"

"Practically," Esther took a bite of her bagel.

Megan assumed that this was the end of the conversation.

A few minutes later, she was startled by the sound of Esther's voice. "Boston has several ethnic pockets. There's the Puerto Ricans, the Blacks, the Italians, the Jews, and so on. Naturally, I grew up in a Jewish neighborhood."

Megan nodded. "That's very different from where I grew up. There was not much diversity in Kaysville, Utah."

"Some people thrive on diversity."

"I think I would like to thrive on diversity," Megan wistfully stated.

"Would you?" Esther asked, her expression clearly indicating that she was doubtful and still withholding a final decision until she could gather the pertinent information.

Megan twisted her hands, uncomfortable with such close scrutiny. No longer able to bear Esther's intense stare, she quietly defended herself. "Okay. I think I would like it for a little while, but at heart I'm really the homebody type."

"I see," Esther stated calmly, staring out over the Commons.

"I like quiet things like being in nature and simply appreciating it."

"And sitting outside, reading a good book," Esther mused.

"Or reading curled up in front of a fire," Megan sighed. "I enjoy those kinds of things. I think I'm a bit old fashioned. I love the old masters: Rembrandt, Raphael, and Rubens. And with sculpture it has to be Michelangelo or Bernini. I can't stand modern art."

Esther chuckled. "I see that as a sign of good taste. Anyone can throw a few blobs of paint on a canvas, but it takes a master to paint portraits and beautiful landscapes. And only a great artist can take a piece of marble and chisel out a work of art." Esther turned her head away from the park and faced Megan. She paused a moment as if she were struggling to make a decision. Finally, Esther quietly confessed, "I'm a little puzzled though."

"By what?" Megan asked. "By how modern art sells?"

Without answering, Esther glanced down, dug into her lunch bag, and withdrew an apple. Still occupied with her lunch, she quietly admitted, "No. I was thinking more of you. I'm confused. You see, I can't help wondering if you're really sure what kind of life you want." Esther's dark eyes lifted from her apple and securitized Megan. Suddenly, without preamble or a smidgen of diplomacy, Esther flatly stated, "I find myself asking, "What's a homebody like you doing taking a job in Boston?"

Megan was surprised that she wasn't offended by Esther's stark question. Maybe it was because underneath Esther's direct approach, Megan detected a genuine warmth and sincere compassion. All these feelings touched something within Megan that bypassed her usual instinct to flee from anything remotely close to personal. Instead, she answered with complete honesty. "Sometimes life doesn't give us the things we want or expect. I've always wanted a cottage in the country. But the job's in Boston."

"And you have to go where the job is," Esther repeated the well-known saying and then added, "but there's more to it than that, isn't there?"

Megan didn't know how to answer. The need for shelter and protection tasted like acid in her throat. When she answered it was with a question. "What makes you say that?"

"It's really very simple." Esther announced, and then in a slightly more mellow tone said, "You have the image thing down to perfection, which suggests you're either a scheming social climber, ambitiously making your way in corporate America, or you're hiding from something and really only want the simple country life." Esther looked intently into Megan's eyes. "I choose hiding. You say that you want the country life, and I believe you. There's also a whimsical softness about you that makes the heartless opportunist not really a possibility."

Megan could not think of a thing to say. Esther didn't act as if she minded. She simply sat calmly munching on her apple and gazing out over the pond. Apparently she was admiring the brilliance of the sun reflecting off the frozen water. The beauty of the scene was totally lost on Megan. Her mind whirled with conjecture, confusion, and insecurity. As Megan sat pondering Esther's words, attempting to understand, she was overwhelmingly impressed by Esther's ability to observe, evaluate, and draw people out. It was a commendable talent, and one that terrified Megan.

Benton Kilgallen looked at his sister oddly. "You want me to go with you to some girl's apartment?"

"Yes," Amber cheerfully announced. "I need you to help me move my stuff. Well, at least some of my things. Dad's coming with his truck next Saturday. I could really use your help then too. Can you come again next Saturday?"

Benton caught a hold of Amber's ponytail and gently tugged. "Hey kid, you're monopolizing my weekends."

Amber tossed her eyes heavenward and scoffed. "It isn't as if you have a social life."

"How do you know I don't have a hot date next weekend?" Benton demanded, dropping Amber's hair.

"Because," Amber shot back sassily, "there are no LDS girls in Worcester, Amherst, or Lowell that you consider hot."

"Maybe I'm converting some cute chick out there." Benton's honey brown hair fell in his eyes, and he brushed it carelessly aside. "Or maybe one of my students is falling in love with me. You know what a handsome professor can do to a young girl's heart."

"Ben, you wouldn't even notice if some girl fainted at your feet." Amber rolled her eyes and sighed. "You'd probably step over her and say a polite, 'Excuse me,' and, 'Don't forget your paper on the French Revolution is due next week.' And then you'd walk on as if nothing had happened."

"Is there a point to all this?" Benton asked patiently.

"Yes," Amber shoved a cookbook into an open box. "You will help me move next Saturday!"

"Ah, a command performance. Sorry kid, but I really do have plans."

"Benton William Kilgallen!"

"I'm still not coming, but Amber, you had better watch it. You sound just like Mom."

"Did you find a parking space?" Amber asked, choosing to ignore his last inflammatory remark.

"Yes, it was a miracle."

"Then haul these boxes down and don't forget to lock the doors," Amber bossed. "Remember, this is Boston."

Benton snickered with a teasing smile. "And Lowell is so safe?"

"Did you come here to bicker or help me?" Amber demanded in a strained voice.

Benton instantly sobered, sensing Amber's frustration. "It's hard isn't it, all your roommates getting married?"

Amber's chin came up, because at the same time she appreciated his understanding, she also resented it. "I'm pretty much used to it by now." Amber made an effort to shrug off her disappointment. "You learn to live with what life hands you, no matter how much it hurts. I'm beginning to think that I'll probably never get married. Sometimes I'm okay with it and others . . ."

Benton slipped an arm around his little sister and hugged her close. "Hey, kiddo, you're not to worry. Look at me. I'm older and still unattached."

"Ben, I'm twenty-five and I've never been in love. I've never really had a boyfriend."

"Ah, come on now. What about that boy who moved into our ward when you were in high school? You'd stand in the church parking lot talking to him for hours."

"We were only friends," Amber disgustedly announced. "I'm the kind of girl that the guys tell their problems to." Amber sank down onto one of the kitchen chairs and sighed, "Ben, have you ever been in love?"

When Benton didn't answer, Amber looked up at him. The expression on his face surprised her. Benton was always mellow, the perfect absent minded professor, but now he appeared to be stiff and tense. He was still rather distant, but not in his usual bumbling way. Instead he stared across the tiny kitchen with an intense expression on his face.

As if he had traveled some far distance, he focused on Amber and tried to make light of his lapse. "Once. It was a long time ago."

"You never told me. Was it here, when you were in graduate school?"

"No. It was when I was at the Y."

Amber watched him shift restlessly. "What happened?"

"Nothing happened."

"Something had to have happened," Amber insisted.

"It's a pretty ridiculous story. She was the fairy tale princess and I was the frog. I never turned into the handsome prince, so she ran off and married someone else." Benton clapped his hands. "End of story. Time to get moving, literally!"

"Wait! One more question."

"I'm sorry my allotted time for questions has expired. Good luck. Your final exam is on Friday," Benton teased, hoping, without much faith, that Amber would let the subject drop.

She didn't. "Did you—I mean—did she know how you felt?"

"No. I'm sure she didn't." Benton ran his fingers through his hair absentmindedly, which only left it sticking up. "I'm not the cutest guy, and prince charming was a real looker."

"Oh, Ben, you're handsome," Amber cried in his defense. She came up out of her chair and gave him a hug.

"Lost your contacts, have you?" Benton joked as he gently unfolded Amber and stepped back. "Let's get this stuff moving. Do you like your new place?"

"It's unbelievable. I think I've died and gone to heaven. Wait until you see it."

Benton's first sight of the apartment complex made him agree with Amber wholeheartedly. The outside of her new building was certainly impressive. Benton continued to admire the architecture as Amber searched for her key. "I know it's here somewhere." She began handing Benton things out of her backpack. There was a comb, a water bottle, some lip gloss, a tube of hand cream, and her iPod with the earphones dangling. Benton carefully balanced the items on the top of the box he was holding. The lip gloss was a bit of a problem; it kept rolling. He was so concentrated on trying to keep everything from falling off that he didn't hear anyone approach. The first thing he saw was a pair of fabulous legs. Next he heard the most delectable laugh he'd heard in years.

"Amber, let me help you. I have my key."

It must be Amber's roommate. As Benton was about to look up, the lip gloss started to roll. He shifted the box to his raised knee and attempted to balance himself on one leg while he caught the lip gloss with his free hand. His face flushed a deep red as he considered what an odd spectacle he must present. It was, at this moment, when he caught a clear view of her roommate's face. He stared in a stunned fashion while time warped around him.

Amber's roommate seemed unaware of his strange comatose state. Her key was inserted in the lock and a buzzer blared as the door opened. The sound woke Benton from his dreamy condition. He lowered his aching leg and balanced the box on his closed hand. He was grateful for the two girls' chatter as he climbed the stairs behind them. He knew introductions were coming soon and felt a spurt of excitement ripple through him.

It had been a long time since Benton had seen a girl that attracted him like this. He had attempted over and over again to fall in love, but there was always something lacking. If the girl was good-looking, then she'd be ditsy or boring. If she fulfilled his desire for intelligent conversation, then there was no chemistry, or spark of attraction. The one exception had been Ally. She was cute enough and made thought-provoking remarks. The one thing that held him back was her lack of commitment to the gospel. She wore immodest clothing and seemed to take living the gospel lightly, as if it were a fun but nonessential part of life. Her belief was not infused into her soul. Sometimes Benton wondered if he was being too picky. He wasn't twenty-four anymore.

With a start, Benton realized the girls had already gone into one of the apartments. Picking up his speed, he headed for the open doorway. "Where do you want this?"

"Oh, Ben, I forgot," Amber cried, "You haven't met my new roommate."

Benton looked over and through the menagerie piled on the box. Over the top of the iPod with its dangling earphones and around the water bottle, he enjoyed one more appreciative glance at Amber's beautiful roommate. He attempted to smile, but somehow his lips stuck together and refused to cooperate.

"Let him put the box down, and then you can introduce us," Megan wisely counseled.

"My room's in here," Amber cheerfully directed Benton to the spare bedroom. He followed silently, feeling like an awkward lackey. Before he turned to meet the roommate, he set Amber's box on the floor up against the wall and wiped his sweaty palms.

He turned, faced the two girls, and waited. Anticipation tingled across the back of his neck and rippled down his arms. He waited for something special and only heard Amber quietly stating, "This is my brother, Benton Kilgallen."

"It's nice to meet you," Megan politely extended her hand.

For one wildly insane moment, Benton considered kissing her hand and saying something outrageously romantic. Instead he took her smooth fingers in his and held them far too long. A flood of memories assaulted him as he stood frozen, reliving the past. He was young, inexperienced, and had no idea of what to say. The past and the present melted and blurred together.

Megan tried to wiggle her fingers free, causing Benton to drop her hand and step back. "Sorry, I was thinking of something else," he apologized, shrugging his shoulders nonchalantly while a chill of disappointment shriveled up his soul.

"I'm Megan Spencer."

His smile finally came. It was a bit tight, but at least it was visible. "That's nice." He brushed past Megan saying, "I'll run down to the car and get the rest of the boxes."

Amber watched Benton leave with a perplexed look on her face. She turned to Megan and hastily assured, "He's really a nice guy! He's been out of the social scene for awhile."

"You make him sound like a hermit," Megan laughed walking back into the living room.

"He sort of is," Amber chuckled as she followed Megan. "He reads way too much."

"What does he read?" Megan felt a spark of curiosity flickering somewhere distant in her mind.

"History books. Ben's obsessed with history." Amber had moved toward the front door. "I should help him."

Megan wondered if there was something wrong with Amber's brother. Sinking down onto the living room couch, she thought maybe he was just socially inept. Her skirt rode up and she irritably yanked it down. A wave of exhaustion swept over Megan. She hadn't realized how many social functions her new job would entail. One of the CEOs of the Silverton grocery chain had insisted on a Saturday luncheon to introduce the managers to their new legal counsel. Schaffer, Cronin, and Schaffer had a different way of doing business than her Salt Lake firm.

Megan's mind wandered. She processed details of her work,

wondered about her new roommate, and then allowed her mind to jump tangentially around. She didn't realize she had fallen asleep until Ben was standing above her, offering a mug of hot soup. The steam rose tempting her with its delicious aroma. Megan suddenly remembered that she had hardly touched her executive lunch because the pressure to smile and appear perfect had been horrendous. The soup and the fact that someone had tossed a blanket over her brought a sting of tears to her eyes. It had been a long time since anyone had taken care of her. The hairline crack in Megan's meticulously manufactured image widened and the desire for close human contact began pouring in.

"Thanks," Megan whispered determinedly, trying to seal up the crack.

Benton handed her the mug, "No problem. I'm a whiz with a can opener and the microwave." He headed back to the kitchen while Megan's eyes followed him. A second later, Benton reappeared with another steaming mug. "For Amber," he mumbled as he passed the couch on his way to the spare room.

Megan decided that Benton might be a little different, but he was kind. A million years ago kindness had figured prevalently in her life. It had ebbed and washed over her so consistently that Megan had thought everyone lived with kindness and consideration. All of that had been before Scott, before law school, and before work—but mostly before Scott. She wanted to remember a time when Scott had not calculated the result of performing some thoughtful act. None came to mind.

That was unfair, Megan chided herself. She had buried the good times because they made her forget the bad times and filled her with the desire to go back to the beginning when Scott had been more . . . Megan caught the direction of her thoughts and halted them immediately. Pain was all that was left, and an empty aching heart. She could not live with the choices Scott had made. Their brilliant future had splintered into jagged shards of glass.

"Are you all right?" Benton stood looking down at Megan. Her translucent skin looked deathly pale.

The genuine caring in Benton's expression released the tears

Megan had been so carefully holding back. She felt like an idiot and expected Ben to hastily depart. Men weren't good with tears and women's emotions. Instead of running away, Benton approached the couch, sat awkwardly on the edge, and took her hand. There was an odd atmosphere of security that reached deep inside of Megan, loosening some of the heavy tightness that was wound around her heart. No words of comfort were offered, only the soft, gentle clasp of his hand. Of course, all of this made Megan cry even harder. She had been alone for so long and now suddenly she felt safe and protected. The tears continued to fall, washing away little chunks of the pain.

Finally Benton spoke. "It's going to be okay. Most things just take a little time."

After months of bleakness, Megan felt a whisper of hope. Benton's thoughtfulness made her want to believe that somewhere out there peace and happiness waited for her. He was right. Time had become her friend.

"I'm sorry. I'm not very good at this," Benton apologized.

"No, you were fine."

"You're still crying," Benton protested. "Now, if I were really good at this I would have said something funny, and you'd be laughing by now."

Megan looked at him for a moment and debated whether to be honest. Something in his face made it easy for her. "Thanks for letting me cry. I needed it. I promise I don't usually cry the first time I meet someone."

Ben mumbled something under his breath and looked away. Megan didn't catch what he had said, but the way he had said it and his odd attitude made her wonder if there wasn't something seriously wrong with him mentally. The weird look on his averted face made Megan even more uncomfortable. What had Amber said, something about him being out of the social scene and a hermit? Was he crazy? Was he lucid or certifiable?

Before Megan could control the expression on her face, Benton turned back and looked at her. Immediately he defended himself against what he saw reflected in her eyes. "No, I'm not crazy."

Megan opened her mouth and shut it without speaking.

Benton smiled his first natural, unaffected smile. It was wide and warm, lighting up his eyes to a glowing bronze. With a little start of surprise, Megan thought he was rather attractive in a subtle, unassuming way. She stared at him, amazed that she hadn't noticed before. It was a mistake to look too closely at anyone. She couldn't afford to take chances. Yet there was a thick, honey quality to his brown-sugar eyes that reached into Megan's shattered heart and soothed it.

Ben looked away first. Megan sensed his embarrassment when he realized he was still holding her hand. He immediately dropped it and rose to his feet. "Eat the rest of your soup. It'll make you feel better." With an awkward lift of his hand, he returned to help Amber with her unpacking.

After Ben and Amber had left, Megan wandered into the kitchen. All the mugs had been washed and were drying in the dish drainer. Megan was almost positive that Amber hadn't gone back into the kitchen.

When the phone rang, Megan absently picked it up. "Hello." The quiet coziness of her condominium instantly disintegrated. His voice had that effect on her. A small, strangled portion of her mind wondered how he had gotten her phone number. In a slow but convoluted manner, Megan figured out that her mother had given it to him along with her address.

"Did you get my letter?"

"Yes."

"I've really been working hard on everything. You know what I mean."

"That's good."

"I would really like to see you."

A strong feeling of relief flowed through Megan. It was the best thing she had ever done to move away. The distance was her friend. "It's a long ways," Megan flatly stated.

"You could fly out for the weekend."

"I'm too busy with a case."

"You never used to be too busy for me. And I'm so lonely.

You can't imagine how much I miss you." His voice had a needy quality that made Megan hesitate. The urge to help him, the desire to be needed by him again, and the hope that maybe this time it would be different all crept unbidden into her mind. With a surge of determination, Megan suppressed these emotions. She would not go back.

"Things have changed. It's not the same anymore."

"But it could be. If you'd just give me another chance," he pleaded. "That's why I want you to come home for a weekend."

"Scott, I'm not going to come. I can't."

For a few seconds there was no sound on his end of the line. When he finally spoke again, it was with a softer, more persuasive tone, but it was still designed to increase the pressure on Megan. He tried to tempt her with promises of the fun they could have, of expensive dinners, exciting movies, or simply wonderful times talking and enjoying each other's company.

For the next ten minutes Scott continued his eloquent pleading, interspersed with tidbits about her family and about their need to see her as well. Megan had done her best to be kind and firm, but the strain was growing far too heavy. Feeling overwhelmed and aching all over, she said that she had to go and politely terminated the conversation. Even now, half an hour after she'd hung up, Megan still couldn't stop shaking. In an agitated haze, she wandered through the kitchen and fingered one of the clean soup mugs.

Megan could not help comparing the two divergent men. Ben Kilgallen might be a dull, rather strange person, but he was kind and considerate. Whereas Scott . . . Megan attempted unsuccessfully to end this line of reasoning. Pacing aimlessly around the kitchen didn't seem to help. She couldn't keep herself from worrying about what Scott would do. Even though she had tried to keep from upsetting him, she knew she'd failed. When Scott was angry, he could be cruel and vindictive. Megan abruptly stopped walking and reminded herself that she was safe. Scott would have difficulty seeing her. He wasn't around the corner or in the neighborhood anymore. Distance was her friend, offering security. That part of her life was finished. She had no desire to return to the disappointment and the despair she associated with Scott.

Chapter Three

As the weeks passed, Megan immersed herself in her work. Her spare time was so minimal that she sometimes forgot she had a roommate. The firm and the law library became her habitat. Megan felt a sense of euphoria over the Silverton case. It was developing nicely. She only allowed herself one little distraction: the pleasure of a walk in the Commons with Esther and Jane.

Megan marveled at how much she had come to enjoy the two ladies. On the first day they met, Megan had only consented to having lunch with them to prove to Esther that she wasn't a snobbish person, addicted to the hierarchy of office politics. Slowly and quietly, without Megan realizing how it had happened, she found herself developing more than a superficial relationship with Jane and Esther. Their conversations were interesting. They made no demands on her and rarely required any privately personal details. Both women emitted a motherly kind of love and concern that unwound Megan's tightly wrapped emotions. Unwittingly, Megan accepted their therapy and flourished on their walks together.

Megan sometimes wondered if Jane and Esther had befriended her because they were a bit lonely. Tressa hardly ever walked with them anymore. At first, Tressa had been so caught up in the details of her wedding that she had begun using her lunch hour to run special errands. Now that the wedding was over, Tressa worked through lunch so that she could go home early to spend time with Alex. As the weeks had gone by, the remaining three women had settled into a content threesome.

Their walks had even grown into an occasional weekend outing. Esther loved to go the ballet. One of her favorites was *Cinderella*. Since the Boston Ballet was performing it during a time when her husband, Norman, couldn't get away from work, Esther suggested that Jane and Megan accompany her. In her forthright way, Esther had invited, arranged, and organized the entire activity. Every once in a while, Jane would mumble something like, "Wouldn't it be more fun to all get together and watch an old movie?" Nevertheless, the activity was scheduled, tickets were bought, and travel arrangements were made. Esther chauffeured them to the Saturday afternoon matinee, parked her car in the firm's parking garage, and ushered them into the Wang Center.

Apparently, Esther was a connoisseur of ballet. At intermission she delightedly praised the intricate footwork. "And did you notice," she said enthusiastically, "how everything blended together in perfect artistic harmony?"

Jane looked a little puzzled. "What do you mean?"

"The colors in the scenery and in the costumes complemented each other. The movements and the dance fit the music. And to tie it all together, the music and the dance were also perfectly suited for the scenery and the costumes. It made one beautiful artistic whole. And their arms, did you notice their arms, how light and airy they were?" Esther sighed with complete satisfaction.

Megan listened and enjoyed. It was an education since she hadn't been to the ballet since she was a child. As the afternoon wore on, Megan began to wonder if it was the ballet she was enjoying so much or Esther's dynamic enthusiasm over everything related to the performance. Even Jane appeared to be enjoying herself. She sat in her chair, focusing on the stage as if she were trying to absorb everything about the performance. She tilted her head from side to side, observing the movement and colors from different angles. Once again, Jane reminded Megan of a rounded, little bird.

After they had dropped Jane off at her house, Esther turned to Megan and asked, "What did you really think?"

"I loved it, and I also learned a lot from you."

Esther didn't say anything. Megan thought she might be a little uncomfortable with the compliment. She was trying to think of an appropriate remark when the chimes on her cell phone rang. Digging her phone out of her purse, Megan said, "If you don't mind, I think I'll take this. It's my sister in Utah."

Esther nodded, "Go ahead. It's no problem."

"Hi, Kristy, how are you doing?"

Her sister's voice sounded tired and concerned. "I'm fine."

"Are you sure? You don't sound very good." Megan's eyes clouded over, worrying that something might be wrong at home.

"No, I really am fine. It's you I'm worried about. Scott asked me to call."

Megan stiffened and felt irritation tingle down her arms. "That was nice of him."

"He's really concerned about you."

"There's nothing to be concerned about." Megan looked at Esther, who appeared to be more interested in the traffic than in the phone conversation.

"He feels like there is. Dan and I have him over to dinner all the time. He's great with the kids and he's such a nice guy. Megan, I don't see how you could have—"

"I'm glad you and Dan have him over to dinner. That's nice. But this is between Scott and me."

"He says he needs you and can't understand why you left. He's so lonely and would do anything to get you back."

"Kristy, I really don't want to talk about him."

"He wants to know if you'll fly back here to see him. He says that any weekend you can come is fine."

Megan felt trapped and manipulated. It was the same thing again, only this time Scott had Kristy doing his bidding. "I don't want to see him."

"Are you sure?" Kristy almost sounded as if she were pleading. "We're all so worried about you."

"I'm sure. And don't worry. I'm doing great."

"Megan, I really think you should . . . "

Megan quit listening and bit her lip. If it had been anyone else but her sister, Megan would have hung up. With Kristy, this was not an option. Megan was positive that an abrupt end to the conversation would crush Kristy's sensitive feelings. "Maybe we can talk about this some other time. Right now I'm with a friend, and I need to go."

"I just wanted to make sure you were okay. With the way Scott was talking, I thought maybe you were really down. I want you to know I'll always be here to help you."

"I appreciate that, but I've got to go. Bye," after hearing Kristy's good-bye, Megan snapped her phone shut. She glanced over at Esther and wondered what her astute friend would make from hearing the one sided conversation.

Esther turned her head, looked at Megan, and gave her a firm nod. "Sometimes families can be a bit much."

"You must have a sister," Megan said.

"I do."

There it was again, that relaxed silence that Megan enjoyed so often in Esther's company. It was strange how sometimes Esther pried and asked the most probing questions and other times like this, the quiet washed serenely around them. Naturally the quiet couldn't last. Esther broke it by starkly inquiring, "The 'him' you were talking about on the phone probably doesn't like the ballet, does he?"

"No, he doesn't."

"I didn't think so."

Generally, curling up on the couch and reading was a favorite pastime for Megan. Only today it didn't seem to soothe or distract her. The silence in the condo seemed oppressive. Amber had gone to her parents' home for the weekend, robbing the apartment of her cheerful presence. Invariably, Amber would come wandering through the living room asking Megan what she was reading or exploding with the exciting details of some event that had just happened. Amber had a refreshing way of filling their apartment with her bubbly optimism. Megan missed Amber's influence. The silence hung like a dark mist over her.

Megan tried to focus on her afternoon at the ballet rather than on Kristy's phone call. But somehow her conversation with her sister took precedence. It reminded her of the numerous times Scott had used a third party to put pressure on her. It was always done under the guise of helping her when in reality it was a manipulative process that he had perfected in order to get what he wanted. The role of kind-hearted victim seemed to come to him naturally. He played it so well that everyone always believed him and refused to see what was really going on.

Megan wondered what Esther would think if she met Scott. Would she see through his artificial exterior? *"The 'him' you were talking about on the phone doesn't like the ballet, does he?"* Recalling Esther's words made Megan smile. It was a fleeting smile that was almost immediately chased away by the thought that Megan wasn't sure what Scott liked anymore. He had lived a secret life for so long that Megan wasn't sure what was real and what was done to hide the truth.

In the early days of their relationship, Scott and Megan had studied regularly. They had played racquetball in the mornings, packed picnic lunches and gone hiking in the afternoons, and attended plays and concerts in the evenings. Every moment was overflowing with togetherness and fun. They had shared laughter, academic discussions, and hours of talking about silly things as well as crucial issues. At some indefinable point, their life had changed. The peace and compatibility had all drifted away until there was only arguing. The choice of what DVD to watch had become a huge obstacle. The memory of Scott waving an R-rated DVD in front of her made Megan flinch.

Scott persuasively claimed, "It's only rated this way for a little violence. You can look away when the bad part comes."

"I really don't want to watch it."

"Listen, some PG-13s are a lot worse than Rs. You know that."

"Scott, we agreed to be careful about what PG-13s we watch, so why are you trying to watch that DVD?" Megan motioned toward the distasteful movie.

"I've heard it's not that bad, and it's supposed to be really exciting."

Megan quietly stated that she was not going to watch the movie. Before allowing Scott a chance to think up a more convincing rebuttal, Megan walked out of the room. She prayed that her example would encourage him to return to their old standard. Unfortunately, Megan's refusal did not have the desired effect on him. Instead, watching R-rated movies became one of his favorite pastimes.

Resting her elbow on the arm of the couch, Megan leaned her head on her hand and thought, *It's no use reliving the past. I have to forget it and make a new life with new friends, like I did today.* For some reason after that, it was easier to think of the ballet and how much Esther had enjoyed the dancing. There was also Jane. Poor Jane had only wanted to watch a classic movie, but the magic of Cinderella had reached out and captivated her.

In the next few weeks, Megan found herself spending more and more time in Jane and Esther's company. An hour's break with these two women seemed to help her focus better on work. As she walked on the perimeter of the Commons with her friends, Megan was filled with a strong sense of appreciation for the unique relationship between these two older women. The contrast between Jane, the romantic, and Esther, the realist, was amusing and entertaining. It enlivened Megan's life.

Unfortunately, this uncomplicated amusement was soon to dissipate. Without a single premonition, Megan unsuspectingly walked the same asphalt paths she had traveled for weeks now. They were talking and everything was following their normal tradition. Without warning, Esther shattered Megan's serenity by one question: "How long are you going to hide in your work instead of living life?"

Megan stiffened; the truth of Esther's words sliced through her newfound peace. With distinct relief, Megan heard Jane's cheery response. "It's like in the movie *Without Love*," Jane sighed. "Katharine Hepburn is terrified of any kind of romantic involvement; and then along comes Spencer Tracy."

Esther's smile was a bit gritty. "Yes, well, that's all very interesting, but—"

"She needs a man!" Jane enthusiastically concluded, delighted with her cleverness.

Megan's discomfort dramatically increased, causing her verbal skills to become nonexistent and her mind to swirl in unproductive circles.

"What do you think?" Jane almost bounced as she walked. When no one responded, Jane bubbled blithely on. "Unfortunately good men are hard to come by." Undaunted, Jane determinedly forged ahead. "Where can we find the right man?"

Esther shuddered. "It's more complicated than that. Even if we could find Megan a suitable man, perfect in every way, there would be a problem."

"You're talking as if I'm not here," Megan quietly pointed out. "What if I don't have time for a man right now?"

Esther looked down her nose at Megan, disbelief written legibly on her face. Without realizing it, all the women had stopped and were grouped together in a small huddle. Esther shifted her eyes away from Megan's face and flatly pronounced, "There. You see the problem clearly."

Jane appeared to be baffled while Megan stood stiffly erect, hoping they would drop the subject.

"It's a matter of trust," Esther quietly informed them, looking directly at Megan. "You want the quiet country life, but I think that you're afraid to take a chance and trust in anything."

The words were so painfully accurate that Megan had difficulty maintaining her implacable facade. She forced a soft smile on her lips and lightly agreed. "Most people want someone in their life." Megan felt certain Jane was fooled, but Esther was an entirely different matter.

Dissatisfaction and concern lurked in the shadows of Esther's eyes as she appraised Megan. "I see."

Megan was afraid that Esther did see. Despite the emotional cost, Megan could not allow any trace of her feelings to reflect on her face, so she prayed for serenity.

Jane's next comment diffused some of the tension flowing between Esther and Megan. "I suspect it's really more like the movie *The More the Merrier*. Constance settles for Mr. Pendergast because he is safe."

Megan had become accustom to Jane's constant referrals to romantic comedies from decades past. In truth, Megan preferred Jane's gentle ramblings to Esther's accurate lampoons.

"We need a Bill Carter!" Jane triumphantly announced.

"A Bill Carter?" Esther cried, "Who's Bill Carter?"

"The man Constance marries in *The More the Merrier*."

"I thought you said she married Mr. Pender-something." Esther was becoming confused.

"Constance was going to marry Mr. Pendergast, but an older gentleman interferes, and she marries Bill Carter," Jane cheerfully elaborated.

Esther snorted loudly. "I'm glad you told us."

Ignoring Esther's lack of appreciation, Jane quickly summarized, "It's really related. All we need to do is be like the older gentleman in Constance's life. We need to interfere!" Jane fastened her perky, blue eyes on Megan and smiled.

Megan's carefully constructed image crumbled as her mouth dropped open and her eyes darted wildly from side to side, searching for an escape. A terrifying feeling of panic battered her. She wanted to say something, but the effort of breathing in and out was taking all her concentration.

The horrible tightness in Megan's chest was eased slightly by Esther's next words. "Maybe she would rather we didn't interfere."

"Nonsense!" Jane adamantly insisted, pivoting to face Esther. "Just like Megan said, most people wants someone in their life."

"But there are times," Esther was struggling to keep her voice tightly restrained, "when we need time and space to ourselves."

"She needs a good man!" Jane single-mindedly persisted.

"Then may I suggest," Esther pointed out, momentarily losing her temper, "that Megan and I begin searching for a suitable gentleman for you. Jane, your husband has been dead for ten years!"

Jane blinked while her eyes widened into huge ovals. "I . . . I . . ." she sputtered, floundering around like a bird with a broken wing.

"There, you see?" Esther patted Jane's arm sympathetically in order to make up for the stinging bluntness of her previous words.

Although Jane was still flustered, she refused to be diverted. "Yes," she cried rallying, "but I've had twenty-six years of memories with Thomas to warm my heart. A love like that doesn't come along twice." Jane gulped in a deep breath. "But you, Megan, are young and vital. You're not sitting on the floor playing with your grandchildren on Saturday afternoons." Jane's voice rose with emotional intensity. "Megan, you need a man to make memories with that'll last a lifetime. Now's the time to make those memories!"

Esther and Megan stared in profound silence. Megan was seeing a glimpse of her old dream before it had been crushed and destroyed. The shattering of her expectations had been so painful that this tiny flicker of hope wavered precariously in the winds of her past. Yet it glimmered faintly in the distance and persisted.

Esther's practical nature had finally had enough of the romantic gibberish. "I suppose that was a line from one of your old movies."

"Actually," Jane proudly proclaimed, "I made it up myself. Although I must admit, I was influenced by the older man in *The More the Merrier*. In the movie he asks Constance if she keeps a diary. He says that people who keep diaries don't have time to live life, or something like that. It's just what you were saying before, Esther, about Megan hiding in her work and not living life." Jane rubbed her forehead and seemed to lose track of what she had been saying. "I wish I could remember the older man's name in the movie."

Esther rolled her eyes and grabbed Megan's arm. As she dragged Megan away, Esther grumbled good-naturedly, "It's time to get back to work."

Jane followed absently in their wake. Her brow was crinkled with the concentrated effort of recalling the older man's name. As they entered the lobby of Schaffer, Cronin, and Schaffer, Jane joyously called out, "Mr. Dingle. His name was Mr. Dingle."

Esther shuddered and marched determinedly over to the elevator. Pressing the up button, Esther sarcastically said, "Wonderful, I don't think I could have gone through another day without knowing his name was Mr. Dingle."

"Wait a minute! The young man's name was Joe Carter, not Bill Carter."

Esther's face was so caustically stiff and Jane's so cheerfully triumphant that Megan couldn't help but laugh. She was still chuckling when she entered her office.

A sense of gratitude swept over Megan as she sat behind her desk. Esther and Jane were good for her. Although both women were old enough to be her mother, they had become her friends and enlivened her life. She silently thanked Heavenly Father for the blessings of her friendship with Jane and Esther. Suddenly it occurred to Megan that it had been a long time since she had talked to the Lord like this. In the past, her communication with Him had been through prayers of desperation that were carried to heaven on waves of pain and disillusionment. This prayer of gratitude left such a sweetness that Megan could almost taste it.

Chapter Four

As Megan climbed the stairs to her condo, she shook her head, trying to clear out all the details of the Silverton case. She was exhausted, but apparently not exhausted enough to escape from her own mental processing. Every pertinent piece of information must be weighed, evaluated, and properly sorted. All the cases she had read in the last few weeks followed her up the stairs and they demanded her attention.

Megan stopped on the landing, pulled out her key, and tilted her head to the side. What was that she had just heard?

Childish laughter seemed to be coming out from behind her door. Megan decided that it was a crazy illusion brought on by her overtaxed brain. Or maybe it was coming from one of the neighboring apartments. A sliver of memory penetrated Megan's thoughts. Hadn't Amber asked if it was okay if she watched her three nephews this Saturday afternoon?

Megan recalled Amber saying, "My sister needs me to babysit the boys. You see, they live up in Maine, and it's hard for them to get down to the temple. The boys will only be here long enough for Rick and Diane to do a session. Right afterward, they want to go to Wooster to see Mom and Dad." Before Megan had a chance to answer, Amber had rushed on. "I know they're boys, but they really are well behaved."

Megan couldn't help smiling. "I'm sure they are."

"I'll have Rick and Diane bring some movies. The boys will just sit in front of the TV all the time they're here. They aren't allowed to watch much TV. Diane is always saying there are much better things for children to do. She only lets them watch select DVDs. So it'll be a treat for them to space out in front of the TV." Amber paused and appeared to be concerned. "But if you think it's not a good idea, I'll call Diane and tell her something has come up and I can't watch the boys."

"It's okay." Megan really didn't think it would be a problem. "I probably won't be around anyway. I thought I had this case under control, but lately it's taking some turns and getting pretty complicated."

Amber twisted her ponytail around her finger and anxiously suggested, "Maybe if you're so stressed, it's not a good idea."

Megan shook her head, "Don't worry about it. I really don't mind. Besides, I like kids."

"You're sure?"

Megan remembered reassuring Amber one last time and then had promptly forgotten about it until now.

The laughter on the other side of the door broke out again as Megan tried the handle. The knob turned easily, releasing the latch soundlessly. Megan pushed the door open and stepped onto the marble entryway. She froze.

The sight in front of her touched her so deeply that she almost cried. It was not Amber who sat on the couch with the boys, but Ben. It was almost like a dream or some beautiful scene out of a children's movie.

There was a toddler curled up on Ben's lap. The child was asleep with his thumb almost falling out of his mouth. His clutch on a blankie had relaxed and his fingers were spayed out over the silky binding. On each side of Ben, two older boys where snuggled up close. The younger of the two boys was giggling while the older boy was indignantly protesting, "That's not how the story goes."

"It's not?" The comical look on Ben's face made it obvious that he was having some difficulty keeping a serious face.

The older boy sat up straight and gave Ben a suspicious look, but he didn't comment. Ben turned to the younger boy and asked, "Josh, what do you think? Isn't this how the story goes?"

Josh's only answer was another round of uncontrollable giggles.

"Well, let's see, where was I?" Ben pretended to scan the few words at the bottom of the page and continued, "Clifford goes to Uncle Ben's house."

The oldest boy was trying hard not to laugh. He made a stern, grumpy face and cried, "Uncle Ben, that's not how it goes."

Before Ben could answer, Josh piped up, "But Zack, I like it. It's funny!" His curly little head bobbed up and down against Ben's arm.

Zack rolled his eyes and collapsed back against the couch. With a quick look at Zack, Ben pretended to read again, "Clifford loved to go to Uncle Ben's house. No big, red dog like Clifford could help but want to be with Uncle Ben."

Every few seconds, Ben would sneak a quick peek at Zack to see how he was taking all the teasing. Zack sat completely still, but the corners of his mouth kept quirking up. Zack would immediately force his lips down again, frowning determinedly. The quirking-up time was easily beating out the down time.

"Uncle Ben's house was the most wonderful—"

With glee, Zack interrupted. "You don't have a house. You live with Grandma and Grandpa!"

"I don't live there all the time. Sometimes I live in Amherst. Anyhow, where was I? Oh, yes! Uncle Ben's house was the most wonderful place where all dogs and nephews loved to—"

Zack couldn't contain himself any longer. His short, stubby finger reached out and tapped boldly on the picture of Clifford at the library. "It's not a house," he insisted. "See all the books? There's lots and lots of books, so it's a libarry."

"Oh, really," Ben politely studied the picture. "Well, I thought your Uncle Ben had a lot of books. He likes to read. It could still be his house."

Zack tilted his head at an angle and lifted his light, gray eyes up to his uncle. "Please, will you read it right?"

"No more teasing?"

"No more teasing," Zack repeated solemnly.

The strap of her leather briefcase dug into Megan's shoulder, making her realize how long she had been standing there watching the scene before her. Despite the discomfort of her shoulder pack, she couldn't seem to look away.

The baby's cheeks were that sweet, rosy red of slumbering children. Josh's curly, brown head was nestled so lovingly up against Ben's shoulder that it made Megan's heart ache. There was also Zack staring up at Ben. Teasing or no teasing, it was apparent that Zack adored his uncle.

The real thing that caught and held Megan spellbound was Ben. The love he had for his nephews filled the room. It dripped off the lamp shades and ran down the walls, showering Megan's condo with peace and security. Ben's face almost glowed and his eyes sparkled with pleasure. There was no doubt that he was enjoying his nephews.

The isolation of Megan's situation became almost unbearable. She felt years of loneliness freezing her to death. She functioned in this world, but she never partook. Empty, empty was all she ever felt. Megan wanted to reach out and touch Josh's curly head, to hug Zack's precocious little body, and the baby . . . she wanted to hold him and feel the rhythm of his breathing as she snuggled him close.

Instantly, she felt the darkness of fear stretching out and snatching away all the love and all the security. This was not her family. She did not belong. In the manner she had used to cope for years, Megan began to recoil all those tender feelings of love and warmth deep down inside of her. The effort was so intense that she shut her eyes to block out the pain. A moment later, Megan opened her eyes feeling like she was in control again. Her fragile composure was marred by suddenly realizing she was staring right into Benton's eyes. He had just looked up and seen her standing there.

Her whole body flinched causing the leather strap over her

shoulder to slip. Her briefcase went crashing to the floor. Hastily, she bent to pick it up. Ben looked like he was about to jump up and help her, but then seemed to remember his littlest nephew. He slowly rose, holding the boy against his chest.

By the time Ben had gently placed the toddler on the couch, Megan had collected her briefcase as well as her emotions. Her mask was tightly in place, concealing anything she might have been feeling. She was trying to think of some ordinary thing to say when Zack blurted out, "Who's that?"

Ben calmly answered, "She's Aunt Amber's roommate. She lives here."

"You live here?" Zack stood up and took a closer, more interested look at Megan.

"I do."

Zack pointed in the direction of Megan's office. "In that room over there, there's a TV."

Megan smiled, "Yes, there is."

"Can we watch it? We brought our own movies."

At the mention of movies, Josh jumped off the couch, and his chubby little legs ran across the room until he came to a tote bag resting on the floor. "This is a good one," he cried, yanking out a DVD with Veggie Tales characters printed on the front.

"I'm sure it is," Megan nodded in agreement, "but it's up to your Uncle Ben. He's in charge."

"It's okay with me."

"I don't want that one!" Zack complained. "We don't get to watch TV much and Josh always wants to watch the same stupid one."

Ben turned to look at Josh. He was holding the DVD tightly to his chest and his stubborn, little face showed no indication that he was willing to compromise. Ben sauntered over to the bag, knelt down, and began taking out other Veggie Tale DVDs. He held up one movie and asked, "I've heard that the tomato sings in one of these. Is it this one?"

"No," Josh pointed at another case, "this one."

Ben looked first at Zack and then at Josh. "I'd really like to hear the tomato sing." Ben looked wistfully at the picture of the tomato and the cucumber. "Do you mind if we watch this one?"

Zack was quick to agree. "Any one but that other one."

Josh fingered the cover to the case of his favorite DVD reluctantly, but said nothing.

For good measure, Ben repeated, "I'd really like to hear the tomato sing."

Suddenly Josh's eyes took on a calculating look. "You'll stay and watch the whole thing with us?"

For a fraction of a second, a horrified expression flickered across Ben's face. He quickly recovered and agreed. Megan almost laughed. She was positive that Ben was thinking of some way out of his current dilemma. He'd probably fall asleep. She could see the boys determinedly waking him up in time to hear the tomato sing.

After Ben had settled the boys in front of the TV, he slipped out of the room with the excuse that he had to check on the baby. One quick peek at the toddler satisfied Ben that the boy was still sound asleep.

Ben immediately headed for the kitchen where Megan stood fixing herself a sandwich. Out of the corner of her eye, Megan watched him wait patiently. It was difficult not to smile, because Ben's expression and posture made it obvious that he was feeling awkward. Megan couldn't suppress her smile much longer. She had watched Ben making up silly stories instead of reading like a normal person and heard him profess that he wanted to hear the tomato sing. Best of all, she had enjoyed the dazed look that had appeared briefly on Ben's face when his nephews had insisted that he stay and watch the entire DVD.

Megan's amusement was tempered by something sweeter and more pure. A feeling of happiness and safety filled her chest and reminded her of her childhood when all was right and the ugly side of life had never shown itself close to her neighborhood. Naturally these emotions were brushed aside and left unacknowledged. Bending her head, Megan concentrated on preparing her sandwich.

Ben simply stood in the open archway shifting from one foot to the other.

Megan didn't glance up from her sandwich. "Are you hungry?"

"No."

"How about the boys?"

"I think they're okay."

Megan still didn't look up. She screwed on the lid to the mayonnaise and stuffed the lettuce back into a plastic bag. The silence was beginning to bother her. She raised her head and stared at Ben.

He squirmed. "You're probably wondering why I'm here."

Megan turned her head away and smiled. He was kind of cute when he was so uncomfortable.

"Well, Amber called me early this morning and asked if I could drive over and watch the boys. Someone at her work got sick so she had to cover for them. Rick and Diane had already left, so I got to babysit."

"It seems like you're pretty good at it." She said looking back at him.

Ben looked surprised. His cheeks appeared to be overly heated while his eyes wouldn't meet Megan's.

"They're cute kids," Megan finally filled in the silence.

"Yeah, they are."

Well, this was really an in-depth conversation. Apparently normal communication was something that eluded Ben Kilgallen.

"Are you sure you don't want something to eat?" Megan repeated her offer.

"I'm sure."

Megan wondered how long they were going to stand here making inane comments. One thing she knew for sure was that she didn't have time for this. She needed to relax and unwind. This tense, awkward situation was not helping. "I've got things to do. I'll just go to my room and let you enjoy your nephews."

"Yeah, they're good boys."

Megan almost laughed. They had been over this before just

minutes ago. As she walked past Benton, out of the kitchen, she couldn't resist saying, "You'd better get back in there. If you miss the tomato singing, you're going to be in big trouble."

Chapter Five

Megan set her briefcase down on the desk and turned to face Amber. "I really don't want to go tonight."

"You work too hard and too long," Amber's voice was filled with compassion. "Come into the kitchen. I made dinner tonight."

Megan respectfully declined. After a month of watching Amber fix macaroni and cheese or another quick meal out of the box, Megan had no desire to sample Amber's cooking.

"Are you sure?" Amber asked standing in the doorway. "I made lasagna. I had a lot of time this afternoon, so I cooked."

Megan's eyes brightened at the mere thought of a homemade meal. "I think I will have some. Lasagna sounds wonderful. Give me a second to change and I'll be in."

As Megan hustled into her room and found a pair of jeans and a soft sweatshirt, the aroma of dinner heating in the microwave drifted into her room. Dressing in record time, Megan rushed into the kitchen and sank into a chair. Amber set a plate of lasagna in front of her and handed her a fork.

"This looks great. Thanks so much." Megan took her first bite and sighed.

Amber slowly lowered herself into the chair across from Megan and began to curl the tip of her ponytail around her index finger. For several seconds, she watched Megan and finally found enough courage to confess. "About tonight—"

"I really don't want to go," Megan repeated, setting her fork down.

Amber's fingers twirled her hair even faster. "I think there's a problem."

"Do you need to borrow my car? If you do, I don't mind. You're welcome to use it tonight."

"It's not a transportation problem." Amber let her hair slip through her fingers and leaned across the table. Her expression was apprehensive. "It's a little more complicated than that. You see, Kayla has the flu. She was up all last night and is still pretty sick today. So we're not having the party at her house."

"That's too bad. I'm sorry she's not feeling well."

"Me too," Amber agreed, resting her chin on her hands.

Swallowing a delicious mouthful of lasagna, Megan innocently inquired, "Then the group is not getting together tonight?"

"No, they're getting together," Amber assured.

"Oh, where?"

"Here." Amber shifted back in her chair restlessly. "Jason called and asked if we could hang out here and without thinking I said yes. I know, I should have talked it over with you first, but I just forgot. You know how it is."

"It's okay." Megan massaged the back of her head and wearily stated, "I'll stay in the study and work on my computer."

"You could watch a movie in there too." Amber felt guilty for disrupting Megan's evening. "I'm really sorry."

"Don't worry. I told you before you moved in that I wouldn't mind your parties."

"Megan, can I ask you something?"

Megan stiffened her shoulders and then systematically forced herself to relax each muscle. She agreed with a phony, languid, "Sure."

"Do you feel a part of our group? I mean, do you feel accepted?"

"Yes, I do. Everyone has been really nice."

"Then why do you avoid being with us?" Concern shadowed Amber's blue eyes.

"Amber, I'm older."

"Not really," Amber immediately challenged.

"I'm older than all of you."

"That's not true. Greg and Mark are older too. And Ben is coming tonight. There's also Ally Whitesides. She's close to thirty." Amber's eyes closed to suspicious little slits. "So it's not your age."

"At night, I'm tired. Work takes everything out of me." It was true, Megan told herself. Yet a tiny voice whispered that it was only a sliver of the truth.

Amber appeared satisfied. Her next statement stunned Megan. "I need your help. Will you help me?"

Cautiously, Megan asked, "What do you need my help with?"

"With my brother, Ben," Amber earnestly replied. "He used to date Ally, and she won't stop bothering him." Amber's hand returned to her ponytail and she began twisting it again. "I would love to see Benton get married, but I don't think Ally would make him happy. The bottom line is that Ally would take anyone that came along. She's so desperate to get married that she doesn't care whether it's right or not. I really do understand her dilemma, but Ben deserves someone who will really love him. And that's not Ally."

"It's his choice," Megan gently suggested.

"I know. I kind of hoped you'd distract Ben so Ally won't attach herself to him."

"Amber, if he's interested in Ally—"

"He's not!" Amber's voice was firm and final. "It's all over between them, only Ally hasn't accepted it. And Ben," Amber hesitated. "Well, Ben is one of those sweet, nice guys who doesn't want to hurt anyone."

A picture of Ben flashed through Megan's mind. He was holding a steaming mug of soup, and his brown-sugar eyes glowed with understanding. "She takes advantage of his kind heart."

"Will you help me?" Amber quietly asked.

"I don't see how I can. I'm going to be in my office working out some snags in my case."

Amber smiled sadly. "If I think of something, I'll let you know." Amber rose slowly. "I appreciate the help. Thanks."

The party had been underway for several hours. During this time, Megan had privately shut herself in the study, where she poured meticulously over her notes. She had a stack of volumes piled beside her and a headache almost as high as the towering books. Leaning her elbow on the desk, she rubbed her throbbing temples.

The muted sounds of laughter, music, and dialogue from a movie filtered into Megan's office, comforting her. She was alone, but not alone. A roommate had been a good idea even though Amber was sometimes too inquisitive and too perceptive. There was that expression on Amber's face when she said, "I think there's a story here."

When Amber first made her story comment, Megan had met Amber's blunt curiosity with a nonchalant shrug. "Maybe, maybe not."

The second time Amber had probed, Megan hid her alarm behind gentle teasing. "Amber, you'd find a story anywhere. If two strangers walked down the same street and accidentally bumped into each other, there would be a story there."

Amber had been effectively diverted. Tilting her head to one side, she had enthusiastically cried, "Well, of course! Maybe they knew each other before, a long time ago, or maybe it would be fate."

Megan had listened, half-amused and half-apprehensive, fearfully anticipating Amber's next attempt to intrude her personal life. Even now, as Megan sat at her desk listening to the sounds of the party, she wondered how long she'd be able to stop Amber from coming too close. Her survival and her ability to cope depended solely upon her vigilant refusal to develop any kind of meaningful relationship. She was safe as long as she continued to hide behind the image she had created.

A soft tapping sound on the door interrupted Megan's depressing thoughts. It took a second before her mind made the connection that someone was knocking. The door slowly opened and Amber's brother peeked into the room. He smiled weakly and mumbled a hesitant, "Hi." When Megan didn't make any disparaging sounds, Benton came in and closed the door softly behind him. He carried a plate laden with snacks and a drink that was balanced precariously on one side of the dish. "I figured a rejection would be less likely if I came bearing gifts. How about a study break?"

It reminded Megan of when he had brought her the soup. "Do you make it a habit of feeding and taking care of ladies?" she teased.

"I don't know," Benton returned, lightly matching her teasing tone. "Do you think I could make my fortune catering to ladies?"

"Absolutely. You'd make a million."

"If I could be that successful, I'd limit my clientele to beautiful ladies like yourself."

The total absence of mockery in his voice and the sincerity in his expression made Megan uncomfortable. It had been a long time since she had considered herself attractive. Scott had taken all that away from her. Nothing was ever good enough. Measuring up was an impossible feat. She shifted restlessly in her chair and looked away.

Benton quietly disclosed, "I have a confession to make."

Megan's eyes immediately flashed back to his face. Her guard dropped for a moment and she looked apprehensive and troubled.

"I've sinned," Benton acknowledged with mock humility. "I have come with ulterior motives."

Megan, who prided herself on the concealment of her emotions, looked terrified. Benton met her frightened eyes and smiled encouragingly. "You see, I need a place to hide out."

"Hide out?" Megan repeated blankly. She couldn't understand what was wrong with her. A few simple words from Ben and she found herself befuddled and frightened. He was only attempting to joke with her. Yet some strange invisible tension snapped between them. What had happened to the awkward professor who made her feel safe and secure?

With a small shock of surprise, Megan realized that Ben was refusing to make eye contact. Absorbed in some strange fascination with the glass he was recklessly twirling, Ben stared straight down at the plate. He looked bumbling and absentminded. He hadn't answered her question, which irritated Megan. The precariousness of the swirling drink also worried her. The moment Megan noticed that the patch of brilliant red on the back of his neck was creeping slowly up toward his face, she softened. Rising swiftly, Megan saved the drink from immanent danger of spilling and also took the plate out of his useless hands.

"I repeat," Megan patiently reiterated, "hide out from what?"

"It would probably be more correct to ask from whom?" Benton unhelpfully suggested, staring at his empty hands.

Megan's earlier conversation with Amber drifted through her mind. She was pretty certain that the answer to Ben's question of "from whom" was Ally Whitesides. For some reason, Megan found this information reassuring. The crackling tension between them subsided into an acceptable hum. Ben was safe, and safety was all Megan was interested in. He had not come into the office to pursue her, but rather to flee from the unwanted attentions of Ally. In an instant, Megan decided to aid him.

"I believe I understand your dilemma," she quietly concluded.

Benton's eyes jerked up and met hers. "You do?"

"Uh-huh." A mischievous glow lit the blue sparkles in Megan's gray eyes.

Benton observed the light in her eyes and looked wary. "If you don't mind, I'll sit here and read." He pointed to a comfortable chair by the television while he scanned the bookshelf for interesting titles. After making a selection, Benton settled into the armchair and flipped open the book.

Megan had resumed her seat at the desk and was examining the treats Ben had brought. She picked up a mini carrot and twirled it between her fingers. "Want to talk about it?"

Benton didn't even glance up from his book. "Nope."

He was so intent on appearing relaxed that it struck Megan as humorous. Her mirth caught her as much by surprise as it did Ben.

Benton's normally amiable face clouded over with uncertainty. A tangle of light brown hair fell across his forehead as he raised his head to look at Megan. "What's so funny?"

Some long lost impulse to be silly reared up inside of her. She giggled like a child. "I think there's a story here!" she laughed.

Benton groaned and raised his eyes toward the ceiling. It was no help. She was still laughing when he glanced back at her. "You've already been Amber's roommate too long."

Megan continued chuckling. It was so delicious to feel the years of strain and stress come gurgling hysterically out in laughter rather than tears. She had already shed enough tears to be dehydrated for the rest of her life.

Benton watched her quietly. When her amusement subsided, he thoughtfully repeated, "I think there is a story here."

A flame of steady, earnest concern burned in his eyes, warming Megan. It began to melt her instinct to flee. Her laughter died away as she stared mesmerized at Ben.

"Want to tell me about it?"

Instantly, Megan's defenses clicked back into place. Despite the warmth and security she had felt, she whispered, "No."

"I understand."

She thought he might. It was almost as if they had exchanged secrets and shared their most intimate thoughts.

As if nothing important had taken place, Ben returned to his book. Megan simply stared at him. It was probably a good two minutes before she turned back to the open book on her desk.

An hour passed in this peaceful solitude. The only sounds in the room were the gentle rustle of pages turning and the occasional scratching of Megan's pen. Although neither occupant of the room seemed to have noticed, the noise of the party had died down. Megan was absorbed in her work while Benton stared at the two books he had selected from her bookshelves.

The two volumes were rather alike. A master photographer had produced both artistic works. The glossy pages throughout the books depicted a quaint coziness of years gone by. There were picket fences with rose-covered archways, lilac trellises, and window boxes rioting with pink impatiens. The houses had steep pitched roofs with small paned windows that reflected the golden glow of the sun. Each picture had the same quality whether it was a tiny house on the seashore, a retreat in the woods, or a haven set in grassy green meadows. The photographs evoked images in Benton's imagination. He could see women in long flowing dresses, children playing on quilted blankets with porcelain dolls and wooden boats, and a man and a woman reclining contentedly in wicker chairs.

Benton carefully closed both books and placed them on the shelf. Sitting back in his chair, he folded his hands across his chest and pondered. It was interesting what one could learn by examining someone else's bookshelf. The irritating part was he knew he had been affected. He cursed himself for being a fool.

Chapter Six

Megan shivered in her coat and tightly clutched her gloved hands together. The cold stung her cheeks, but the walk was invigorating. She couldn't help smiling at Jane and Esther's bickering. They were arguing good-naturedly over something. Megan wasn't quite sure what, since she hadn't been paying attention.

"Megan," Jane caught hold of Megan's coat sleeve, "you don't mind, do you?"

Megan was about to confess that she hadn't been listening when Esther curtly grumbled, "Of course, she minds. It's none of our business."

"But we're her friends," Jane insisted still clutching Megan's sleeve. "It's our duty to help her."

"We've been through this before." Esther flatly stated in a tired voice. "Besides, it's too cold today. We should have gone to the lunchroom."

"You absolutely cannot be private in the company lunchroom," Jane hastily informed Esther. "We must be discrete."

Megan's lips curved up in amusement. "What are we being discrete about?"

"You!" Jane said.

Megan swallowed apprehensively. "Me?" The chill in the air hit her front teeth and made them ache. It was nothing to the chill caused by Jane's next words.

"The Spring Charity Gala. You need a date." Jane peered up at Megan. "You did see the company memo on your email?"

Megan looked down at the ground. "I hadn't planned on going."

"All employees are required to go, especially the attorneys," Esther calmly informed Megan.

Megan's eyes shot up in surprise. She was about to protest when Jane perkily announced, "The Charity Gala, the company picnic in August, and the Christmas party are the most important social events at the firm." Jane's sunny smile froze Megan's heart. "I guess we don't call it a Christmas party anymore do we?"

"It is now called a December holiday party. Apparently some non-Christians protested. Frankly, I think it was stupid. I'm not Christian and I love the parties," Esther shrugged her shoulders. "Some people are so easily offended these days."

"Well, the Gala," Jane warmed to her original topic, "is the most fabulous dance."

"How nice." Megan plastered what she hoped was a serene look on her face.

"Isn't it though?" Jane looked far away and dreamy. "The Gala is a formal affair. They hire a live band. It's so heavenly. That's why we must get you a date."

Megan's intricately constructed facial expression crumbled. "I don't think—"

Ester interrupted in a concerned voice. "It's not wise to go alone. There's always a lot of alcohol, and some of the men at the firm are not very nice after they've had a few drinks too many."

Megan stopped walking and felt as if the sky were closing in around her, squeezing. The image was shattered and Megan's mind was forced to face stark reality as Jane reached into her purse, produced a slip of paper, and thrust it into Megan's hand.

Esther crinkled her nose and asked, "What's that?"

"The list," Jane patiently explained.

In a state of nervous apprehension, Megan read out loud, "Phillip Connors. Michael—"

"Phillip Connors!" Esther erupted. "You made a list of potential dates, and Phillip Connors is at the top of that list?"

Unmoved by Esther's sudden intensity, Jane stoutly fired back, "What's wrong with Mr. Connors? He's divinely handsome."

Dropping her hands to her sides, Esther narrowed her eyes and said far too sweetly, "He is fabulously good looking, but Megan would need a body guard to protect her from him!" Esther took a deep, ragged breath and continued. "I thought the idea was to ensure Megan's well-being. Who else is on the list?"

Megan looked away from her two feuding friends and read, "Michael Jaffe."

"My nephew? Leah's son?" Esther gasped.

"Well, yes." Jane appeared a little flustered. "I don't know a lot of single men, and I thought your sister's son would be a good candidate."

"Michael's having an identity crisis right now." Esther's face grew even more sober. "My sister says he's playing around with some religious cult. She's threatening to disown him."

Jane's eyes glistened as she squeezed Esther's arm. "I'm sorry. He was so darkly handsome and seemed to be such a nice young man."

Looking as if she were uncomfortable with Jane's open sympathy, Esther immediately gave a brittle smile and moved the conversation forward. "Thank you for your concern, but we need to return to the issue at hand. It is only about three weeks until the dance." Esther covered her mouth with her gloved hand. Her brow furrowed and her eyes had a far away look as if she were doing some deep thinking.

Megan had reached her maximum tolerance level. "I can find my own date," she stiffly announced.

"Well, of course you can," Jane soothed. "It's just that you haven't lived here very long."

Esther squirmed and looked guilty. Nevertheless, she resolutely confessed to Jane, "I know I haven't helped you in coming up with a list, but . . ." her voice faded out and died away. Concern was evident in Esther's face as she glanced over at Megan. Her eyes were warm with understanding and compassion. The next moment her expression changed. It clouded over with uncertainty and then slowly cleared. Brusquely, Esther yanked up her coat sleeve and examined her watch. "It's time to get back to work, but how about this? I'll get together with Jane and we'll come up with some acceptable men. As soon as we can compile a list, we'll talk about it."

Megan frantically tried to think of something to say. She appreciated their kind efforts, but taking a date to the Gala, let alone being set up on one, was the last thing Megan wanted. "I really don't think—"

"It's all right," Jane interrupted soothingly. "We don't mind. We're glad to help. Give us a few days and we'll have a list of eligible bachelors."

Megan was effectively silenced. She smiled tightly and worried all the way back to the office. One hopeful thought did intrude into Megan's sober reflections. Today was Friday. She wouldn't have to face the dreaded list until Monday. Sighing with relief, Megan was able to smile sincerely and say goodbye to her friends.

Benton's hands were so sweaty that he had to rub them discretely on the sides of his jeans. If this didn't stop, he was going to have to take drastic measures. He'd tried talking to her, but Ally didn't seem to understand plain English. Benton hated these kinds of romantic entanglements. He felt like an insect at the mercy of a praying mantis. The green prongs of his jail were slowly closing. The noise and the music of the party seemed to be growing more distant.

"Ally," Benton tried desperately to extricate himself from her clutches.

"I've heard you have a new teaching position," Ally leaned in closer and smiled.

He smelled the familiar scent of her perfume as he jerked

his eyes away from her tight sweater. Taking a step backward, Benton leaned his head against the kitchen wall. The minute Ally had walked into Jason's apartment, she had cornered him. Reluctantly, he answered her question. "Yes, I've been offered a full-time position in Amherst."

"That's quite an honor!" Ally leaned in until she was only inches away from his face. "Shall I call you Professor?" She was tantalizingly close, but Benton was not moved. Actually, he wretchedly wanted to be moved—far away from her. And yet he felt pity for Ally. She only wanted someone to love her and make her feel special. How many times had he wanted the same thing?

He shook his head and forced himself to answer her question. "I don't think so, but I am pleased with the offer." Benton wished he could see around or through Ally so that he could make some excuse to escape. It wasn't possible because she had him literally backed into the corner and was blocking his view. The longer he talked to her, the more she would get her hopes up. He craned his head to the side and tried to see over her raised arm.

"That's why you taught at UMASS, Lowell wasn't it? You taught part time at both Lowell and Amherst so you could make a name for yourself. That was very clever of you." She tossed her head and some of her thick, dark brown hair brushed Benton's cheek. "Now that you'll only be teaching at one college, instead of spreading yourself between two, will we see more of you?"

Benton angled himself so that he could see a portion of the kitchen floor beneath the arm Ally had rested on the wall beside him. "I've been in Boston most weekends lately," he mumbled.

"I know." The two words radiated with innuendo. Without saying anything, Ally had effectively made it clear that she understood that his frequency in Boston had everything to do with her.

Benton smiled weakly, realizing that his immediate removal was imperative. With dramatic relief, he caught a glimpse of an ironed crease up a jean pant leg. He couldn't comprehend how, but he knew instantly that it was Megan Spencer. Ducking under the arm that Ally had placed on the wall to trap him, Benton grabbed Megan's hand. "Are you ready to go on the walk you promised me?"

Megan blinked and glanced curiously up at Ben. He was making all kinds of strange faces, beseeching Megan to help him. Behind Ben, Ally was saying happily, "A walk in the snow. I love walks in the snow."

Benton pivoted to face Ally while still maintaining his hold on Megan's hand. He determinedly lied, "I'm so sorry. Megan wanted to try out some of her strategy for the . . . the . . . a case she's . . ."

"The Silverton case," Megan inserted, apparently deciding to help Ben. "I won't keep him long."

An exhilarating surge rocked through Ben. He squeezed Megan's hand and offered, "Shall I get our coats?" He had no idea what Megan's coat looked like, and he couldn't have cared less. He was free.

As Megan and Benton sifted through the coats piled on the floor behind the couch; Benton could feel all the questions Megan was dying to ask. He was willing to oblige, the second they were alone.

As soon as the front door to Jason's apartment swung shut, Megan began chuckling. When she got her amusement under control, she teased, "You should have seen your face. It was a marvel in pathetic desperation. I think that you owe me an explanation."

"Sure, on one condition."

Megan looked narrowly up at Ben and inquired, "And that condition is?"

"I get to ask one question."

"One question?" Megan nervously inquired.

"Yes."

"Is it personal?"

"Not really," Benton assured her. "I guess the real question is how badly do you want to know why we're traipsing down a rickety flight of stairs to go outside and freeze in the snow?" Benton halted on the stair below Megan and looked up at her. His brown eyes were asking all kinds of impertinent questions.

Instead of finding the situation threatening, his teasing nature reassured Megan and made her realize how lonely she was. It seemed like forever since she'd had a friend.

The seriousness of her expression bothered Benton. They stood silently staring at one another as Benton felt something heavy and disturbing in how she was reacting to one tiny question. She must have been hurt badly. The gravity of the damage did not deter him because he felt the Spirit helping him understand. He recalled the healing power of the Savior's Atonement and felt tears sting his eyes.

Megan watched him while a feeling of comfort and peace settled over her. For a brief instant, she trusted. "I'll answer your question." The minute the words were out of her mouth, she regretted them. Fear surged in, washing away all of Megan's trust in one cresting wave. She shivered and looked wildly around.

Benton gently took her hand and started back up the staircase. "It's too cold to walk outside. Let's go up a few floors and sit on the landing."

After they had settled themselves on the floor, Benton, with his back to the wall, and Megan on the first step, Benton began explaining. "Last weekend when I came into your study, I was hiding."

"From Ally Whitesides."

Benton raised his eyebrows. "I guess it was pretty obvious."

"Yeah, that and your sister."

Benton shook his head and sighed, "Amber! Well, anyhow, I'm trying to avoid Ally. It is becoming rather difficult. And yet, I really don't want to hurt her feelings."

"She is pursuing you pretty aggressively."

Benton looked down partially embarrassed. "To be fair, I have to admit that I encouraged her in the beginning." Benton lifted his head and sheepishly confessed, "At first, I was interested. She's cute, has this crazy sense of the ridiculous, and at the same time, she's intelligent."

Megan experienced a light, heady feeling and flippantly deducted, "You like smart women."

Benton's eyes twinkled. "I do."

"But Ally was too smart." Megan was enjoying herself.

Benton rested his elbow on his knee. "Not exactly," his eyes roved around the small landing and then rested on Megan. "Have you ever considered the Mormon man's dilemma?"

Megan was intrigued. "I can't say that I have."

"Well, I've heard the woman's side repeatedly," Benton lightly informed her. "I hear it from Amber and from my other sisters, and I do sympathize."

"But the man's side?" Megan probed, the blue flecks in her eyes sparkled with interest.

"Believe me, it is just as obnoxious only in a different way." Benton was warming to his subject. "One of the older prophets said something to the effect that if a man was not married by twenty-five, then he was a menace to society. I'll be twenty-nine in August. And I have tried."

"And?" Megan encouraged, fascinated by the male perspective.

"You want to know how I've tried?" Megan nodded, signaling Ben to continue. "Sometimes it hasn't been easy. I was a little shy when I first got off my mission."

Megan's eyes went wide in an exaggerated way and she teased, "A little shy, huh?"

"All right, I was terrified of girls. I'd hardly dated before my mission. There aren't very many LDS girls in Worcester. So I was uncomfortable around any girl that wasn't one of my sisters." Benton sighed. "This is getting long and boring. To put it simply, I went away to school and for the first time, I became seriously interested in a girl."

Something tingled inside of Megan and she whispered, "She was really special, wasn't she?"

Benton's eyes glowed like bright pieces of amber glass. "I think she was." He paused a second and then added, "It's funny how things work out."

"What do you mean?"

"I didn't have the courage to do anything. I sat around hoping that things would work out. I mostly just watched and waited."

"And?"

"She fell in love with someone else and married him." The light in Ben's eyes died out, leaving them flat and dull.

Megan slipped her coat off before she quietly asked, "Are you telling me that no other girl ever measured up?"

Before responding, Benton pulled his jacket off, folded it neatly into a square, and sat on it. "I don't know what I'm saying. There were things I liked about that girl that I haven't found in any other girl. It was a long time ago and maybe it was part of a young man's dream. What I do know is that I've never felt like getting serious with any other girl. I've really tried. I especially made an effort with Ally. Like I said before, she was cute and intelligent, but the magic never happened. There was something missing on my side. It took me a while to understand what was going on. While I was realizing that Ally wasn't what I really wanted, she became more and more intense in our relationship.

"I'm afraid I might have hurt her badly. I know she still wants to date me, but I can't do it. You see, as time went on, I kept discovering things about Ally that disturbed me, things that I personally couldn't live with. For example, I couldn't picture Ally teaching our children the gospel. She lacks commitment." Benton looked embarrassed about disclosing such negative information about Ally. "She's really a nice girl, and I do think highly of her."

"I understand," Megan acknowledged. "If you're sincerely committed to living the gospel and you marry someone who thinks the gospel is a pleasant way of life, but that's all, it makes things difficult."

Benton stared at Megan, wondering if she realized how much she had just revealed about herself in that statement. She obviously did not, because she blithely continued on. "Have you dated a lot of different girls?"

"I have."

"And?"

"It's been nice and every once in a while I think maybe this can go somewhere, and then it just sort of fizzles out."

They sat in companionable silence, absorbed in their own personal thoughts until the noise of Jason's guests departing echoed up the stairs and disturbed them.

"Do you think Ally's left by now?" Benton scooted forward and peered anxiously down the stairwell. He looked so awkward in his crouched position that Megan chuckled.

Benton glared up at her and hissed, "It's not funny! I stay with Jason when I'm in town. I am not going down there until I'm positive that Ally's gone."

Megan pretended to be disgusted. Unable to maintain her poise under Ben's pathetic, puppy-dog expression, she conceded, "Oh, all right. I'll go down and check. If Ally's gone, I'll come out and tap on the stair railing a couple of times. Otherwise it looks like you're stuck up here for the rest of the night."

As Megan stiffly rose, Benton forestalled her with a simple request. "Will you answer my question first?"

She had forgotten. The cozy, secure atmosphere vanished as fear clogged Megan's throat and made waiting torment. She nodded. Her relief was so profound that Megan almost laughed when she heard his question.

"Why do you iron your jeans?"

Chapter Seven

As Megan looked around the snug café, she decided that she approved of Esther's and Jane's taste in restaurants. Her approval of the list was another matter. Jane was waving the offending article in the air as if she had triumphantly climbed Mt. Everest.

Eyeing the paper warily, Megan firmly stated, "I've already told you, this is not necessary. I don't need a date. I'll go to the dance, put in an appearance, and leave early."

"But," Jane earnestly insisted, "I want to see you dancing with some handsome young man." Jane spooned a large heaping of dressing on her green salad. "It could eventually lead to something; romance, marriage, happiness. Now, let's take a look at the list. Of course, Esther and I have expanded it. Mr. Connors and Esther's nephew are only the beginning."

"I appreciate your efforts, but—"

"We know that," Jane smiled lovingly. "There's Eugene Martin. He's a friend of my sister's daughter. My niece has promised me a picture of Eugene. I should have it by tomorrow at the latest."

"That's very kind of you, but I—"

"Oh, wait until you hear about the next man on our list," Jane smiled. "He's so handsome. For the last six months, I've rented out my basement apartment to him. His name is so cute!"

Esther put an end to Jane's gushing. "This entire list worries me. How do we know these men are any better than the employees at the firm? They might be just as likely to have a few drinks and become obnoxious."

"Oh, no!" Jane contradicted hastily. "Mr. Purity is the sweetest, most kind gentleman. He does repairs for me and always pays his rent on time."

"That settles it," Esther snorted. "Repairing things constitutes perfection."

"Oh, but he is such a nice man!"

"That's what they say about serial killers too," Esther tartly pronounced. "I want Megan to be safe. Maybe she should come with us. I know Norman wouldn't mind."

"Mr. Douglas Purity is not a serial killer," Jane sputtered. "Besides, there are other men on the list. Let me see . . ."

"I really couldn't accept your help anyway," Megan anxiously intervened.

"Why not?" Jane cried, her round face showing signs of disappointment.

"Because," Megan's mind whirled desperately searching for an answer, "because I . . . I've met someone." Megan hated the lie the instant it left her mouth.

Esther's eyes narrowed skeptically as she watched Megan under heavy lids while Jane gushed excitedly, "You have?" It was obvious that Jane was delighted, her whole face glowed. "Where did you meet him?"

This was becoming worse rather than getting better. Megan stalled by faking a secretive smile. It bought her a little needed time while Jane oohed and aahed. Unfortunately, Esther merely maintained her flinty gaze.

"This is so wonderful," Jane almost bubbled.

Without blinking, Esther said, "It had better be."

Megan was trapped, caught, and sinking in quicksand. In the midst of her frantic searching, Megan saw his face. Instinctively, she knew he would help her. Besides, didn't he owe her one for rescuing him last Saturday night?

"His name is Ben, and he's my roommate's brother."

"Ben, that's a pleasant name," Jane enthused, her eyes bright with anticipation. "And you are seeing him?"

"Yes." *At church and when he visits his sister.* It was still a lie. One falsehood always led to another. A tiny depressed voice began whispering inside of Megan's head, *What's one more lie when your entire life has been a lie for the last six years?* Despite the truth of the words, Megan felt pain as one more falsehood pierced her tender spirit.

Esther's eyes were penetrating too deeply into Megan's private, secure space. Deciding that if she were going to do this she might as well make it good, Megan said, "We went to a party last Saturday night and sat on the stairs and talked. He is fun to be with. I really enjoyed myself." With a little shiver of shock, Megan realized that her last two statements were the truth.

Esther's expression relaxed as she gently concluded, "He's of your faith, isn't he?" When Megan agreed, Esther shifted so she could see Jane clearly. "Being of the same faith is important to Mormons."

"I don't see why!" Jane looked dubious.

"Well, it is," Esther firmly reiterated. "That's why I wasn't thrilled about the list. I admit that I did help you, but I had reservations."

"What's wrong with a good Catholic boy, a Jewish boy, or a Lutheran for that matter?" Jane inquired sincerely confused by all this fuss over religious preference.

Megan answered Jane's question with understanding and patience. "When you feel strongly about religion, it's best to share those beliefs in marriage so that you have the same goals and direction in life."

Jane seemed to be immune to the topic of strong religious beliefs. She appeared bored, and eager to move the conversation in a more exciting direction. "It hardly matters what religion the men on the list are since you already have a boyfriend." Jane shrugged her shoulders, dismissing the subject as inconsequential.

The word *boyfriend* bothered Megan. Her discomfort was expressed in the manner in which she scrutinized her bland vegetable soup.

Jane didn't seem to notice as she was cheerfully stabbing her lettuce with her fork. "I'm so glad you've found someone," Jane sighed, and then lifted a bite to her lips. "I told you before about the movie *Without Love.*" Jane paused and rested her elbows on the table. A piece of lettuce dangled precariously from her fork as she dreamily resumed. "Both Tracy and Hepburn have been hurt in love, so they begin a relationship without love. Has your boyfriend been unlucky in love? Is he older?"

"He'll be twenty-nine in August," Megan cautiously responded once more studying the smooth texture of her soup.

"I'm positive," Jane delightedly purred, "that he has been hurt just like you've been hurt." Megan wrenched her eyes away from her bowl and stared at Jane. For a second, Jane faltered under Megan's surprised gaze and then steadied. "Well, Esther said that she thought you might have been hurt, and Esther is always right. I've learned never to argue with Esther. She always wins."

Esther glanced over at Megan and their eyes met. The corners of Esther's mouth began to twitch. It was contagious. Megan's eyes started to glitter with suppressed merriment. They could not stand it. Simultaneously, they burst out laughing.

Jane looked quizzically from one to the other of them. Apparently she decided to ignore their strange outburst. "Well, you do, Esther. You're always right. It's some kind of instinct you have. I swear you watch people so much that you don't miss anything. Oh, never mind." Jane happily chomped on her salad.

After swallowing, Jane miraculously returned to her original topic of conversation. "So Ben is older, more mature, and has been hurt badly? Maybe he was simply unlucky in who he chose to love. Do you know what happened?"

"I don't know," Megan thoughtfully replied. "I really don't know."

"You've asked him to the company party, right?" Jane pressed, her eyes shining. It was clear she was thinking of all the delightful possibilities an evening of romance afforded.

"I haven't yet," Megan could feel the tension knotting in her shoulders.

Esther opportunely stepped in. "There's no hurry. The dance is still a ways off."

Megan smiled feeling grateful for Esther's intervention.

Acknowledging Megan's gratitude with a single nod, Esther asked the group in general, "What do you think about the new web service the law library is offering? They say we'll be able to research cases in half the time."

As Megan sat at the kitchen table eating dinner, fragments of her conversation with Esther and Jane kept running through her mind. Surprisingly enough it was not thinking of ways to ask Ben to the Company Gala that occupied Megan's mind. Instead, she was haunted by the question Jane had unwittingly asked. Was Ben unlucky in love? Had he been in love and it turned out badly? Megan could not stop thinking about it.

She meticulously recalled every word Ben had spoken while they sat in the stairwell. He had admitted that he had met some girl that had affected him deeply. Megan remembered asking, *"Are you trying to tell me that no one else ever measured up?"*

Hadn't Ben said that he had tried but had never found that same magic? There had also been something sweet and endearing about the way Ben's eyes had glowed when he talked about that girl. Megan stared across the kitchen and only saw Ben's expression.

It was too bad there weren't more LDS girls in the area. A desire to help Ben find the perfect wife filled Megan. She began sorting through all the eligible women she knew. The numbers were pathetically small. In the last few years Megan had intentionally cut herself off from friends, both single and married. It had been easier that way.

Megan toyed with the mini-pizza on her plate and wondered if Ben was afraid of a serious commitment. Perhaps he was content being the absentminded professor. If that were the case, it made him a safe friend. A serious commitment was the last thing Megan wanted. Maybe she could make an arrangement with Ben. She would protect him from Ally and in return Ben would take her to the dance and protect her from the list. Megan liked the plan. In fact, the desirability of the idea continued to grow until she actually became eager to implement it.

Ben Kilgallen, however, was not cooperating. At the ward games night, he was glaringly absent. Megan cheerfully played games with her new friends, but found herself distracted. Every time anyone went in or out of the cultural hall, Megan looked up.

As Amber and Megan drove home, Amber commented on Megan's vigilant door monitoring. "Who were you looking for? All night you kept watching the door."

Megan was uncomfortable. She couldn't very well say, "Your brother." In what she hoped was a neutral tone of voice, Megan answered, "Nobody in particular."

"Joe Fielding doesn't usually come to very many activities."

Joe Fielding? Megan searched her brain trying to fit the name with a face. Slowly it came. She had talked to a tall, thin man after church last Sunday. He must be Joe Fielding. Deciding that some response was necessary, Megan casually said, "Oh, really?"

"Yeah, but he comes every Sunday," Amber hastened to reassure. "He might have to work on the weekends."

"Some people do." Megan was grateful that the conversation had turned in a new direction. Yet she still wanted to know where Ben was this weekend. "Maybe he spends a lot of time with his family, like your brother, Ben."

Since Amber was still focused on Joe Fielding, Megan's attempt at fishing for answers went nowhere. "That's a possibility. I think he is a native of this area." Then in a helpful voice, "Do you want me to try and find out for you?"

"No. It's not that important."

As Megan parked the car, she had to bite her tongue to keep from asking about Ben. Just because he had come to Boston for the last two weekends in a row didn't mean he came every weekend. He might only come to Boston occasionally for the activities. *Which means,* Megan thought dismally, *that I have no idea when I'll see him again.*

There was always Amber. But somehow Megan couldn't bring herself to ask Amber for her brother's phone number. Amber might get ideas. All of that would lead to questions and complications that Megan was unwilling risk.

As Amber shut the door to the condo and leaned against it, she studied Megan closely. "Have I offended you?"

Megan was halfway across the living room. At the sound of Amber's words, she whirled around and faced her roommate. "No! What makes you ask?"

"Well, we've been roommates for several months now and we never talk."

"We were just talking in the car on the way home," Megan pointed out.

"It was all light and not terribly important."

Megan unzipped her jacket and started to take it off. Amber's intensity was making her uneasy. At the same time, a silly, irrelevant thought popped into Megan's mind. What did it matter anyway? The life she was so carefully hiding was over and done with. This was her new life, the one she had promised herself in those dark, lonely hours. Was she afraid to reach out and start living it?

Surely her new life should be filled with close friends rather than acquaintances. She had Esther and Jane, but even Megan's interactions with them had been just barely below the shallow surface. She had not let anyone into her personal world for so long that it was difficult to remember how to develop close relationships.

Megan tossed her jacket on the couch and looked at Amber leaning on the door. With a silent prayer in her heart, Megan whispered, "I haven't had a friend for a really long time."

Amber appeared to be stunned as if she were having difficulty believing that she had heard Megan correctly. "But you have everything: good looks, a wonderful career, and a beautiful condo."

Megan smiled a sad upward twist of her lips.

Amber pushed off from the door and approached Megan. "Oh, I see," she cried looking as if she had been enlightened. "In order to get where you are with law school and your career, you haven't had time to make friends."

Megan was saved from having to answer by the telephone ringing. As Amber rushed into the kitchen to pick up the phone, she grumbled, "Who'd call this late?" Immediately, Amber put on her best telephone voice. "Hello? . . . No, I'm her roommate . . . Sure, no problem." Amber turned to Megan with her hand over the mouthpiece of the receiver. "It's some guy named Scott. He sounds nice. You had better . . ." the rest of the words wilted in Amber's throat as she stared at Megan's face. Megan's cheeks had turned a pasty white and her eyes had a glassy expression. "Are you all right?"

"Fine," Megan said between clenched teeth. She took the phone and spoke as she walked toward her bedroom. "Hi, how are you doing?"

Amber couldn't help but hear the panic in Megan's next words. "No, don't do that! It won't be worth your trouble." As the door to Megan's room shut, Amber only heard a fragment of the next sentence. "I'm never coming . . ."

Without much difficulty, Amber decided the last word she hadn't heard was probably *back*. Megan was never coming back. Apparently, Scott wanted Megan to return.

Later that night, Amber wandered out into the kitchen. She was having trouble sleeping and thought a glass of milk might help her. As she passed Megan's closed door, she heard muffled crying. Amber's gentle heart was wrung by the sound. She didn't know what to do, so she prayed that somehow she would be able to help her friend.

When Megan finally saw Ben again, she had to chuckle. It

was so unexpected and the situation so comical that laughter was the only possible solution.

Since the church coat alcove had been overcrowded, it had been difficult to locate a vacant hanger. Megan had finally found a hanger and was in the act of squashing all the other garments to one side to make room for her coat when she'd seen Ben's face peering out. He was crouched down, hiding behind the rack of winter clothing. His cheeks turned a brilliant red, but he still managed to laugh.

"I know it looks odd."

"You're hiding!" Megan supplied for him. He nodded, his face resuming a more natural color. "What do you plan to do now?" Megan asked.

Benton pushed through the clothing, smoothing down his sandy colored hair. "I need a partner in crime," he teased.

"Ah, and I look like a suitable candidate?" Megan scoffed while still smiling.

"Indeed you do." His brown-sugar eyes glittered dangerously.

Oddly enough Megan didn't retreat. She felt comfortable, lighthearted, and almost giddy. "And what crime are you thinking of committing?"

"I'm going to perpetrate a lie," Benton boldly announced with a devilish twist of his lips.

Megan felt like chiding him as if he were a second grader. Before she could, he grabbed her hand and pleaded. "Please walk into sacrament meeting with me. Sit with me. Let me hold your hand."

"You're already holding my hand," Megan glanced down at their intertwined fingers for emphasis.

Benton looked craftily down at Megan and laughed, "It looks like I'm doing pretty good."

Megan tried to wrench her fingers free, but Ben held on tightly. "Wait a minute and just listen!"

In the distance, they could hear the organ playing the prelude music. Benton glanced toward the chapel and hastily explained,

"It's Ally, again. I know most of it is my fault, but I get a little paranoid. I don't want to hurt her feelings, but—"

"All you have to do is tell her you only want to be friends," Megan recommended.

"I've done that."

"And?"

"It didn't work!"

"What do you mean it didn't work?"

"Simple. She agrees and says she's okay with only being friends, but the minute Ally sees me, she comes running. I think she has a different idea of what friendship means than I do."

"Are you sure you made it clear that you have no romantic interest?" Megan persisted.

"As clear as I can without being downright mean," Ben calmly informed her. "That's why I think she needs a visual sign."

"Holding my hand and being seen with me?"

"Yes," Benton looked deep into Megan's eyes and whispered, "I need your help."

Something warm and tender encircled Megan. She felt and was cognizant of some slender thread that bound them together. He needed her and she needed him. The list was still balanced precariously over her head. Megan had thought of this same solution herself. "You want me to pretend to be your girlfriend?"

"Exactly," Benton resolutely declared.

"Great!"

Ben looked surprised and seemed to be shaken by Megan's firm and enthusiastic reply.

"You see, I have a similar problem," Megan said.

"You do?"

"Uh-huh," Megan almost laughed. She hadn't felt this carefree for half a decade. "You see, there are these two older ladies at work."

Benton's expression showed that he was absolutely confused. Megan couldn't stop herself from giggling. "They are trying to match make."

Benton nodded, eyeing Megan warily.

"No, really," Megan insisted without seeing the smug, satisfied expression underneath Ben's pretense of skepticism. She smiled, not realizing that his teasing had brought a relaxed, happy glow to her face.

"Esther and Jane think that everyone should have some one."

Benton squeezed her hand and with exaggerated eagerness he teased, "I agree."

"Ben!" she cried.

"I thought I was helping," Benton's fake look of innocence was not convincing.

"You know you're not."

"Well, go on. Two old ladies are terrifying you," Benton in mock solemnity pronounced.

"They're not that old!" Megan rolled her eyes and then finished seriously, "But they are rather determined. You see, the firm is having a formal dance in about two weeks."

"That's nice," Benton blandly commented, but this time, the teasing glint in his eye registered with Megan.

She dug her fingernails into the palm of his hand. Immediately, he dropped her hand and searched his skin for damages.

"It's not nice," Megan chided, "and you know it. Esther and Jane have come up with a list of possible dates for me."

"And you are considering one," Benton stated in a matter-of-fact manner while his eyes were gleaming with amusement.

"Actually, I told them I didn't need the list."

Benton's joking manner fell away as he inquired, "Why did you do that?"

"Because I lied."

"You did?"

"I did. I know it was wrong, but it was necessary. You see, I told them I already had a boyfriend and that his name was Ben. I figured since I rescued you from Ally that the least you could do was rescue me from Jane and Esther's list." Megan's voice died away as she watched Ben hesitantly.

"It looks like we're partners in crime," Ben cheerfully observed.

"It certainly does," Megan agreed with relief.

Benton grabbed Megan's hand again and pulled her out of the coat alcove. "Let's get started. We're just in time to make a grand entrance into sacrament meeting."

Chapter Eight

Both Benton and Megan knew an explanation was due the minute they entered the condo and saw Amber sitting on the couch, waiting. Her arms were folded across her chest and her foot was tapping an impatient rhythm on the carpet.

"That was quite a performance," she stonily asserted.

"We were rather good, weren't we?" Benton cheekily claimed obviously proud of himself.

"And the reason for this was?" Amber challenged.

"Self-preservation," Benton announced. "A simple matter of self-preservation."

"And you agreed to this?" Amber turned to Megan.

"I most certainly did," Megan confirmed. "You remember Tressa's friends at the firm, Esther and Jane?" After Amber nodded, Megan continued. "Well, they have come up with a list of eligible bachelors to take me to the company dance. Ben is saving me from the list, and I am saving him from Ally."

Amber was about to protest that a deception like this was devious and beneath them when she saw the expression on Benton's face as he helped Megan with her coat. There was no need for Ben to be acting, yet his expression was unaccountably warm.

Turning toward Megan brought another curious observation to Amber's attention. This did not seem like the same Megan who had cried last night, neither did this woman seem like the same tired and listless girl who had forced a smile and called a cheerful good-bye when Amber had left for an early church meeting. Megan's cheeks were tinged with pink, making her appear more youthful and carefree. A new thought played and replayed in Amber's head. *Who is deceiving who?*

Saving all these fascinating questions to ponder later, Amber rose and casually said, "Well, the whole thing is crazy, that's all I can say."

It might have been all Amber could say, but her thoughts ran rampant as she helped Megan fix Sunday dinner. Who was Scott? Was Megan running away from some disastrous relationship? Her crying certainly supported that theory.

There was also Benton. Amber kept remembering the day Ben had helped her move. He had confessed that he thought he might have been in love once. Was he finally looking beyond the girl he had admired while he was at the Y? There certainly seemed to be something vibrating in the air between him and Megan. The longer Amber watched them, the more questions crowded her mind. It definitely made for an interesting Sunday afternoon.

That night, as Amber lay in bed, she pondered a difficult question. Did she want Benton and Megan to become serious? The worst part was that her own needs made her feel selfish and uncomfortable. She wasn't sure if she could stand to see another roommate marry. Yet, if Megan married Ben, there would be a quiet sweetness that would balance out the aching bitterness. Ben had been looking for a wife for a long time, longer than she'd been searching for a husband. Amber concluded that she could suffer through losing one more roommate if it were for Ben. With this decision made, Amber found peace and drifted off to sleep.

As Megan critically viewed her appearance in the mirror, a little tremor of anxiety shivered down her arms. The last two weeks had soared by, leaving Megan unprepared for this formal date. Actually, it was the date itself, not the formality of the ball, that bothered her. It had been years since she'd been on a date with anyone besides Scott. Megan's tremors increased and her stomach fluttered.

Why was it that anxiety did this to her? It was only Ben. She was safe since he was a friend and nothing more. They were performing a service for each other. She didn't need to worry. Ben was definitely not pursuing her. Megan hadn't even seen him since the Sunday they had agreed to pretend to be dating. Other than one phone call in which he finalized their plans for the Charity Gala, Megan hadn't heard from him.

"Wow," Amber lounged in the open doorway to Megan's bedroom, "that royal blue is a fabulous color on you."

"Thanks." Megan took another quick glance in the mirror and tried to breathe normally.

"The dress is classy and modest," Amber leaned one hip on the door jam. "You and Ben will be the best looking couple at the Ball. It's like Cinderella," Amber teased, "only I've always pictured you more as Snow White."

"I'll take that as a compliment." Megan picked up her gauzy shawl. "I think I'm going to freeze."

"The price of beauty," Amber commiserated. "Hey, there's the door. I'll get it."

Megan said a silent prayer before following Amber. Ben stood holding a corsage box in the open doorway. For a few seconds, Megan stared at him. There was a sweet, hesitant look on his face that reminded her of some past memory. It was illusive, but not unpleasant. This sensation plus Ben's appearance calmed all the discontent rumblings in Megan's stomach.

Appreciation gleamed in Ben's eyes. "I fear its Beauty and the Beast tonight. You look too good to be true."

"I think you and Amber must have watched too many Disney cartoons when you were kids. Amber thought I was Cinderella or Snow White."

"I guess we should get our stories straight," Benton laughed. "Shall I call you Snow or Belle?"

"What if I prefer Cinderella?"

Benton looked critically at her feet. "No glass slippers. Sorry, Cinderella is out."

Megan pretended to be offended while Amber slipped unobtrusively out of the room. When Amber returned from the kitchen with Benton's boutonnière, Megan and Benton were laughing and deciding which dwarf was their favorite.

"Grumpy," Megan insisted. "He's so crabby, but there's that cute little sparkle in his eyes."

"Not Dopey?" Ben was amazed. "I thought everyone loved the underdog. He tries so hard."

Amber shook her head and handed Megan the florist box. "You're going to be late."

Benton's eyes widened. "And I'm double parked. We'd better go."

"Be home by midnight," Amber jested.

"Yes, Mother," Benton cheerfully responded.

"Midnight's good," Megan enthusiastically agreed. "I might turn into a pumpkin."

With a wave and an echo of laughter, the couple departed. While Amber watched them from the open doorway, she felt something funny and wasn't sure if it was a premonition or the Spirit. Whichever it was, Amber felt positive that this was going to be a fabulous night for Megan and Ben.

The teasing had left both Megan and Benton feeling completely at ease. By the time they reached the Charity Gala, their camaraderie had increased dramatically. Megan found herself openly sharing amusing details from her childhood while Ben added humorous incidents from his youth.

They danced. They smiled. Later they spoke to Megan's business associates and friends and then danced again. Across the room, Esther and Jane watched while Esther's husband, Norman, tapped his foot in time to the music. He turned to his wife. "Would you like me to bring you something to eat?"

Esther smiled warmly at him, "That would be nice."

"And Jane, would you like anything?" Norman politely inquired.

"Yes, that would be wonderful. Could you bring me a little of everything?"

As Norman turned to leave, Jane leaned across the table toward Esther and sighed, "She looks so happy. Isn't it divine?"

"To be honest with you, I'm rather surprised," Esther confessed, still observing Ben and Megan through narrowed eyes.

"Why?" Jane was puzzled.

"Because, I halfway imagined that Ben was someone Megan had made up so that we'd stop pushing the list."

Jane almost gagged on her punch. She wiped her lips and cried, "You're kidding?"

"No, I'm not. However, he looks real enough."

"He certainly does." Jane dreamily studied the couple. "There's something about him. He has that look, that special something. I can't figure out what it is." Jane leaned her head on her hand and stared. "I know!" she cried, "He's like Jake Robinson. Remember you said that Mr. Robinson looked like a Rabbi. Well, this Ben has the rabbi look."

Esther regarded Ben, studying him seriously. After a few more seconds of this careful consideration, she asserted, "I believe you are right. He appears to be a gentle, religious sort of man. But," Esther cautioned, "sometimes it's easy to be fooled."

"No, he's perfect for Megan," Jane concluded, once more sipping her punch.

"I still think there's something not quite right here," Esther advised. "I don't believe that Megan is as carefree as she pretends to be. All these months while we have walked in the commons and sat over lunch, it seems to me that she's been holding herself back. She's not very open. We really don't know that much about her. And it's not just what we call the 'New England Reserve.' It's more like Megan has secrets she's hiding."

"Nonsense," Jane began, but almost immediately something changed. She clamped her mouth shut and her eyes narrowed.

Focusing on the dancing couple, Jane enthusiastically exclaimed, "It is exactly like in *Without Love* again, isn't it?" Jane mused, "She's afraid because of old emotional wounds."

"It's possible," Esther agreed, but then thoughtfully added, "I don't really know what the problem is with Megan, but don't you think if this young man continues to move slowly and is always there for her, she'll give in and fall in love?"

Jane's eyes were round with wonder. "Wouldn't it be wonderful? What do you think happened to Megan? I mean, what caused her to be so closed up and—? It had to be a man, don't you think?" Jane's tender heart throbbed sympathetically.

"I don't know," Esther shook her head sadly, "but whatever it was, she's not willing to trust again."

Megan felt like she was waltzing in a dream. His hand was on her waist and her fingers were intertwined with his. The band was playing soft tunes from the 60s and 70s. Megan felt her spirits rising on a tide of pure pleasure. It was almost as if she could feel the years of loneliness withering up and blowing away. Those dark days danced and twirled behind her in the breeze from her flowing skirts. With each circle of movement, those awful times were pushed farther and farther away. Megan looked up at Ben and felt wonderful. She had been dead and cold for so long that the tingle of emotion was almost like a firebrand. Instead of panicking, Megan felt thrilled by the surge of vitality. She was alive!

Throughout this rising emotional tide, Ben's eyes held hers in an understanding manner. Unspoken words flashed between them. Calmness, balm, and soothing flowed over Megan.

"I've tried so hard," she whispered as they danced.

By some miracle he heard. "You have," he affirmed.

Embarrassment flooded her senses, causing Megan to look away and bite her lip. It was too late. She had laid herself open, exposed the suffering in her heart and at the same time, forged a bond with Ben. It would never be the same again. Megan was thrilled and terrified. She told herself that she needed a friend and silently allowed Ben to glide her around the dance floor.

Later that night, before entering her condo, Megan leaned against the doorway and tried to explain. "You don't know what this means to me."

Benton nodded, "I think I might."

She closed her eyes and whispered, "Ben, I'm not what you think I am."

"And what do you think I think you are?" Ben convolutedly inquired.

"A typical LDS girl."

"I've never thought that you were the typical LDS girl. There's more to you than that stereotype."

She fingered the gauze of her scarf and raised her eyes to his. "For the first month I lived in Boston, I didn't attend church."

"I'm sure there were reasons," Ben reassured.

"I've been through the temple, made promises and covenants, and I thought about becoming less active and never attending church again." Megan wrenched her eyes away from him.

"No one is perfect. Everyone makes mistakes. It's what you do about the mistakes that count," Ben patiently pointed out.

"You mean repentance."

"Yes, repentance is for the little things as well as the big things." He leaned back against the door casing and said, "I think the question is, have you repented and decided to be active and faithful?"

He asked the question in such a way that Megan knew he believed she would be active and faithful. "Yes, but the faith part is hard," Megan whispered.

"Is it?" Benton's lips turned up in a half smile. "Sometimes life is hard and doesn't turn out exactly like we thought it would."

Tears glistened on the tips of Megan's eyelashes. "In Young Women our leaders always told us to keep the commandments, marry in the temple, and have an eternal family. If you did that then life would be wonderful." She paused so long that Ben wondered if she'd be able to finish. "But sometimes it doesn't turn out like that."

Benton nodded solemnly. "Some women never marry. Some divorce. Some couples are childless. Illness unexpectedly strikes or death robs you of time with your loved ones." Benton shifted and shrugged his shoulders. "It's called trials. Not my favorite word, but they're a reality."

She closed her eyes trying to stop the tears from spilling out.

"And Megan, it's because of our trials that we become the people that we are."

Megan opened her eyes and regarded Ben thoughtfully.

He smiled crookedly and continued solemnly. "Although, I don't know exactly what things you've suffered through, I'm impressed that you've tried to face your struggles and still remain active in church. It seems to me that you have chosen your commitment to Christ over the pain of your trials." Benton looked embarrassed, but still persisted. "Now, here's the real test for me. It's to find happiness in the small things; a fat, fluffy snowflake; a sister who loves me and thinks I'm handsome; and a car that runs no matter how old it is. What I'm trying to say is, enjoy every moment of happiness, because trials will come. Drink up the good times and keep trying to do what's right."

Peace flowed through Megan's soul. "It's been a wonderful evening. Thank you so much."

Lightheartedly, Benton quipped, "I doubt you'll ever go out with me again. We've discussed our favorite dwarf from Snow White, I've stabbed you with the corsage pin, trod on your foot, and to top the evening off, I've lectured you on your doorstep."

Megan couldn't help but smile and say exactly what she felt. "I'll go out with you again." As swiftly as her courage came, it vanished. She fled into the apartment, hastily shutting the door behind her.

Benton whistled as he walked down the stairs.

The next day was Sunday, which filled Megan with misgivings. Since the Company Gala had lasted until late into the evening, there was a good chance that she would see Ben at church. It was too soon. She wasn't ready. In her mind, Megan reviewed everything they had said and done. She could not imagine what had prompted her to be so open.

She had laughed, joked, and confided some of her most private thoughts and emotions. With a wave of relief, Megan was grateful she hadn't told him her biggest secret. The fear that flowed through her now was that if she persisted in seeing Ben, she would eventually open up and tell him everything. It was far too easy to confide in him.

She could avoid seeing Ben by staying home wrapped up in a blanket, pretending to be sick. Two things about this option bothered Megan. The deceit. The falseness of it ate at her soul like acid. Pretense was her past: covering for Scott, praying that he would change. Her whole life had been a lie. There would be no more lies.

The other part about pretending to be ill that disturbed Megan was that Ben would be concerned. He'd probably come home from church with Amber to see how she was doing. Megan could picture Ben making her a mug of steaming hot chicken soup.

As Megan dressed for church, she admitted she could not afford to miss the spiritual uplift that Sunday worship afforded. Her attendance at church, her prayers, and her scripture study were helping her to heal. These little acts seemed so bland and non-consequential, but underneath there was a slow, continuous current that moved her toward peace. In the past, she had overlooked the importance of these simple actions, but now it was different. Megan felt the power surge that lay beneath righteous commitment.

The first sight of Ben standing in the church foyer shook Megan. She was afraid of him. Ben looked up and saw her expression. Determination glinted in his eyes, along with a desire to lighten her burdens. With a purpose, Benton pushed through the crowd.

Lightly clasping her upper arm, Benton implored, "Megan, save me."

Afterward, Benton wondered if it had been divine intervention. His initial plan had been to exaggerate Ally's persistence in pursuing him. He was therefore completely astonished when he looked up and saw Ally swaying across the foyer toward him. There was no need to act panicked. Benton was terrified. Once again, he had the same irrational desire to hide in the coat closet. It was too late. Ally had already seen him.

"Please," he begged his voice piteously pathetic.

Megan had trouble not laughing. There was a mutinous, stubborn look on Ally's face. It was like a scene out of some ridiculous farce.

Megan had pity, and her hand closed over Ben's fingers. She gave him her most dazzling smile. He stood transfixed, petrified. He was in heaven. Megan was looking at him like—a tiny clink of reality snapped in place. It was all an act for Ally's benefit. Megan didn't mean it. Benton stood like a benign idiot and allowed Megan to lead him off to Gospel Doctrine Class.

Chapter Nine

Amber invited Ben and Jason over for Sunday dinner. It was not a grand affair since it had been a spur-of-the-moment decision. Rummaging through the cupboards and collecting whatever they could, the girls managed to assemble a respectable meal.

After they had finished eating, they sat around the table laughing and talking. The close, intimate circle that they created charmed and delighted Megan. She had not felt this at ease for years. Something had altered inside of her last night, but it had not altered enough to effect a permanent change. This morning she had been willing to revert back to living in a hollow shell. As she watched Jason move the salt and pepper shakers around to explain his story, Megan decided she didn't want to return to her old way of escaping.

Her heart soaked up the cuteness of Jason's ridiculous tale, the coziness of Ben and Amber's laughter, and her own wonderful sense of belonging. Ben's words from last night filled her mind. *Find happiness in the small things.* This was happiness. A radiant glow of contentment settled over Megan's features. It was as if she were having a reunion with her old friends, Peace and Joy.

Distracted by some small movement, Megan looked up from the table and met Ben's eyes. His expression seemed to be telling her that he knew what she was thinking and experiencing. Since his smile was so kind and undemanding, it reassured Megan, and thoughts of feeling threatened did not surface. She smiled back, and tranquility filling her soul.

Throughout the remainder of the afternoon, Megan continued to be an integral part of the group. It no longer seemed imperative that she conceal her past and remain aloof. Confidence and a tiny belief in herself budded and began to flower.

While Megan was experiencing these emotions, Amber watched her with confusion and surprise. She and Megan had been roommates for several months now and had never indulged in the late-night talks where roommates tell all. Instead, Megan stayed busy, distant, and cool in a way that Amber suspected was deliberate. No one was allowed into Megan's inner sanctum. The entrance was bolted and always kept carefully guarded. Yet today, in some mysterious way, Megan had cracked open the door and was allowing little rays of light to filter in.

Amber was digesting this significant change when she inadvertently stumbled on another piece of this intriguing puzzle. She turned to ask Benton a question and caught an unobstructed view of his face. It was almost as if she were seeing her brother for the first time, he looked so different. Although he had always been happy in a quiet, gentle way, now his happiness was resplendent. For a moment, Amber chuckled inwardly over the old-fashioned term. Resplendent seemed like the only appropriate word to describe the change in Benton's appearance.

She whispered, "Ben," in amazement. His gaze reluctantly shifted to Amber. Slowly the glorious illumination faded and left Ben's eyes the usual brown-sugar color. He smiled. He was the same old Benton she had grown up with, her mellow, absent-minded brother. For a moment longer, Amber stared at him, unable to forget the intensity she had seen warming his eyes.

"Hey, kiddo, where are you?" Ben softly touched Amber's arm. "You called my name."

"I did." Amber forced her mind back to the present. "We're having a party next Friday night, here at our place."

Megan glanced up, surprised. She and Amber had not discussed throwing a party.

"Can you come?" Amber asked.

"Not on Friday night, I need to get an exam written." Benton smiled, "Maybe some other time."

"We could change the party to Saturday if you could make it," Amber encouraged, hoping to promote the relationship she saw developing. Losing a roommate no longer seemed so important.

"I could come on Saturday," Benton confirmed.

"Great." Amber was thoroughly delighted with herself. It was time her brother found someone special. That other girl from years ago was going to fade fast with Megan Spencer around.

"I'll pull out the old sleeping bag and throw it on the couch for you," Jason cheerfully offered.

"That sounds good," Benton rose and smoothed the front of his slacks. "I should be going. I need to get back and take care of some things."

They all stood and moved toward the living room. Amber's mind was racing frantically. "Hey, Jason, why don't you come back into the kitchen and help me scrounge up a care package to send home with Ben."

Jason followed Amber obligingly. Amber stopped in the kitchen doorway and snuck one quick peek at Benton. He winked at her.

"That was a little contrived, don't you think?" Megan tilted her head and looked up at Ben.

"Amber's strength was never subtlety," Benton chuckled. "I think she wants us to have a private moment together."

Megan looked anxiously toward the kitchen. "It's because of the Ally situation that Amber imagines there's something between us." When Ben didn't respond, Megan glanced back up at him. For the first time his mild, unhurried manner was irritating. Ben simply looked at her and waited. Megan's irritation grew. She wanted him to say something. Finally, Megan impatiently suggested, "We should tell her we're only friends."

"I wouldn't recommend it."

Megan eyed him suspiciously. "Why not?"

"I think it is Amber's most hated phrase. She's liable to go off on one of her little tirades about how that is the most worthless phrase in our LDS society." Ben's lips quirked up in amusement.

"Why is that so funny?" Megan was not particularly entertained.

"You won't like it," Ben warned, his eyes sparkling with humor.

"Try me." Megan commanded not realizing how far she was straying from her usual behavior.

"Amber's roommates always say, 'We're only friends,' right before they get engaged."

Megan's mouth dropped open. Benton chuckled. "You have very nice teeth." Megan snapped her mouth shut while Ben went right on laughing.

She gave him a disgusted look and quietly demanded, "Then what do we do?"

"Not a thing."

"Nothing?" Megan was clearly dissatisfied. "But I have to live with her."

"If you're so worried, explain to her in detail about Ally and the list. She might not have understood the day we told her."

"All right, that sounds good."

Benton smiled even wider.

"What's that cheesy smile for?" Megan demanded.

"For someone who never told anyone anything, you've come a long way in a few months," Benton waited for Megan's reaction. When it came, it was surprising.

Instead of defending herself or trying to cover up her past withdrawn behavior, Megan met Ben's eyes squarely. "I have, haven't I?"

Benton knew he shouldn't do it, but he had to touch her. A kiss would send her running like a terrified animal. He couldn't afford that, so he leaned forward and smoothed a strand of silken hair off her porcelain cheek.

Benton was so moved by the single stroke of her skin that he almost didn't catch Megan's next words. "Thank you. I haven't had a friend for a long time." Benton felt a heavy weight press against his heart, crushing his dream.

Unaware of the strength of Ben's emotions, Megan blithely continued on. "Both you and Amber have been so wonderful."

Words would not formulate in Benton's mind. He stood stiff, trying to adjust to this major setback. It was like a bad joke. Here he was, the friend, when he wanted so much more.

One thing Benton had always been was patient. Momentarily this character trait had failed him, but it immediately returned. He nodded, dropped the hand that wanted to encircle her waist, and waited.

That night Megan did something she had promised herself she would never do again. It was silly and endangered her emotional health. The day she had packed up her belongings and moved to Boston, she had slid one picture of Scott into the side pocket of her luggage. She had known at the time that it was a stupid thing to do, but had done it anyway. The photo had lain there untouched for months. Tonight it called to her.

Something about spending the afternoon and evening with Ben, Amber, and Jason had ignited a need in Megan to see Scott's face one more time. She dug through her closet, shoving her clothes to the side so she could reach the spot where she'd pushed her luggage to the back. While locating the suitcase with the article in it, Megan chastened herself. Repeating over and over again the futility of looking at his picture, she still continued her quest.

There was no letup of this strange urgency until she was sitting on the floor and staring into his printed face. His dark brown hair and shimmering almost-black eyes looked so good to her. How could she have forgotten how handsome he was? He looked absolutely perfect, exactly like he had the day she'd knelt across the altar from him. Megan remembered the hope and the excitement. Everything white, everything pure. There relationship had been untainted by things that were to come later, things that Megan had not expected, things she had taken a long time to understand and believe.

How could this have happened? Why had she felt the Spirit telling her that it was right to marry Scott? Why hadn't she seen the signs? Why had she believed so willingly everything Scott told her?

Through a mist of tears, memories flowed through Megan's mind.

She was wandering out of her and Scott's kitchen and into their small living area. She had heard the doorbell and wondered who had come to visit. Scott was standing with his back to Megan in the open doorway. A young law student who was in several of their classes was saying something intently to Scott. Megan couldn't make out the words, but the whole situation made her feel uneasy. The woman handed Scott a folder while at the same time he dug out his wallet and extended some bills. His voice was clear and appreciative as he said, "Thanks. I couldn't do this without you."

The young woman looked down at the bills she had taken. "This is too much."

"You deserve it," Scott insisted.

"Are you sure?" she looked up at Scott in that way women always did. It felt like a chunk of Megan's heart was being sliced off.

She wanted to storm across the room, to slam the door shut, and to demand why this girl was coming to their apartment. Instead, she covered her emotions and called out in a perfectly calm voice, "Hi."

Both their heads turned to look at Megan with surprise. There was a startled, guilty look on the woman's face that immediately made Megan shiver and feel queasy. She braced her hand on the back of the couch and attempted to appear normal.

"You know Tracy," Scott confidently swung the door wider. "She just came by to drop some things off."

Megan couldn't help it. Her eyebrows lifted skeptically and her fingers dug into the fabric on the camelback sofa.

"She was correcting one of my papers." He said it coolly and as if it had no great significance. His casual dismissal of the situation

made a heavier wave of nausea wash through her. Scott no longer asked her to look over his papers. The camaraderie and assistance they had shown each other in the first year of law school had vanished. Megan remembered when she and Scott had spent hours with their heads together going over the sentences, the ideas, and the presentations of their arguments and proposals.

The loss of these precious and enjoyable moments wounded Megan deeply. She had so little time with Scott anymore and now he had chosen to spend time elsewhere. The intense pain made tears sting her eyes. She hated it when she cried, especially in front of Scott. He never allowed her to forget that crying made her eyes puffy and turned them a disgusting, blotchy red. With an inner strength that she seemed to be drawing on more and more each day, Megan maintained a calm expression and even uttered a few appropriate words.

Scott insisted that Tracy had just been leaving. Cheerfully false good-byes were exchanged before Scott closed the door.

Megan erupted, all constraint worn thin. "Why did you pay her?"

Scott dropped his hand to his side. "I don't get it. What's the big deal?"

"What did you pay her for?" Megan's voice was as deathly cold as it had been volcanically hot a second before. Control had returned, freezing, mindlessly cold.

"I told you. What is this? An inquisition?" Scott flung himself down on a chair. "She checked over my paper."

"But usually we all check over each other's papers. It's what we all do as study partners, and there's never any money involved," Megan pointed out in a voice that was too quiet and controlled to be normal.

"All right, I didn't want to embarrass Tracy. But she's having a hard time right now. She's separated from her boyfriend, and he won't give her any money for her kid." Scott turned his most charming smile on Megan. "Sweetheart, I don't understand why you get so upset every time I try to help someone out. I'm just being a good priesthood holder."

It didn't feel right, didn't taste right. Scott was out of his chair and across the room. His arms pulled Megan close. Pressing her head to his shoulder, Scott whispered, "It's okay, honey. Tell me what the problem is?"

"We never have any time together anymore. Why don't you let me proofread your papers like you used to?"

"I've been trying to give you a break. I know school has been getting to you. I hoped not doing my papers would take some of the pressure off you. Let's go out tonight. You need to get away."

And of course the next day a dozen red roses had been delivered to Megan with Scott's name scrawled across the card.

Megan pulled the edge of her sleeve down and gently wiped the tears off Scott's picture. She was about to place it back in the suitcase when the thought of red roses became overwhelming. She could almost smell their strong scent. Memories of how a dozen red roses had been delivered after each of Scott's indiscretions seared Megan's heart. Suddenly she wanted to scream and throw things. "Roses aren't really red," she cried, disillusioned. In her mind, Megan saw full fragrant blooms tied together with glittering ribbon and dangling cards written with a profusion of lies. Seeing beyond the artificiality of what red roses were supposed to signify, Megan whispered, "They don't symbolize love and faithfulness. It's all lies and distortion. Roses aren't red."

Along with the falling tears an intense anger boiled within her and rolled like lava down to her trembling fingertips. Her hands took over. They tore and tore again until Scott's perfect face lay in tiny pieces at her feet.

Chapter Ten

All week Benton kept remembering standing at Megan's front door, wanting to hold her close to him, but knowing he had to wait. The following Saturday morning as Benton drove toward Boston, he was wondering how long he ought to wait. Since last Sunday, he had done a lot of thinking and praying. He wanted some assurances that the risk he was about to take would be worth it. Unfortunately, the Spirit seemed particularly illusive.

Why is it when you pray and pray for an answer that the Spirit sometimes plays hide and seek? And why at other times when you don't particularly want an answer, the Holy Ghost bolts one down to you? Ben shook his head and remembered how he hadn't even prayed about Ally. He had hoped and thought things might work out. Her lack of commitment and style of dress bothered him, but he had felt like that could change. Besides, she had other qualities that attracted him, like her crazy sense of humor and the way she appreciated everything they did together. She thought of fun things to do like swinging in the park at midnight, and dancing in the rain. At the same time, Ally was well educated and thrived in the academic world, which Ben was certain he couldn't live without.

Things seemed to be progressing nicely when suddenly, in the middle of this hopeful relationship, the Spirit had firmly manifested itself. She was not for him. It was followed by a series of troubling thoughts, one of which Benton had voiced to Megan. Ally would not raise their children in the manner Benton desired.

That answer had been clear. But what about now? Was he wasting his time and putting himself out when it would be more consistent with his nature to sit back and do nothing? Would he be creating new problems? Megan had a fragile appearance that bothered Benton. He was unwilling to take a chance on pursuing her unless he had some strong spiritual assurances.

It was on the outskirts of Amherst, Massachusetts, when he noticed it. He slammed on the brakes and skidded to a halt. In an afterthought, Benton realized his stupidity and darted a fearful glance in the rearview mirror. Thank heavens the road was deserted this early on a Saturday morning. All he needed was to be hit from behind.

With more care this time, Benton reversed his car and turned into the weedy driveway. He stared at the steep, pitched roof, at the arched windows, and at the riot of wild rose bushes valiantly sending their leaves forth in hopes of spring. The whole place was a mess, run-down and unkempt. It would take a fortune, or hours of work to restore the little cottage. Actually, the more Benton looked at the house, the more he reconsidered his first impression. The house was a good size, a family home.

Benton switched off the ignition and stared at the cottage. A second later, he slowly opened the car door and got out. There was a flagstone walkway that was so overgrown with weeds it was difficult to see the individual stones. He took a few steps down the path and stopped.

A scent of fragrant peace whispered around him. Benton closed his eyes and savored the feeling. The most beautiful images flooded his mind. He knew they weren't real, but it was as if he was seeing the future. The door of the cottage burst open. A little girl with a tangle of light brown curls came tumbling out, followed by an even smaller girl. The two children came dancing down the neatly trimmed path, giggling and smiling. They stopped in front of Benton and reached their arms up to him, calling out a joyous "Daddy!"

The blare of a horn caused Benton to snap his head around toward the driveway. An ancient pickup truck was parked behind his car and an older gentleman was climbing out of it. He didn't look pleased and curtly yelled, "You looking for somebody?"

Benton felt something warm on his cheek and quickly wiped it away. He stepped back towards his car and faced the man, "I'm sorry. I was just looking at the house."

The man's eyes narrowed as he stared closely at Ben, "Why?"

Still thinking about what he had seen in his mind, Benton answered, "It looks like a nice house to raise children in."

"You think so?"

"Yeah." Benton smiled, thinking of the two little girls running down the path towards him.

"Ellie would like that." The older man's face lost some of its harshness, but he continued to stare at Ben with an intent, appraising look. "It's pretty run-down."

Benton nodded, looking once more at the straggly grass, the healthy weeds, and the determined roses. The older man followed Ben's gaze. "You like rose bushes?"

"Yes." *And little girls running out of the house, down the walkway*, he thought.

"Ellie loved roses. she had a dozen different kinds blooming all over the place. Sometimes I come over here and try to do a little gardening, but mostly I just sit here and remember how it was."

"It must have been beautiful." Ben tried to picture the yard covered with roses.

"It was." He gazed out across the yard and then extended his hand, "I'm Mitch Brown."

"Ben Kilgallen."

Mitch nodded and then said, "I love this place. I really should come out here more often and work in the yard. My wife would love that. It would get me out of the house and out of her way.

She keeps trying to make me go into town and play Bingo or some other fool game. I'd rather come here." After a short pause he added, "I was hoping someday to fix up the place, make it look like it did in the old days."

"That would be good."

"Do you ever watch those TV shows on Saturday mornings where they fix up old houses? I love to watch the way they remodel everything."

"I've watched a few of those shows with my dad," Ben quietly admitted.

"With your dad," Mitch repeated with a little catch in his voice. Clearing his throat he stated, "Well, I love those shows. All my life, I've done construction jobs on the side. There's something satisfying about building and repairing things."

As far as conversations went, this one didn't seem to amount to much. Yet, underneath it all, a strange strand of compatibility was forming. The older man rubbed his receding hairline and asked, "You want to see the house?"

Benton nodded. Both men moved down the unkempt path towards the front door. The older man's loneliness permeated the air as the key turned in the rusty lock. He repeated needlessly, "It didn't used to look like this."

"I know," Benton couldn't get the picture of neat flower boxes, fresh paint, and two little girls skipping down the path out of his head. "Did you and Ellie have little girls?" Benton irrelevantly asked.

"Heck no!" The man erupted into laughter, "Ellie was my sister. Myra and I live in town."

Benton wasn't sure what to think. The image of the girls had been so real. While Benton toured the house, Mitch began to reminisce. "Me and Ellie, we grew up in this house. It was a good life. We were happy here." The older man's memories made the chunks of plaster on the floor and the worn floorboards seem less pitiful. During their walk through the house, Benton learned a variety of things.

Ellie had taught second grade and loved children. She was

a spinster and had taken over the house after their parents died. Caring for the house and teaching school were Ellie's passions until cancer ended her life.

At the conclusion of their tour, Ben and the older gentleman stopped in the living room and stood, lost in their own private thoughts. Fingering the old-fashioned woodwork around one of the windows, Mitch quietly told Ben, "I tried to get my oldest son to buy the place and come live here. But he's too caught up in the big city. There's not enough excitement and nightlife here for him. He thinks it's dull and gets bored a half hour after he gets here. Lately he doesn't come that much anymore. I guess Amherst is too quiet for him."

"Amherst is quiet, but I like it." Ben gazed at the hardwood floors of the living room and thought of how much money and effort it would take to get this house into shape. The front room floor wasn't too bad, but it would still take a lot of money and a lot of time. Sometimes money and time were worth it when . . .

Mitch dropped his hand from the woodwork, "You live around here?"

"I rent a room from some friends in Amherst. I teach at the University." A strong peaceful feeling warmed Benton's heart. He heard himself asking, "Have you ever thought of selling this house?"

The old man's eyes penetrated deep into Benton's soul, "I always wanted to keep the house in the family. That's why I never sold it. This house is full of good memories for me. We had parties for the Baptist church in our backyard. that's where I met Myra. And the boys played here with Ellie when they were little."

Ben nodded, understanding, but feeling disappointed at the same time.

Mitch seemed to be struggling with some strong emotions. He mindlessly rubbed his thinning hair. "This is also where Ellie died. She looked pretty bad at the end."

Benton didn't know what to say. He nodded, thinking how hard it must have been for the older man to watch his sister die.

Mitch seemed to shake off his melancholy past and force

himself to return to the present, "There are a lot of memories here," he said nodding his head, "but Myra says the house is only getting more run down."

Benton felt the two little girls again. It was as if they were dancing around the room, laughing and playing. Behind the girls, the walls were clean, neat, and homelike. Nothing elegant, just cozy and warm.

"Houses should be for children," Benton breathed out, desiring a family so badly his chest ached.

"You have kids?"

"No, I wish I did."

"Ellie would have liked you."

"I think I would have liked her too."

A man was supposed to want sons, wasn't he? Benton trudged up the stairs to Amber and Megan's condo, shaking his head. It had been the oddest day of his life. The image of two little girls had plagued and delighted him all day. Never before had he had an experience like this. It was almost as if he had seen the future.

For quite a long while now, Benton had wanted to settle down and marry. Those two little girls, who danced circles around in his mind, should be his. Life had definitely not followed his time line. Benton stood ringing the bell and chuckling. Maybe God had not received his memo. His amusement died away the instant the door opened.

"Why hello!" Ally's thick brown hair swung over her shoulder, and her face lit with delight. "What a wonderful surprise. I didn't know you were in town again."

"Yeah, I'm here."

Ally leaned against the doorway barring his entrance and prolonging their conversation. Only Benton had no conversation.

"We've been having so much fun. We're playing a group game."

Benton's only response was a weak twist of his lips.

Ally instantly became serious. "You know, we never talk anymore. I miss it."

Ben did not want to hurt her, but he didn't want to encourage her either. He chose to remind her of their past conversations. "Things have changed. Remember, we've talked about it."

"True, but you are always coming up for the weekends. It must mean something," Ally persisted.

"I like to see my sister," Benton flatly stated.

With great relief, Benton heard someone call out, "Ally, you're blocking the door. Let whoever's out there come in."

Benton pushed forward. At the last instant, Ally gave way. As he fled across the room, Benton's main goal became escape. He headed immediately for his sister and gave her a loving hug. Amber squeezed him back giggling, "You look terrified."

"I am."

"It's not good. Look natural," Amber commanded, her eyes sparkling with good humor.

"Where's Megan?"

"Your little buddy in crime had to work tonight," Amber cheerfully informed him, watching for his reaction.

"On a Saturday night?"

"You worked last night writing up some kind of exams. I believe that was Friday. Hot date night, remember?"

"All right, she's working," Benton grumpily agreed.

Amber took pity on him. "They've set a court date, and it's sooner than Megan anticipated. Listen, if I distract Ally maybe you can slip into the office and hide out." Amber scrunched her mouth to one side and suggested, "This is becoming a habit. Why don't you tell Ally it's over?"

Benton stiffened and crabbed, "I have at multiple times and in multiple places. She doesn't want to hear it."

Megan had forgotten about the party until she reached her front door. Laughter and energy bubbled out of the apartment, greeting her as she walked in. It was not pleasant. Her mind and body were so exhausted that she couldn't handle company right then. She immediately decided to change her clothes, sneak into the office, and unwind by watching a movie.

By some miraculous means, Megan made it to her room, slipped into casual clothes, and picked up a DVD. She was furtively making her way to her study when Amber stopped her. Shoving a plate of food into Megan's free hand, Amber quietly informed her, "There's a terrified beast cornered in your office. Feed him and he's your friend for life."

Momentarily, Megan was puzzled until her eyes landed on Ally who sat dispiritedly on the end of the couch. The poor girl looked as if she were about to cry. "I think she really likes him. Ally obviously doesn't realize it's over, does she?"

"It doesn't look like it." Amber glanced toward Ally, "She's bright, determined, and ambitious. Unfortunately, all that is focused on Ben. Poor boy, He swears he's told her no repeatedly."

"I think he might have," Megan sympathized as she headed for the office cautiously balancing the plate of food.

Benton had strategically positioned himself so he couldn't be seen from the doorway. He was not taking any chances as he watched the door open.

"Oh, Beast, are you in here?" Megan teased taking several steps into the room. Benton kicked the door shut. "Ah," Megan cried mockingly, "Amber said there was a terrified beast cornered in here."

Benton was about to protest and defend his maligned manhood when he saw the plate. He hadn't eaten since breakfast and could smell Amber's chicken enchiladas. The protest died on his lips. "You must be Beauty if you've brought me food."

"And a DVD," Megan slipped the DVD out from under her arm.

"*Sense and Sensibility*," Benton groaned.

"I'm a great Jane Austin fan," even as she said it, Megan marveled at herself. This was how she had been years ago: open, talkative, and excited about life. Soaring high on this delightful sensation, Megan forgot she was exhausted. "It's the men in those cute knee pants that I really love."

Benton placed a hand on his head dramatically. "I believe I'm going to faint."

"Oh, this is great," Megan laughed. "I've never seen a grown man faint before."

"Then prepare yourself."

"Wait! Before you faint, I need to know why. Is it because I mentioned men's knees?"

"No, although that was really deplorable. In reality, I'm starving to death," Benton eyed Megan critically before formally announcing, "and you, madame, still hold the plate."

Benton faked a backward faint, only he misjudged the position of the overstuffed chair. He crashed onto the floor and went down with a surprised grunt. Megan quickly set the plate down and bent over him. Her concern grew as she noticed his eyes were closed and he wasn't moving.

"Ben, are you okay?"

Benton didn't know what kind of perfume she was wearing, but it certainly smelled good. He tried to lie perfectly still, but was afraid his nose was going to twitch.

"Ben, answer me."

Benton cracked open one eye. She was very close. Oh, this was delicious!

Quickly snapping his eye shut, he moaned. Megan leaned closer. A length of her hair brushed his cheek, and he was lost. As if his arms had a will of their own, they circled around Megan and pulled her close.

He wanted to kiss her, but knew he shouldn't. So he held her tight and laughed.

Megan beat against his chest with her fists. "You sneaky, underhanded beast!"

Benton loosened his grip and demanded, "Before I let you go, you must promise, no *Sense and Sensibility*."

Megan stiffened, "Absolutely not! This is my house and my office and I'll watch whatever I want."

Benton pulled her back tight against his chest and smartly quipped, "I see. What you're really saying is that it's been a long time since a man has held you and you've forgotten how wonderful it can be."

The teasing atmosphere between them evaporated in a hot, humid mist and was replaced by crackling tension. Benton released her and sat up. Megan scooted toward the door, rested her head back, and closed her eyes. Benton thought maybe he should apologize, but he wasn't sorry. Megan had felt marvelous in his arms. He could say he was just playing around, but it wasn't true. Lying to her was something Benton didn't feel right about doing. Unable to think of any acceptable alternative, Benton patiently watched and waited.

The shadows in the room along with Megan's usual reserve made it difficult to discern her emotions. Megan's eyes were closed, so reading anything there was impossible. Benton wanted her to speak, to tell him how she felt. Only silence greeted his desires.

Without a word, he rose and picked up his dinner. Ten minutes ago, he had been starving. Now Benton toyed with the enchiladas and salad on his plate and had trouble forcing himself to swallow. It disturbed him that he had upset Megan. Worse still, he was irritated with himself for not being patient and giving her the time she needed.

Eventually Megan opened her eyes and slowly stood. Benton tried to think of something to say. Feeling like an idiot, he mumbled, "Amber makes good Mexican food."

Megan smiled weakly. "When she cooks, it's great. I'm not fond of her mac and cheese."

Benton forced a laugh and thought, *So we're not going to talk about it.* He offered the only apology he honestly could. "I didn't mean to offend you."

"I know," she lifted her hands listlessly. "Ben, I have a lot of things I'm trying to make sense of in my life right now."

Benton nodded, thinking that he too had a lot of things he was trying to make sense out of in his life, mainly Megan.

"Well then, I don't think you want to watch *Sense and Sensibility*, so what would you like to watch?"

"*Sense and Sensibility* is fine," Ben shrugged and fingered the edges of his plate. "I should probably go anyhow."

Megan looked guilty. "It's still really early. You're welcome to stay. I don't want to run you off."

"No, it's okay," Ben balanced his fork on the plate. "I'll take this back into the kitchen and say good-bye to Amber."

"Are you sure?"

"Yeah, I need to go."

"No, I mean about running the plate into the kitchen? It'd be safer if you bolted for the front door."

Benton's eyes widened. It was obvious that he had forgotten about Ally. "She's a nice girl, but I'll let you take my plate back to the kitchen. Thanks."

The distressed look on Ben's face made Megan want to laugh. Forgetting her recent discomfort, she cheekily offered, "Do you want me to check and make sure the coast is clear?"

Benton gave her a disgusted look and shook his head. "I think I can handle this." He pulled his jacket off the back of the chair and slipped out the door.

Megan watched him leave. She was half relieved and half disappointed. If he had stayed a moment longer, she might have lost control and told him everything. Confiding in Ben would be a disaster. Megan's previous experiences in seeking understanding had not been positive. Once she'd broken down and attempted to ask her sister for advice. Kristy had only laughed and scolded her. "Scott's a dream," she had said. "Naturally he has a few faults, but he's so handsome and so fun that you should just forget about the little things." Later, after the divorce, Megan had tried to explain to her mother and to her sister. Both women had shaken their heads and seemed unable to believe that Scott was anything less than perfect. Kristy had become disgusted with Megan and yelled, "You're crazy to let him go. You wouldn't know Mr. Perfect if he stood right in front of you."

Would Ben yell too? Probably not, but most likely he would

say, "Divorces are caused by two people." No, it was better to remain silent. Bishop Carden had been the only one who had listened and understood. Megan remembered the sad, pained expression on his face when she had told him how Scott had become cruel and petty when she had consistently refused to watch R-rated movies with him. After Scott had angrily inserted his latest inappropriate DVD in the player, he had pivoted around and glared at Megan in an arrogant and threatening manner. Without a word, Megan rose to leave.

Every time before, Scott had allowed Megan to exit the room without any more argument, but not that terrible night. Before she made it safely to the door, Scott had swiftly come up behind her and grabbed her arm. His fingers had dug cruelly into the soft flesh underneath and twisted and pinched until she had begged him to stop. Along with the pain, Megan had been forced to hear the petty, filthy things that flew out of his mouth. After this vile tirade had ended, Scott had shoved her away like she were a worthless piece of trash. The pathetic part, Megan concluded, was that this was not a single, one time loss of control. If only Scott had been truly sorry and repented of his one time abuse. Instead, it had become a repeat pattern, recurring with increased regularity. There was always the petty pinching, the cruel words, and then, of course, the roses.

Throughout this terrible time, Bishop Carden had supported and encouraged her while he had continued to work with Scott. The bishop seemed to hate what Scott was doing, yet he was like a loving father: working with Scott, talking with Scott, and encouraging Scott. Many times Bishop Carden had warned Scott and advised him that his actions were abusive and that they were not worthy of the kind of man Scott really was. For a time, the bishop's words would always have an effect. Unfortunately, the shortness of Scott's periods of repentance was a pitiful thing.

Megan pushed all these disturbing thoughts out of her mind and tried to focus on the positive. Bishop Carden had counseled her to be patient and cheerful, despite her ordeal. Megan had listened and tired to incorporate his advice. Even though it was hard and always seemed to require more than she felt she had to give, she persisted. Cheerfulness in the face of her trails appeared to be an impossible request. Yet the more Megan prayed for a change of heart and the strength to endure and overcome, the more the Spirit had slowly lifted her.

A sense of gratitude flowed through her, rinsing away some of the disappointment and anger she felt. The Lord had not abandoned her, although her path had been stony and hard. She tried to think charitably of Scott and was able to appreciate the fact that he was still living in their old ward. Scott needed Bishop Carden's wise and caring counsel.

And what did she need, Megan wondered? In the first few weeks after her separation from Scott, Megan had needed the calm understanding of Bishop Carden. The Bishop in her new ward was kind, but he lacked the deep understanding that Bishop Carden had gained by standing beside her throughout her turbulent marriage. Her new bishop was a good man, but he didn't know her history. to repeat her whole story to him was too painful to even be considered. So Megan merely remained silent and spent her time pondering the things Bishop Carden had taught her. With a smile, Megan remembered making appointments with Bishop Carden even though he wasn't her bishop anymore. The hours she had spent talking to him on those few occasions had been wonderful.

"What else did I need?" Megan asked herself. "I needed my family to believe in me." As she looked back at her past, she saw that much of the fault lay with her. The pain of her divorce was packed so tightly inside of her that it was hard to share. When her mother and Kristy had defended Scott, all Megan had to do was tell them that he was emotionally and physically abusive and that he was addicted to pornography. They would have seen through Scott's fake appearance and known the truth. Why hadn't she ever said the words that would make her mother and sister understand?

Instead, she had remained silent, unwilling to admit that her marriage was a failure. Failure was something Megan had never faced before. Ever since her first day in kindergarten, school had been easy for her. She had walked through life earning awards and honors, making friends easily, and enjoying the respect which was freely showered upon her. True, she had worked hard at whatever she did, but nothing was ever insurmountable. If you continued to work hard enough, it would come to you. Law school had been the same way. Megan had control of her life. She could do it. She could be successful at whatever she chose, until Scott.

Her plans and hopes to reform Scott once she knew of his addiction had withered away. She was left a nagging, screaming shrew who had no hope and was ruled by fear. Failure hit her hard. She could not change Scott. He must do it for himself. While this was clear intellectually to Megan, emotionally she couldn't deal with her failure to make everything right. In the end, she was the one who had changed by starting to nag and complain. Megan did not like what she had become.

Even after the divorce, she had still clung to unrealistic hopes and tormenting fears. She let Scott manipulate her family without ever correcting his lies. She answered Scott's phone calls instead of not picking up when she saw his number. Megan kept close to her heart the hope that he would change, while she allowed fear to rule her actions. Fear told her that the cycle of pain would repeat over and over again. No matter what she did, it would always end the same way. Scott would offer hollow promises while she demanded and begged for proof that he had changed.

Her marriage was a failure, but worse still were her own emotions. She was embarrassed by her failure to control her thoughts and feelings. How could she explain how she had turned into a screaming fish wife when things became hopeless? It was better to remain silent and pull the tattered remnants of her self-esteem around her shoulders and sink quietly away.

All of these thoughts made Megan realize that it wasn't really her family who had withdrawn from her. Megan faced squarely that she was the one that had withdrawn from her mother and her sister. Her pride and her fear had been the companions that choked out her family. It had been too much to deal with so

Megan had walked away from her family, admitting nothing, and saying nothing to dispel the fantastic web of lies that Scott had spun. What Megan had needed was to tell her family the truth, but she had never had the courage to do it.

At least she had made one correct decision in coming to Boston. It was more than a good career move. It had allowed her to forgive herself for her stubborn pride, to grow more confident, and to reclaim her ability to make friends like Esther and Jane, and Amber and Ben. Lately, Megan had been catching glimpses of the happy, young girl she had been. Yes, Boston was absolutely right for her.

Chapter Eleven

For the next few days, Megan continued to experience emotional and spiritual ups and downs. As she stared out the glass window of her office Monday afternoon, Megan admitted that she had missed seeing Ben at church. No doubt he had gone home early Sunday morning to avoid Ally. Megan was willing to acknowledge she felt a slight twinge of disappointment at not seeing him, but she refused to admit anything more. It was too dangerous to become involved. She knew that caring could lead to pain, disillusionment, and disappointment. How many times had Scott promised it would never happen again? She had tried so hard and prayed for so many hours.

Despite the many setbacks, Scott had firmly insisted that he was going to conquer his problem. Megan had believed him, because she wanted to. The day he brought home several shopping bags full of clothing had been a nightmare that Megan still wished she could forget.

At first, it was the expense that worried her. They didn't have money for one new skirt, let alone half a dozen new outfits. As Megan held up each article of clothing, her heart felt heavier and heavier.

She did not feel comfortable with any of the clothes. They were inappropriate: too low, too tight, too short, too revealing. How many times had she told Scott that this type of clothing wasn't right? How many times had she refused to go into stores that sold this kind of apparel? Megan's head drooped and she whispered, "I can't wear these clothes. My garments."

"Are you kidding? I go out and buy you some pretty clothes, and you say you can't wear them?" Megan could feel a hideous tension rising in the room, suffocating her. She raised her hand to ward off the horrible words she knew were coming. They came anyway. "Don't you see how dumpy you are? No one dresses like you do. You're unsophisticated, and you look plain and ugly. I'm embarrassed to be seen with you. Wear these clothes and look good for a change!"

She wanted so badly to be attractive to him again, to be the center of his life instead of something so insignificant that it was always shoved to the peripheral edge. Once Scott had made her feel like she was the most beautiful woman in the world. There had been concern, glorious time spent enjoying each others' company, laughter, and a sense of well-being. If only they could return to those times, fix whatever it was that had spun them on this horrible tangent.

Lately, all their relationship consisted of was fighting. The arguing stole what little time they had together. They sat parked in front of sleazy stores and fought. When they went out to dinner, they fought over whether Scott was flirting with the waitress. They fought over the inappropriate movies Scott brought into the house. They fought even more when he pressured Megan to watch them with him. On ward temple night they fought over attending a session. Whenever a time was scheduled to attend the temple, Scott had the tendency to become sick and then miraculously heal by the following morning. It was all one long, exhausting circle of disagreement that was escalating a little faster every day.

Scott thrust the offensive clothes into Megan's arms. "Stop thinking about it and wear them. I can't stand what you've turned into. If you'd try to make our marriage work, we could be so happy. It would be like it used to be before you became so prudish."

"I can't," Megan whispered, fearing that he might grab her arm and pinch the soft flesh underneath until he left it cut and bruised.

Megan watched Scott, waiting, and praying that this time would be different.

"You can't what? You can't try to make this marriage work?" His voice was a taunting hiss as he came closer. Scott was close enough to reach out and . . .

Despite the fear that rose up like yellow bile in her throat, she couldn't compromise her standards. "I can't wear those clothes." Without much hope, she pleaded, "Scott, I'm really trying to make our marriage work, but I can't make any more compromises with what I believe in. We were married in the temple. It's what we both wanted and we made sacred covenants, promising that we would—"

"Are you going to preach to me some more? It's too bad I didn't know before I married you that you were a whiney nag on an errand from God. Instead of being some righteous little servant of the Lord, you're a bigoted woman so blinded by your own prejudice that you can't even allow me to help other people. Every time I try to show compassion and help someone you get the wrong idea and think evil things. It's because you won't dress attractively that you become insanely jealous of any woman who has her act together. Megan, you're a prude hiding your own insecurities behind your puritan clothes. It's time for you to grow up and live in the real world where real people take what they want and make themselves into something worthwhile instead of whining about everything."

Megan had backed away and slumped down on the couch. If Scott was describing the real world, she didn't want any part of it. It was so ugly and so different than the life she had envisioned on her wedding day. Scott's voice rose and his exasperation with Megan flared hotter. His tirade was fueling his out-of-control temper.

Megan shuddered, fearing what was coming next. In an effort to survive, she focused her entire being on not crying. Her self-esteem couldn't stand another round of his criticism about blotched faces and puffy eyes. Not a single tear was going to roll down her cheek, not even if he started pinching and tearing at the flesh under her arm again.

A tear dropped and smeared the legal brief she was preparing. Megan closed her eyes and thrust all the painful memories aside. She would not allow herself to think about any of this anymore.

That tragic portion of her life was over and must not influence her anymore. She was building a good life where she was starting to find serenity and security. In an effort to lighten her mood, Megan began searching for things to be grateful for. Naturally, Amber, good sweet Amber, came to mind. It had been a wonderful day when Amber had come to look at the condo.

There was also Jane and Esther. The hours that Megan had spent walking in the commons, chatting in the crowded lunchroom, or simply laughing with them were wonderfully soothing. Esther was strict and blunt, yet at the same time she cared deeply about people. Megan had observed Esther watching people and studying them until she had a good indication of what their hopes and needs were. Armed with this knowledge, Esther extended herself, reaching out to make their lives better. And Jane, well Jane made Megan want to run out and rent old movies. If Megan had the time, she'd see every movie Jane recommended. As thoughts of her friends swirled in Megan's head, the Spirit warmed her soul and sent more positive and happy thoughts for her to contemplate.

The Silverton case was another wonderful thing to focus on. It had suddenly been settled out of court with her client winning the most concessions. The firm loved her. She loved the firm. The more Megan controlled her thoughts and emphasized the positive, the more her spirits rose. By Wednesday night, when Ben called, Megan felt like she had conquered herself, the world, and everything else.

"Hi, Ben," she cheerfully answered, immediately recognizing his voice. "Amber's not here."

"I didn't call for Amber."

Megan felt like she was sixteen. Her heart thumped and hammered out of control until she remembered Ally. He needed her as protection.

"Are you still there?"

Megan swallowed and answered, "I'm here."

"I was wondering."

"Yes," Megan kept repeating to herself that he was her friend and it didn't matter if he needed her to keep Ally away.

"I thought it might be fun to visit Boston's historical sights. If you're free on Saturday, I'd like to show you around." It was Benton's turn to feel the erratic rhythm of his heart.

"That sounds like fun."

Ben couldn't believe the words he was hearing. He sighed and then hoped his sigh hadn't been loud enough for her to hear. "Great. I'll pick you up at one in the afternoon."

"All right."

"And we'll probably be out late. We'll catch a bite to eat somewhere and see Boston by night."

"So this is an all-day affair," Megan surmised.

"A history professor's tour of Boston."

"I'd love that."

"You'll be bored," Benton predicted.

"I doubt it."

"Wear comfortable shoes. We'll walk the Freedom Trail."

From that phone call on, Megan couldn't stop thinking about how beautifully everything was going. She'd successfully closed her case, had friends to enjoy, and was beginning to recapture her old, cheerful self.

The next day, Megan was still bubbling over with enthusiasm as she rushed down to the lobby to meet Jane and Esther. Maybe in six months or a year from now, she'd be able to return to Utah and smile sweetly at everyone. This time it would be real and not rehearsed.

Esther stood tapping her foot impatiently, watching the elevator doors. As soon as Megan stepped out, Esther's eyes started scrutinizing. A slow, steady smile spread across her face.

Megan walked up to Esther. "Where's Jane?" she asked.

"She's sick today." Esther pivoted toward the front doors. "Shall we go?"

As they strolled in the Commons, Megan enjoyed the spring blossoms and flowering trees. "It's so beautiful," she cried, delighted with everything she saw.

"Pretty much the same as yesterday," Esther's lips quirked

up at the corners and her eyes were laughing. "Seems to me that something has happened to you."

"Well, I won my case, of course."

"That was on Monday," Esther succinctly reminded Megan.

"It was," Megan agreed touching a hanging blossom, "but I'm still riding the high. Life is great."

Esther shook her head and dragged a carton of yogurt out of her bag. "Again, I ask, what happened yesterday?"

"It's a combination of a lot of things," Megan insisted as she too pulled out her lunch. "Shall we sit by the pond?"

"Too noisy." Esther pointed to another bench beneath a large, budding tree. "Over there. I want to talk."

After they seated themselves, Esther prodded, "What combination of things have you lit up like a Christmas tree?"

"I thought Jews didn't have Christmas trees."

"Jews see Christmas trees even if they don't have them! Although some less traditional families do have Christmas trees, only they call them Hanukkah trees. Of course we never had one." Esther's eyes narrowed as if she realized she'd been sidetracked. "You still haven't answered my question. What combination of things?"

"Like I said, the Silverton case went beautifully," Megan stalled.

"It's that man you went to the Charity Gala with, isn't it?"

Megan couldn't believe she was blushing. Never one to miss important details, Esther looked smug. "Yes, I thought so. You're going to think that I'm becoming like Jane," Esther sighed, "but there was something about him. I noticed it at the dance."

"Ben's a good man," Megan quietly stated while she was searching for some way to change the subject.

"There's a spiritual sense to him," Esther fiddled with her spoon and made a face. "Jane believes in good looks and romance, but I believe in something else."

Megan's attention was captivated; her desire to switch topics was instantly forgotten. She turned her head to get a better view of Esther's expression.

"There is this feeling that your friend, Ben, generates," Esther confided. "The first time I saw Norman, I felt the same kind of . . ." Esther shrugged, but couldn't keep a smile from creeping onto her lips. "Norman was in the synagogue and there was a feeling of goodness about him."

The presence of the Spirit whispered softly around Megan. She thought of Ben and felt like he was a righteous man. "I think I know what you mean."

"Jane is a wonderful woman," Esther defended their mutual friend. "However, she is not a religious person, or I guess it would be more accurate to say that Jane doesn't look for religious answers."

"I understand," Megan said and then added her own insight. "Jane lives by good principles, but she isn't too concerned about the origin of those principles."

"That's an accurate analysis." Esther took a spoonful of yogurt. "Now, back to what I'm most interested in. Are you seeing Ben this weekend?"

Megan lifted her shoulders and admitted, "Yes. We're going sightseeing. He's a history professor and loves historical sights."

"And you like him?"

"Of course I like him. I wouldn't go out with him if I didn't like him."

"More than like him?" Esther probed, her eyes shining like black obsidian.

Megan stared straight forward and refused to comment.

"Well, you should!" Esther advised rather strongly. "He seems like the homebody, cottage-in-the-country type. I wouldn't pass him up if I were you."

Megan persisted in refusing to respond, but her mind was relentlessly considering Esther's words. After a few seconds of waiting, Esther whispered quietly, "There was another man wasn't there?"

Megan was startled. Without thinking, she answered, "Yes."

The yes was so painfully uttered that Esther paused and her face softened with compassion. After allowing the silence to linger long enough to give Megan a chance to control her emotions, Esther part asked, part stated, "He wasn't a good man, was he?"

The tears stung Megan's eyes. She had gone from euphoric back to Scott. She looked at Esther unable to speak and nodded her head affirmatively. Putting a motherly arm around Megan's shoulder, Esther squeezed gently. "It's going to be okay." After a few seconds more of loving silence, Esther added, "But you have to learn to trust again."

Long after their discussion Megan found herself still contemplating Esther's advice. She couldn't quite accept it. Caring for someone too much was threatening and left you vulnerable. Life was simpler if you remained uninvolved and aloof. Things passed you by and fell around you, but they never came near enough to hurt you. Esther did not understand, although Megan had to admit that some of Esther's comments hinted at a knowledge that was terrifying. Esther sensed things and talked about spiritual matters, which made Megan feel safe and uncomfortable in a mixed, crazy way.

These months away from Utah had profoundly affected Megan. In the past, as soon as someone like Esther had insisted on something more than a superficial friendship, Megan had immediately terminated the relationship. Yet here in Boston, Megan had accepted Esther's friendship, encouraged Jane, welcomed Amber as her roommate, and allowed Ben to become her friend. A tiny, uninvited voice prodded, "Only Ben is different." The stupid little voice irritated Megan so much that she refused to listen to it. Ben was like a brother to her.

Chapter Twelve

During the first part of their date on Saturday, Ben did little to disturb Megan's assumption that he was only her friend. His calm, steady personality buried all of her fears and doubts. They laughed and joked as they hiked the Freedom Trail. Ben told her interesting tidbits about Paul Revere as they toured his house. He shared historical insights all along the Freedom Trail and impressed her with his love of history.

As they sat in one of the pews in Old North Church, Megan turned to Ben and frankly stated, "You must be a wonderful history professor. No wonder UMASS Amherst wants you to teach full time."

Benton didn't answer. He had glanced away from Megan and was staring stoically toward the front of the historic chapel. Megan followed the direction of his vision but couldn't see anything unusual. She turned back to Ben just in time to hear his quiet, "Thank you." It all seemed a bit odd to Megan until she noticed the patch of red on Ben's neck that was rapidly spreading to his ears and cheeks.

His embarrassment only endeared him to Megan. "You're welcome," she said. She couldn't help smiling. "I wish I could take a class from you. Are you teaching any night classes this summer?"

"No, I'm not. But even if I were, it would be too far for you to drive to Amherst after work."

"Maybe. You'd flunk me anyhow," Megan joked.

With a mock serious face, Benton considered, "That would depend on if you did your homework and passed all of the tests."

"Are you a hard grader?"

"You bet." Benton's mouth widened into a smile and his eyes glittered with mischief. "Of course, I might cut you a deal."

"What do you mean by that?" Megan's eyes narrowed.

"You could do extra credit."

"What kind of extra credit did you have in mind?"

"That depends." Ben's eyes crinkled with amusement, but something in their depths made Megan uneasy. She watched him warily as he continued on. "We might—"

She couldn't let him finish. It seemed like everything was about to change. This was too dangerous. "You'd make me do extra credit reports, tons of them," she cried desperately, trying to return their relationship to a more secure plain.

"That's not what I had in mind."

"Long written reports, and oral reports to the class," Megan rushed on anxiously, "and I bet there would be those beastly fill-in-the-blank worksheets."

"Actually, I thought we'd do day trips to historical sights with your own private tutor." There was enough amused teasing in Ben's voice to slightly ease Megan's alarm. At the same time there was a little fission of attraction that sparkled and flashed between them. She wondered for a second if Ben might be telling her that he found her appealing, desirable, and worthy of his attention.

Megan wasn't sure how she felt. She only needed a friend, but the idea that Ben found her attractive on a deeper level touched some hidden, unacknowledged desire she wanted and she didn't want at the same time.

"My private tutor, huh?" she stalled.

"Sounds good to me."

"What would it cost me?" Megan realized the instant the

words left her mouth that this was the real question that was bothering her. Maybe they weren't talking about a hypothetical history class. Was he asking her to explore something deeper and possibly consider becoming involved? What would it cost her? was exactly the right question. Too much, her mind coldly warned. At the same time her heart insisted that it had been too long since anyone had made her feel special.

Megan's unguarded expression revealed her fear and confusion. The mask she normally kept tightly in place was slipping. Ben raised his eyebrows and looked at Megan with a slightly puzzled expression.

Then with a perky smile and an arrogant manner, Benton pretended to be considering her question. "The cost, let me see," Benton fingered an imaginary beard. "My time is quite valuable. And gas, there's the gas money. There's also my extensive knowledge. I know a lot of history."

A breeze of relief blew through Megan, although a little puff of disappointment lingered unobtrusively. Maybe she had misread him.

"However," Benton rambled on, "there are certain things I like. Two things come to mind right away."

"Such as?" Megan eyed him suspiciously.

"Smart women. I think you qualify, don't you?"

Megan scooted an inch or two down the pew away from Ben. "I guess so."

"I didn't think dumb girls graduated from law school."

Ignoring him, Megan asked, "What's the other thing?"

"Chocolate chip cookies."

Megan turned her head toward Ben and stared.

"You do cook, don't you?" Benton's distressed look was obviously faked. "Some intelligent women haven't a clue how to bake."

Recovering, Megan smart-mouthed, "Like Ally?"

"Well, yes! I hate to malign her, but her chocolate chip cookies were so hard and tasteless that I could not continue the relationship," Benton exclaimed with pathetic insincerity.

"I'll bet Ally never even baked you chocolate chip cookies," Megan skeptically challenged.

"Chocolate chip cookies, raisin cookies, brownies, gourmet meals. I almost married her for her beef stroganoff, but I remembered her chocolate chips cookies just in time," Benton sighed forlornly.

"You lie," Megan accused, laughing.

"In a church?" Benton looked around the alcoves and walls of Old North Church. "Shh, one of those marble busts will hear you. Speaking of cookies, there's this wonderful cookie place in Quincy Market. Let's go." Grabbing her hand, Benton pulled Megan off the bench and headed for the door.

Quincy Market was a long, narrow, indoor corridor of food vendors. A thousand different smells assaulted Megan's nose, at the same time a thousand different sounds bombarded her ears. Quincy Market was noisy and chaotic, but fascinating and stimulating.

Benton quickly located his cookie shoppe and bought Megan the most delectable chocolate chip cookies. She could barely hear Ben when he teased, "Only one. It'll spoil your dinner."

For a while, they simply browsed the corridor, examining all the different variety of foods available. Every kind of meal imaginable was arrayed in a casual but vibrant style. Over the noise of the market Megan heard Ben ask, "Do you want to eat here or find some place quieter?"

Megan lifted her shoulders indicating her willingness to comply with whatever he preferred.

"All right then, if you don't mind, I'd like a little peace and quiet."

Megan nodded, her pulses rioting, because at the last second, Ben had cupped his hand to her ear and whispered his decision. For an instant, Megan was angered by her reaction to his close proximity. In the next second, she convinced herself that it was the excitement and vitality of Quincy Market that elevated pulse and sent shivers down her spine. Ben was only her friend.

Later, as they lingered over a candlelight dinner, Megan was not so certain. It wasn't their sparkling conversation that made Megan reconsider, but their companionable silence. Ben had not been very talkative over dinner. He appeared satisfied to lean back in his chair and savor his meal. Megan had found it restful not to be bothered with the burden of maintaining an inconsequential flow of chatter. She ate, observed their fellow diners, and gave herself up to the cozy, mellow atmosphere.

"I like it here," Ben softly informed her.

"I do too," Megan marveled that no more communication seemed necessary. She didn't feel pushed or stressed. It was a wonderfully relaxing sensation, so different from her past relationship. With Scott, she could always feel his critical comparisons and waited nervously for him to point out her most recently discovered fault. She remembered that she didn't stand up straight enough or her hair wasn't cut in a style that Scott thought was attractive. Tonight, with Ben, Megan felt a new emotion: pure contentment. Ben was satisfied with her. She didn't have to be proving her worth and fighting her own insecurity.

Ben asked if she'd like dessert.

Megan chuckled and held up her bag of unfinished cookies.

"Do you share?" he asked.

Megan peeked into the sack and paused as if she were counting cookies. "It's hard," she confessed, "but my mom taught me it's rude not to."

Benton looked down his nose at her and made a disgusted sound in his throat. Megan knew that he knew there were at least half a dozen cookies left. "I'll hold you to that," he threatened.

Since the spring weather was delightful, they walked in the dusky streets and ate cookies. Once again their silence was a balm to Megan's tattered soul. The only thing that troubled her was that she continued to hear Esther's words repeating themselves over and over in her head. "He's the cottage-in-the-country type. I wouldn't pass him up if I were you."

Was there even a choice? Ben was her friend. He might feel nothing more than companionship. And if he did feel more, did she want to be put in the position where she had to choose?

A terrified portion, the broken, shattered part of her screamed, "No!" The mellow peace that surrounded her when she was with Ben wanted its right to vote as well. It kept whispering, "Let this go on forever."

Chapter Thirteen

Sundays had always been Megan's worst days. They were too long and too unstructured, and lacked the normal everyday occupations that absorbed her mind. Work was not allowed. Resting opened too many opportunities to contemplate and reflect upon things that were best left untouched.

As Megan curled up on the living room couch and opened her Book of Mormon, she thought how different this Sunday was. She felt restful and at peace. Her mind was occupied with pleasant meanderings. Setting the scriptures in her lap, she recalled every detail of her date with Ben.

He had told her he was returning to Amherst last night. Knowing Ben wasn't going to be at church hadn't helped. Megan still watched for him. She felt ridiculous. He was only her friend—no, Ben was more than that. He was her best friend. Megan was glad she had worked this all out. Now she could relax, and study the scriptures.

She had just started reading when Amber looked up from the living room floor and unwittingly sabotaged all of Megan's comforting theories. It started out with a perfectly innocent question. "Did you have fun with Ben yesterday?" Amber was sitting cross-legged on the rug, cutting out different shapes from brightly colored scraps of paper.

"I did," Megan answered, marking her place with her finger. "What are you doing?"

"Scrapbooking. Haven't you ever done it before?"

"No, I never had time."

"I'm making scrapbooks for Christmas."

"It's only May. Isn't it a little early?"

"I'm doing it for my whole family." Amber arranged a photo copy of a snapshot on a purple flowered background. "There are seven of us kids, so it'll take a while to make everyone a book. What did you and Ben do yesterday?"

"We visited historical sights."

"No wonder you were gone so long. Ben's crazy about that kind of stuff." Amber held up a sheet of paper and another picture. "What do you think?"

"I like them together. Who's the baby?"

"My oldest sister, Alisha," Amber stared at the photo. "So you weren't bored?"

Megan was still looking at the baby picture and delayed answering for a few seconds. "Are you asking if I was bored with Ben?"

"Yes. Did he bore you?"

"Not at all."

"Sometimes he doesn't talk for long periods of time. It's a little eerie."

"It's a nice kind of quiet," Megan assured.

Amber looked up over the paper she was cutting. "Are we talking about the same Ben?"

"As far as I know, you only have one brother named Ben."

"True." Amber set her scissors down. "Would you go out with him again?"

"He hasn't asked me."

"Okay, if he did ask you out again, would you go?" Amber rephrased her question.

"I think I would. We had a good time, and I enjoyed his company."

"But you're just friends," Amber supplied watching Megan closely.

"Of course we are." Megan picked a tiny spec of lint off her slacks.

"Did he hold your hand?"

"Amber!" Megan protested.

"Well, did he?"

"No, he didn't."

"Mmm," Amber picked up the scissors again, "that's too bad."

"Friends don't usually hold hands," Megan informed Amber succinctly.

"No, they don't," Amber agreed and made no further comment.

The silence became long and uncomfortable, nothing like Megan's quiet times with Ben. Unasked questions vibrated in the air between them. When Megan couldn't stand it any longer, she stood and walked into the office. She wandered around, touching her computer, picking up a book, and haphazardly organizing some papers. Nothing seemed to soothe her jangled nerves.

Megan knew exactly what was bothering her but was unwilling to examine anything loosely connected with Ben. She absolutely refused to ponder why Ben Kilgallen had not attempted to hold her hand. It was stupid and pointless, yet it irritated her. Friends did not hold hands, so why should she care?

Promising herself that she wouldn't think about it anymore, Megan returned to aimlessly drifting around her office. With determination, she approached the bookshelf. She would read a book. Her fingers closed around one of her favorite volumes. It was a series of photographs of cottages. The instant Megan flipped the cover open she was reminded of Esther's words. "He's the cottage-in-the-country type."

Megan wanted to snap the book shut, but instead she gazed with hopeless longing at the cottages. It was a silly dream. Still, she stared, soaking up the comfort she found in the images of serene, quaint cottages. Once she'd told Scott that she wanted to build a cottage somewhere in the country. Turning with a snide look, he'd mocked her and said that she was a ditsy romantic who didn't understand life.

How could she still be a romantic after everything that had happened to her? Even now, a side of her personality clung to the slim hope that one day she'd discover the peace and serenity she saw in these photos of cottages. It was stupid yearning for something that might not exist. This was how she had gotten in trouble the first time. She'd been too young and too romantic, believing in anyone and everything.

Megan tried to see herself as she had been that last semester at BYU. She was a little naïve and definitely an idealist, but mostly an optimist. Even though her two favorite roommates had just married, Megan saw it as an opportunity to sell her contract and move into an apartment that was a shorter distance from campus. She didn't know anyone in the new ward, but it was okay. They were all friends she hadn't met yet.

On Megan's first Sunday at church, she noticed that a crowd of students were animatedly huddled around a table set up in the foyer. They were talking and comparing little cards that someone behind the table was liberally handing out. She asked her new roommate, Jean, what was going on.

"We're having a formal dance and you sign up for a date. The activities committee—or maybe it's the bishopric—anyhow somebody is setting us all up with blind dates in the ward. Look!" Jean tossed her head in the direction of a good looking man. He was about 5'10," lean and muscular, with thick black hair and heavily lashed dark brown eyes. "That's the elders quorum president, Scott Spencer. Every girl in the ward wants her date to be Scott. Come on, we'll go see who I got lined up with and maybe they'll let you sign up late."

As Megan walked by the elders quorum president, she could easily understand why all the girls in the ward wanted to be set up with him. He was a little too gorgeous to be true. Megan took her eyes off the handsome elders quorum president and followed Jean to the crowd surrounding the table. When Jean made it to the front of the line, she eagerly took her card and asked if there was an extra date available for Megan. The girl at the desk was very apologetic. "Let me take your name and I'll try, but there's not much time with the dance being this Saturday."

Jean and Megan moved through the crowd to the other side of the foyer, where Jean asked, "What do you think? Will it be bad or good?" Jean had been holding her piece of paper clutched in her hand and hadn't checked it to see who her date would be.

"You won't know until you look?" Megan peeked over Jean's shoulder.

Jean glanced down at the name on her paper. "Oh, well, I knew I couldn't be that lucky. Martin Miller isn't too bad though. We'll probably have a fun time."

During the next week, Megan hadn't thought too much about the formal dance. She was working hard maintaining her GPA and trying to study for the LSAT on the side. The test was only two weeks away, so an evening when everyone in the apartment would be out was rather appealing to her. She could curl up on the couch and do some intensive studying. Late Saturday afternoon when Megan trudged into the apartment after a marathon study group, Jean immediately cried, "Do you have a formal dress?"

Surprised Megan had answered a hesitant, "Yes."

"Good, because someone from the activities committee just called and asked if you'd go with some guy in the ward to the dance. Katie McKay is sick. She's got a sore throat and can't stop coughing. So I told them you'd go." Jean grabbed Megan's arm and started propelling her toward their room. "Let's get your dress out and we can steam it in the bathroom. We all need to take showers. And one of Katie's roommates sent down the boutonnière she bought. What color is your dress?"

"I have two: a peach colored one and a greenish blue one."

"It'll have to be the greenish blue since the flowers have mint colored ribbons on them."

"What's the guy's name?" Megan asked.

"I can't remember. He's new in our ward too. I think he just got home from his mission."

"Jean, I don't know."

"It'll be great. The rest of us felt really bad you were going to be here all alone while we're out having a good time."

"I really don't mind. I need to study. And I don't even know this guy. It could be really awkward."

Somehow Megan's fears didn't seem to matter to her roommates. They all ran around the apartment, stopping their own preparation to help Megan get ready for the dance. Later that evening when she opened the door to her date, Megan was wearing her own dress, borrowed nylons, Jean's jeweled hair clip, and another roommate's favorite perfume.

Her date was a bit of a disappointment. He seemed to have some kind of speech impediment that hindered any kind of communication. His chubby face flushed a deep scarlet when he saw her standing in the doorway. The suit he was wearing had worn shiny places around the knees and looked like it would have fit him better if he was about forty pounds thinner. Holding out the corsage box, he nodded and creaked out a weak, "Hello."

"Hi," Megan answered taking the box and wishing all of her roommates hadn't already left. She removed the flowers from the box and silently handed them to her date. His hands shook and his palms looked sweaty, but he managed to pin on her corsage without mishap. The process was repeated in reverse as Megan pinned Katie McKay's boutonnière to his lapel.

He said something so quiet that Megan couldn't quite catch it. Assuming that he was asking to leave, she locked the door and turned to go with him. Their walk across the street to the church was accomplished without conversation. Megan suddenly remembered Jean saying that he had just come home from his mission. No wonder he was so scared.

Trying to think of a way to ease his discomfort, Megan allowed him to open the church door for her. "Where did you go on your mission?"

Before her date could answer, the man every girl in the ward dreamed about called out to them. "Hey, Kelly boy, come on over here and join us."

Megan looked up at Scott and felt grateful. He had done her a favor by letting her know her date's name. She'd called Katie McKay twice trying to find out his name, but both times no one had answered. Poor Katie was probably sleeping. Well, now it didn't matter because she knew that either his first or last name was Kelly.

"You've got to come and sit at our table." Scott threw an arm around Kelly and smiled at Megan. "You're a lucky girl. Kelly may not talk much, but he's a good man."

The rest of the evening had passed in wonderful haze. Although Kelly was rather quiet, he was attentive. He made sure she had punch, pulled out her chair, and even danced relatively well. It didn't seem to matter that Kelly didn't talk that much, because his two friends Scott Spencer and Brian Durand kept the conversation flowing. They laughed and joked and were thoroughly enjoying themselves. Scott had suggested they all trade dance partners just for fun. A few moments later, Megan found herself in Scott's arms whirling around.

"You know, Megan, I like to make up nicknames for everyone. What shall I call you?"

Megan had not known how to answer, so she simply looked away and raised one shoulder slightly.

"It needs to be something special, don't you think?" Scott's gorgeously lashed eyes glowed, doing dangerous things to Megan's insides.

She shook her head, trying to dislodge all this flattering nonsense that Scott was filling her mind with. "I don't believe a word you're saying."

"Well, I'm totally truthful. We all have nicknames. I'm the man, Brian's the weather man because he's going into meteorology and we call—"

"You know, that's not what I mean." Megan instantly protested, "You're a player, a guy who flatters and flirts and it doesn't mean a thing."

Scott threw his head back and laughed. It rumbled out of his muscular chest and caused others on the dance floor to turn and stare at them. "You've got it all wrong. I want a nickname for you because, I'm interested, seriously interested. Since your last name is Jones, I think I should call you Jonzie. Do you like it?" His voice deepened and had a breathy catch to it, "Jonzie, I'd love to dance with you for the rest of the night."

His intensity made Megan uncomfortable and yet it was such a heady feeling to be looked at the way Scott was staring down at her. She glanced across the crowd of dancers and saw Kelly dancing with Scott's date. "I'm here with Kelly," she quietly reminded.

"It's only a blind date." Scott smiled showing straight, beautiful teeth.

Megan refused to look at Scott, "Yes, but it's still a date."

"I like your loyalty," Scott hugged her closer than was proper for a brief second. Releasing her a little and then leaning down, he placed his head close to Megan's ear and whispered, "I'd like very much to get to know you better. There's a fireside tomorrow night. Will you go with me?"

"I . . . I'm . . ."

"Just say yes."

And Megan did. She kept saying yes over and over again. She had said yes the day he asked her to marry him. She had said yes to applying to the same law school. She had said yes far too many times until the divorce.

Chapter Fourteen

Megan squeezed her eyes shut and tried to block out the memories of Scott. It was better to remember the divorce, better to remember the long and lonely process of freeing herself from him. Looking back now, Megan wondered how she could have been so stupid and naive. She had not made plans that took in account Scott's anger and his vindictive nature. He had always promised that he would never stand in her way or make it hard for her if she needed to leave him. Scott had seemed sincere when he had said that he owed that much because of all the mistakes he had made. Megan had believed him. She had still believed him on the day she had stood in front of her apartment door and tried to insert her key.

It wouldn't go in and it definitely wouldn't turn. The locks had been changed. As she stood in shock, locked out of her own apartment, Megan looked down at her suitcase and realized everything else that she owned was on the other side of the door. If only she had known what the future held before she'd left for her business trip to St. George.

She and Scott had agreed and talked rationally about her filing for divorce. He had moved his things out and gone to live with a friend in the ward. So why had Scott come back and changed the locks? Why hadn't she asked for his key? She tried calling Scott's cell phone. No answer. She tried her home line and was greeted with a recorded message that told her this number had been disconnected. Megan leaned her head against the door and felt so tired and hopeless. It hurt so bad that she wanted to let herself slide down the wall, crash on the floor, and just lie there, until it all went away.

She had no place to go. Scott had seen to that. Her parents weren't an option. They were so enamored with Scott that her mother had been frustrated when Megan had quietly informed them she was filing for divorce. Without any effort the memory of her mother's disappointed voice sounded in Megan's head. "Sweetheart, don't throw away a good marriage for little things. Stay together and work things out. Temple marriages are forever."

Megan saw herself sitting on the living room couch of her parents' house, twisting her hands and wondering how to help her mother understand without saying too much. She didn't want her mother to hate Scott and at the same time she wanted to defend her own actions. It was hard enough to admit that she had failed in her marriage, let alone to explain the sick relationship she and Scott had developed. She saw herself crying and begging him to stop and change. It was humiliating. "Mom, it's not just little things."

"Yes it is. He's a good man. Make his favorite meals. Show an interest in the things he likes."

Megan's heart wanted to cry out, "Mom, you don't know what he likes. Our whole life is a lie. Can't you see I'm dying inside? When I fix his favorite meals he either doesn't come home to eat them or he sits at the table and complains that he can't stand to look at me because I make him feel guilty. And the next day he sends me roses and promises that everything is going to be better.

"So I'd stay and try again. But now I don't have anything left. I'm empty. I'm a hollow shell of a person. If I try again, I'm not even sure I'll remember who I am. You can't imagine how tired I am of trying and trying to be what he wants me to be. And when it doesn't work, I start screaming and acting like a witch, and that doesn't work either." Instead of saying all this, Megan remained silent, knowing it wouldn't do any good. Scott had been here before her, telling lies, making promises, and weaving beautiful fantasies.

He did it so well. For years now, she had been repelled and then lured back to where he wanted her. Everything that was wrong with their marriage was her fault. If she had tried harder, if she would only be more patient, if she would be less critical of his giving and helping nature, then they would be able to save their marriage.

There were several reasons Megan couldn't tell mother everything. First of all, she couldn't handle defending herself to her own mother. Wasn't it a mother's duty to believe in her children? And shouldn't a mother instinctively know her daughter well enough to know that her daughter would never file for divorce over petty, insignificant things? It was all too exhausting to try and unravel all the lies and deceit Scott had thrown up between Megan and her mother. Another reason that Megan couldn't tell her mother was that Megan was still holding on to the hope that Scott would repent. If he did change then it was better that only she and Bishop Carden knew the truth. Maybe the most secretive reason Megan couldn't tell her mother everything was her own feelings of failure and pride. True, she had tried hard to be what Scott wanted, but there were those other times when she had let despair and fear rule her actions. She had screamed, pleaded, and demanded when she should have clamped her lips shut and behaved with dignity.

The next two weeks had been emotionally and physically grueling. Megan spent the first three nights in a cheap run-down motel in Layton, hoping and praying she wouldn't see anyone she knew. She didn't want to talk, explain, or even think about what was happening to her. The only phone calls she made that weren't business related were the ones she made to Bishop Carden.

Every hour she didn't spend at her job, she spent in locating an apartment. The Lord, through the hand of Bishop Carden, had blessed her. He knew of an older, divorced woman in Bountiful who was renting out her basement. It was unfurnished. Within the week Megan was sleeping on a camping air mattress and sitting on the kitchen floor, when she remembered to eat.

Megan had filed for divorce herself, but it soon become apparent that she needed someone else to represent her. She was not clearheaded, her stomach was nauseous half the time, and she had lost perspective because of her emotional state. The most important thing was to keep her current job. In order to do this, some of the stress needed to be relieved. A divorce lawyer was the only logical answer.

Her first appointment with Susan Talbot was enlightening. A divorced woman in her own right, she came directly to the point and gave Megan excellent counsel. "Take everything out of your name. Although Utah law doesn't hold you responsible for any debt he incurs from now on, it's a mess to untangle. Proving who charged what and who owes what can be costly too. It's easier not to go there."

"I really don't think—"

"He locked you out of your apartment, didn't he?"

"Yes."

"Have you checked your bank account lately?"

"His name's not on it." Megan felt a little uncomfortable revealing this information.

"Well, that's one smart thing you've done. Listen, do you want me to try to get anything back from your apartment?"

"No, it's just things."

"What about your clothes?"

"He dumped them on the porch at my parents house with some sad story about how I had been in such a hurry to leave him that I hadn't taken my clothes. He said he couldn't understand why I'd left him. You know all the stuff about how hard he had tried to make our marriage work and how broken hearted he was. If only I wouldn't do this to him."

"Typical. It's always our fault, isn't it? Another question for you: the apartment, who signed the lease?"

"We both did."

"And the rent?"

"I had already paid the last month's rent before Scott decided to change the locks. He moved everything out and took what was left of our deposit."

"Do you want me to do anything about all that?"

"The dollar amount couldn't have been much. Scott wouldn't have cleaned. All I want is for this divorce to be over."

"All right. I'm on it."

Somehow Susan's unperturbed, realistic manner was reassuring. Megan felt comfortable leaving everything in Susan's capable hands. From then on Megan devoted herself to her employment. She had always been a good attorney, but now she excelled. There was nothing to divert her or to distract her. Work was her life. She had no friends, no social activities, and no hope. Even her family was not allowed to interfere with her career. Her mother still frequently made contact, but Megan didn't have the energy to respond. She crept inside herself and became adept at smiling and pretending that her life was exactly as she wished it to be. It was a lie, but it made things bearable.

There had also been the nightmare of mediation that was required by state law. It didn't seem to matter that Scott had already taken everything of value they had acquired in the years of their marriage. They still had to sit through the hours of petty discussions. Megan tried to shorten it and cut to the important issues, but Scott, shaking his head with feigned regret, always circumvented her efforts.

Image was absolutely vital to Scott's plans as well as to the sustenance of his magnetic personality. He thrived on being admired and in control. Consequently, he sat with movie star procession in his perfectly fitted suit, raising his handsome head and looking so amiable. Smiling and manipulating, he made his weasely way through the session. He appeared to compromise and have Megan's best interests at heart, when in reality his only interest was in maintaining something that had once belonged to him: Megan. If it were no longer possible to possess her, then he would wreak as much vengeance and sorrow as he could. He promised things that Megan knew he had no intention of ever offering or ever following through with. The mediator was quite taken with his performance. Once in the midst of the six-hour session of negotiations, he had even suggested that Megan might reconsider her decision to divorce Scott. He was such a fine man and Megan must regret her rash decision to file for divorce.

When Scott, who complained that he was too financially strained to hire consul for himself, asked for one half of her 401K and stated Woodward v.Woodward (Utah 1982) as the precedent, Megan was too exhausted to care. Susan had rolled her eyes and gave Megan the

I-told-you-so look. By the time Megan walked out of mediation, she felt empty and dried up. Nothing seemed important anymore, not money, not people, not things. All Megan felt capable of doing was praying. She kept silently pleading over and over again, "Please, let it be over."

As Megan staggered out of the building where the so-called mediation had taken place, she gazed across the parking lot and couldn't remember where she'd parked her car. She wanted to sit in the middle of the black pavement and cry. Slowly, a little piece of her mind clinked into place. All she had to do was press the little button on her keypad. In the hollow state she was in, everyday things seemed so horrendously difficult. Unlocking the car, getting in, inserting the key in the ignition, were now all grueling accomplishments.

Just as she shut the car door, her cell phone rang. She should never have answered it and probably wouldn't have if she'd been thinking more clearly.

"Megan, honey," Scott's voice had syrupy sweetness drizzled all over it.

"What do you want?"

"I'm worried about you." This time, he almost sounded sincere.

For a moment, Megan was swayed. But it was only for a moment. Her mind, exhausted as it was, still rebelled and demanded that she remember all the things he had said and done in the last six hours of mediation. If he had really cared, would he be making the divorce as miserable as possible? Would he be turning her parents and her family against her with lies and manipulation? Would he be demanding a chunk of her 401K when he hadn't bothered to add a single contribution to his own 401K?

"I'm okay. I've got to run."

"Why don't we go out to dinner and talk about what we're doing. There's still time to work things out."

Did he mean he would like to take her out to a nice restaurant and then start his usual lecture on how she wasn't charitable enough or how she had such a big problem with forgiveness? No, she couldn't stand it. "I can't. I have other plans."

"Megan, you mean so much to me. I lie awake at nights thinking

about you and wishing we could go back to the way it was."

"Scott, please don't."

"Honey, it's true. I'm changing and getting everything in order like I should."

How many times had she heard this before? If she would only forgive him one more time, give him another chance."I'm sorry, I can't today."

"I'll call you tomorrow."

Megan didn't want him to call tomorrow or the next day for that matter. She couldn't tell him that because she was afraid he'd become angry and start saying hateful things that left her bruised and bleeding emotionally. Compromising, she ended their conversation with, "If you want to."

"Bye. Remember, I'll be thinking of you."

"Bye." Megan clicked her phone shut. In despair, she leaned her head on the steering wheel and wept.

They had never gotten together for dinner. Megan was always quick to have some reasonable excuse; she wasn't strong enough to have dinner with him. Sometimes in the deepest part of her soul, she wanted to give him another chance. It was hard to let go of what Scott had been like before. His brown eyes had glowed with the light of the gospel. He had wanted to please the Lord and keep the commandments. They had worked so hard at law school, played on the weekends, and studied their scriptures at night. Marriage hadn't been everything Megan dreamed about, but she had been content. There were those moments when everything was so wonderful that she thought she'd burst with gratitude. Then there were those times when Scott irritated her so much she wanted to scream. All of it had balanced out into an everyday relationship that was good and solid.

Megan wasn't exactly sure when things began to crumble and change. It had crept in slowly and insidiously until her entire relationship with Scott had been absorbed and then distorted by this new and different way of life. Their new marriage had turned ugly and become devoid of healthy emotion. It had grown monstrous tentacles that had greedily sucked up their pleasant past and left a future full of dread instead of hope, pain instead of joy, and fear instead of love.

Finally it had reached the point that all Megan wanted was for Scott to sign the divorce papers.

Naturally, it could not be so painless. Scott seemed to find a twisted pleasure in prolonging the process, deliberately procrastinating closure, and extending the inconvenience and discomfort with a warped satisfaction. He called Megan regularly, asked for her help with little insignificant things, demanded to know what she was doing, and frequently relayed messages from her mother. Each conversation would start off kind and gentle with Scott attempting to win her back, but when Megan refused to respond, the tone gradually changed. It would grow vile and unreasonable, and always ended with Scott vowing never to sign.

Megan's life consisted of work and an occasional meeting with Bishop Carden. Her spirit and her testimony were mangled and broken. Slowly, with meticulous care, Megan learned to wash out her wounds, douse them with antiseptic, and put band-aids on the most lacerated places. It was excruciatingly painful. Megan loved Heavenly Father, but she had difficulty reconciling what had happened to her. How could a loving Heavenly Father let this happen?

She had kept the commandments and married in the temple. And this was her reward? Bishop Carden had repeatedly talked about time and healing. Megan was just trying to make it through to the afternoon. Nights, she would not think about. Despite all this, she had tried to heed Bishop Carden's counsel. She read her scriptures and prayed. Maybe someday she'd understand and find hope. Maybe someday she'd feel better.

Seven months later, Scott miraculously signed. Megan never knew why he had finally broken down and scrawled his name brazenly across the pages. She had expected to feel relieved, free, and ready to forget the past. Instead, she felt a greater emptiness than before. She thought Scott would stop calling, but he didn't. It was a new kind of pain and a new test to fight her way through.

The day the headhunter had entered Megan's Salt Lake office seemed like an answer to her prayers. Unwittingly, he had offered her far more than a fabulous career opportunity in Boston. He was showing her a way to escape, a way to distance herself from the pain that trailed behind her no matter where she went. There was no need to pray about it. The Spirit was so strong that Megan felt as if her whole body had been lifted off the ground. Peace and hope soared through her, reviving her tired soul. She knew this was what she should do. The Lord's hand was reaching down and pulling her out of the abyss. She was to go to Boston. In record time she had packed her bags and left.

The musical tones of the phone caused Megan to let go of her past and return to reality. For one disoriented moment, she looked around her study and wondered where she was. As she reached for the phone, she somehow knew it was Scott before she heard his voice.

"How you doing, honey?" It was his typical greeting.

Scott's charm oozed over the thousands of miles between them. Megan had an odd, detached feeling as she answered, "I'm fine." It was almost as if Scott was a sad story she had read in some depressing book that she vowed never to read again. Megan decided that reviewing the past for the last hour had been good therapy. She felt like she was seeing things with a clearer perspective, and understanding things in a different manner.

"How come you never answer my emails?"

Megan paused a moment, wondering if she should tell him the truth. She stiffened and finding new courage stated, "I delete your emails without opening them."

There was silence on the other end of the line. Megan waited for his heated outburst. The longer the quiet went on, the more uneasy Megan became. Her newfound courage began to waver.

His answer was surprisingly soft. "I'm sorry you do that. Well, then tell me, when are you coming home?"

Her mind cleared and her courage returned. It was so simple that Megan could not believe she had not seen it before. "I am home," she quietly affirmed, knowing it was true.

"You can't mean that, not after all we've meant to each other," Scott insisted, sounding crushed. "Remember the time—"

"I try not to remember," Megan patiently interrupted. "I

hope things are going well for you."

"Then come home and see how I'm doing."

"Like I said, I'm happy for you."

"Your mom keeps asking when we're getting back together. She says temple marriages are forever."

Megan closed her eyes and swallowed before answering, "Scott, you know I never told my mother the truth about why we divorced. She doesn't understand," Megan took a deep breath, "but you know the truth. A temple marriage requires both partners to honor their vows."

"But I've reformed."

"I'm glad to hear it."

"You sound like an answering machine repeating a recorded message over and over again." Scott's irritation began to penetrate across the connection. Megan was sure his anger was rising.

"Maybe that's because you're not listening." A strong surge of determination swept through Megan. "Every time you call, we go through the exact same thing. Let me state this clearly. I am not coming back. We have been divorced for a year now. I have no intention of ever remarrying you."

"You sound so sure," a pathetic, broken-heartedness trembled across the miles. In the past, he had been rather good at playing upon her sympathies.

Megan's finger traced the cottage on the cover of her book. "I am sure."

"Megan, honey," he began to coax.

"I love my job here. I've made friends. I have a wonderful LDS roommate. It's time for you to accept the fact that I have my own life."

"But I need you back here with me." There was a catch in his voice.

A flash of understanding filled Megan's mind. She wasn't precisely certain if it was the Spirit or not; nevertheless, it made sense and felt good. "Scott, you don't need me. You never have. I wasn't what you wanted at all. You've only tried to change me. I can't be what you want and need. I don't believe in it."

"But I've changed."

"It's too late," Megan's voice rang with finality. "I'm sorry, but it's too late."

"There's somebody else," Scott accused in a harsh, gritty voice.

"If there is, it's none of your business." Megan had never stood up for herself and taken control like this before. She had repeatedly confronted him about his addiction, about his inappropriate behavior with other women, and about his lack of commitment to the church, but she had never demanded anything for herself. A warm peaceful sensation settled over her. Even Scott's frustrated silence did not torment her like it had a few minutes earlier. She waited for him to lash out and shout hurtful things. She didn't have to listen anymore. All she had to do was hang up.

"You always thought you were better than everyone else, little Miss Holier than thou!" Scott's anger radiated across the miles, "You're really just a—"

Very gently, Megan hung up. He would probably call back. She didn't care. It was easy. She'd hang up again. No, she was not even going to be here. Megan rushed into the living room. "Amber, I'm going for a walk. I haven't got my keys, so please don't lock the door." With a tight little smile, Megan dashed out of the condo.

Chapter Fifteen

For an hour Megan walked on a wave of confident euphoria. She had talked to Scott and set down the rules. Not for one moment had she felt like crying. She remembered something Bishop Carden had said, *"One day, Megan, you'll be able to look at this differently. It's really not you that doesn't measure up, but in a situation like this, it's hard not to take it personally."*

Megan had always taken it personally, but not today. As she walked, along, she felt contentedly different. Instead of being full of pain and fear, her heart basked in gratitude to her Heavenly Father. She thought of Bishop Carden and prayed for him. She thought of Scott and prayed for him. A beautiful, liquid peace poured over her soul like running water.

She loved Boston. Everything about Boston was wonderful. For the first time in years, Megan felt positive that she could become whole again. Hope whispered around her. Once again, she felt as if her life with Scott was a horrible book or a bad movie instead of a harsh reality. She was starting to think about her marriage almost as if it were her other life.

The thought that timing was crucial entered Megan's head. She had stayed in the marriage until she'd almost felt a physical release from Heavenly Father, like a release from a trying church calling that stretched you continuously beyond your natural endurance. Without the feeling that it was acceptable to the Lord for her to leave, she would have always wondered, if she had stayed longer, would Scott have changed? It had been in the Lord's hands and she had submitted herself to His timing, to His will.

Now she also began to comprehend the price of staying too long in an abusive marriage. Her spirit was still in the process of recovering from all she'd suffered through in order to give Scott every opportunity to repent. If she had stayed in the marriage too long, could she have been damaged beyond her ability to withstand? There was a delicate balance between when it was right to stay and when it was right to leave. The Spirit and Bishop Carden had carefully guided her through that maze of progression.

Today, Megan had changed her behavior, as well as her perceptions of what was required to interact with Scott. She had taken a step closer to beginning her new life. In her heart she rejoiced, because she knew she was going to be successful. Somewhere in the hills or on the seashore, maybe by a meadow or in the forest, there was a cottage waiting for her, and she was determined to find it.

It would take hours—no, months—of work, but somehow Benton knew it would be worth it. He tried to view it as an investment. Instead, he kept seeing two little girls skipping down the path to meet him.

He signed his name again and again while the weight of thirty years pressed down on him. He'd be almost sixty in thirty years. Benton hesitated over the last signature. While the pen shook between his fingers, he thought of all the money, all the commitment, and all the responsibility. It seemed endless.

A tiny ray of sunlight splashed across the mortgage papers. One of the lawyers said something and laughed. Benton saw everything, yet nothing; he heard, and didn't hear at the same time. Most of all, he knew this was what he should do. He signed the last document, boldly concentrating on the image of two little girls dancing down the steps to his house. Was he going insane? How many men dreamed of daughters instead of sons?

And what about a wife? In order to have sons or daughters, a man needed a wife.

"Mr. Kilgallen?"

Rotating his head to look up at the older gentleman, Ben corrected, "Ben."

"Ben," Mitchell Brown scratched his gray head, "if you wouldn't mind, I'd be willing to help you fix the place up." Mitch shifted his tall, thin frame awkwardly from side to side. "I know it's your place now."

"I'd appreciate the help."

"I promise not to tell you what to do. I mean, you can fix the place up any way you like," Mitch solemnly vowed.

"Thanks," Benton said. "First of all, I need to be pretty practical. I have to live in the house."

"Well, I have some spare time this afternoon."

"Then we'd better get over to Home Depot right away."

Mitch's smile took ten years off his leathery face. "You can follow me. I brought my pickup."

In the next few weeks, Benton came to thank Heavenly Father repeatedly for Mitch Brown's assistance. The older man was a virtual handyman. He could sweat pipes, rewire electrical outlets, hang sheetrock and mud dry wall, fit molding and lay tile, along with a dozen other crucial jobs that the old house radically needed.

As Benton worked on his new home, he often found his thoughts dwelling on Megan. Unintentionally he chose colors and styles that reminded him of her cottages. Benton was inadvertently creating something out of the pages of her books. He liked it. By the end of the week, he'd been able to move in. There were still a million more repairs to finish, but one bathroom and one bedroom were livable.

Having a home of his own was wonderful. For two years, he'd spent his time living between his parents' house in Worcester and the Stratton's home in Amherst. With these dual residences, he'd been able to teach two nights a week at UMASS Amherst and days at UMASS Lowell. It had been hectic but had led to the fulfillment of his dream of becoming a full-time professor at Amherst.

The quaint small-town atmosphere of Amherst had enchanted Benton from the beginning. He knew he was lost forever the moment he walked into the Amherst public library. The center of the building had a conservatory-like glass dome for a ceiling. Benton couldn't help himself. He'd selected a book and sat reading, enjoying the natural light in the domed solarium. History permeated the old brick library. Yes, Amherst was Benton's kind of town. It was small yet it was teaming with the college life. Academics, history, and beauty all made Amherst his village.

Benton hadn't seen Megan for three weeks. He'd thought about her more than he cared to admit. Caution ruled his actions. He was afraid to move too fast and at the same time he was leery of upsetting his comfortable life. He could think of at least five reasons why he should disappear and never see Megan again. These reasons were all clear, logical, and methodically thought out. Benton ignored every single one of them.

At the end of the first week that Benton was confined to hard labor in his cottage, he had escaped to the library where he promptly got on the internet and located the site of his favorite cookie shoppe in Quincy Market. Before he could lose his courage, he'd ordered two dozen chocolate chip cookies and had them sent to Megan Spencer on Chestnut Street, Cambridge, Massachusetts.

It was a stupid thing to do. What had he been thinking? Frankly, he'd been remembering Megan holding the cookie bag close to her chest, peeking into the sack and then refusing to share. They had laughed so hard they'd had to stop walking to catch their breath. It was a memory Benton thought he might never forget. He had not felt like this for years, not since his college days. Look at what had happened then! Because he had been slow and unwilling to fight for her, the woman he had loved had married someone else. Once again, Ben was scared. So he stayed away, worked hard on his house, and sent cookies.

A week after sending the cookies, Benton was still wondering if he should have sent roses or some other kind of flower. For some reason roses didn't seem quite right. What if she didn't care that much for chocolate chip cookies? Despite his misgivings, Benton found himself strangely drawn toward the notion of sending cookies again. As the night wore on, Benton attempted to ignore these promptings.

He restlessly tangled himself in the bedsheets until he couldn't stand it anymore. He'd wandered through the house and flipped the lights on and off, fighting the urge. He'd sat in the dark and thought of all the reasons why it was a ridiculous idea. At 2:00 AM he'd given up and gone to his computer. As soon as he got online, he hit the web site he wanted. This time it was easier to find. Instead of chocolate chip cookies, he had ordered a variety pack to be delivered. Who in the world sent cookies to a girl? Ben shut down the computer and decided he was an idiot.

As Benton climbed back in bed, he was surrounded by an odd, comforting peace. There was one crucial aspect that was different from his past experience. This time he was doing something, even if it was only sending cookies. Benton knew in his heart that it was time to go back to Boston. He had to see her again.

Megan stared at the box of cookies on the kitchen counter and smiled. This time it wasn't all chocolate chip cookies, but an assortment. She lifted two mint chocolate cookies out of their distinctive tissue paper and dropped them into a sandwich bag. She'd have cookies with her lunch. A second later, she stuffed four more cookies into another plastic baggie. She hoped Jane and Esther would enjoy them.

She was grateful that Amber hadn't been home on both occasions when the cookies had been delivered. The idea of explaining that Ben had sent cookies didn't appeal to Megan in the slightest. She could picture Amber saying, "There's a story here."

As if thinking about her had made her materialize, Amber walked into the kitchen. Megan quickly offered her cookies. "Take all you want," she said.

"You sure do like these fancy cookies." Amber lifted the lid and peeked inside.

"I do," Megan agreed, moving toward the door. "I'll see you tonight."

There was something sweet about Ben sending her cookies. When she had arrived home last night, the caretaker had opened his door and handed her the box of cookies. "These came for you, Ms. Spencer."

The instant Megan had seen the logo, she knew it was more cookies from Ben. Other men sent flowers or candy, but not Ben. She knew why he had sent cookies. They were a reminder of that day at Quincy Market.

Sometimes the afternoon and evening she had spent with Ben grew out of proportion. It took on a dreamlike quality that suddenly diminished when she remembered he hadn't held her hand or come to see her for three weeks. He hadn't even tried to call.

Megan vowed that she would not think about Ben anymore. She was able to keep her promise the entire morning, right up until she had lunch in the Commons. Even then, it wasn't really her fault, since Esther and Jane led the conversation around to him.

Jane munched gratefully on her cookie. "These are delicious! Or is it just that I've been on a diet for too long?"

"No," Esther confirmed, "they're good."

"Where did you buy them?" Jane asked picking up every single crumb that had fallen onto her skirt.

"I didn't buy them."

Esther raised her eyebrows. "Then I want the recipe. Norman loves cookies."

"I didn't make them either. They were sent to me," Megan confessed, blushing.

Jane caught on immediately. "By him," she surmised excitedly. "Ben sent them."

Megan's colored heightened.

"Usually men send flowers, a dozen red roses, or something

like that," Jane sighed, her romantic heart touched.

"I hate red roses," Megan passionately announced. "My ex-husband always sent red roses after he'd been . . ." Megan clamped her mouth shut, realizing what she had inadvertently revealed.

Jane stared with huge oval eyes while Esther turned to Megan and quietly stated, "He wasn't the cottage type, was he?"

The shock appeared to be wearing off because Jane demanded, "What do you mean he wasn't the cottage type?"

Esther read the embarrassment and discomfort in Megan's eyes. "I mean," Esther informed Jane, "the warm, homebody type like Norman."

It was true. Scott had not been a home and family man. Even in the beginning, he'd liked adventure and excitement too much to be willing to subject himself to the everyday boredom of doing dishes, washing the cars, and mowing the lawn. From a distance, Megan heard her own voice saying, "He was extremely handsome, sophisticated, and charming. I have learned to beware of men like that."

"And you were really young," Jane helpfully suggested.

"I was."

"And probably idealistic and romantic," Jane added for good measure.

Megan nodded her head sadly. "But I won't make that mistake again."

"Of course not," Jane assured. Suddenly her entire demeanor changed. Jane's eyes emitted sparks and her nostrils flared. "You knew!" She accused turning on Esther, "You knew Megan was divorced and you never told me."

Esther held up her hand. "I really didn't know. Megan and I had several conversations where we discussed the kind of life Megan wanted, but she never told me she was divorced. Of course, I've wondered. Jane, you and I've both talked about how we thought Megan must have been hurt badly in the past."

Jane subsided slightly, but still grumbled, "All right. I still think you should have said something. Warned me that you thought Megan might be divorced or something like that."

Esther lifted one shoulder in a noncommittal manner and said nothing.

"It's really not important," Megan insisted hoping to defuse the situation.

"But of course it's important," Jane instantly protested. "It explains why you're living *Without Love,* like in the movie. You've been hurt and you're afraid to risk." Jane heaved a huge, shuddering sigh. "I'm sure everything will turn out all right."

While Esther and Megan stared, Jane bit into her second cookie. With her mouth full she gurgled, "He sends cookies. How original! I like it. They should have a hero in a movie that does that. I mean, that sends cookies."

Esther rolled her eyes and began to eat her last cookie while Megan tried not to laugh.

"So when are you seeing him again?" Jane wanted to know.

"I'm not sure."

"You're not sure?" Jane looked confused.

"I haven't seen him for three weeks."

Esther was the only one who appeared to notice that Megan was counting the days. She raised her eyebrows and silently digested this revealing piece of information.

"But he sends cookies," Jane mused. "Why don't you call him?"

"I don't know," Megan hesitated, feeling awkward.

"Wait! What do you think about this?" Jane smiled broadly. "You should thank him for the cookies. Call and thank him for the cookies."

Megan glanced at Esther for some kind of confirmation. Esther paused a moment and then nodded. "I don't think it would hurt to call him. You should thank him for the cookies." Esther stared intently at Megan, "But calling him isn't the real issue, is it?"

Megan was afraid to answer. She wasn't precisely certain what she was feeling since there was a jumble of emotions rambling around inside of her.

"The difficulty is," Esther softly concluded, "that you want a sign, like Gideon and the golden fleece in the Books of the Prophets. You want to be positive you're not making the same mistake again."

The tangle of Megan's emotions unraveled as she accepted the truth of Esther's words. She was about to comment when Jane asked, "Is that a movie, *Gideon and the Golden Fleece*?" Jane scrunched up her brow trying to remember. "If it is, I don't think I've ever seen it."

Chapter Sixteen

For the last half hour, Megan had sat in her study staring at the phone. Once, she even picked it up and dialed the first four digits of Ben's cell. Acquiring Ben's phone number had seemed like an insurmountable task since Megan refused to ask Amber for the number. Amber was bound to ask all kinds of deep, probing questions. In the end, locating Ben's number had been ridiculously easy. Amber had taped a bright purple 3x5 card on the back side of the cabinet door above the phone. Her friends, her doctor, her dentist, and every other important person in Amber's life were listed along with the corresponding phone number.

The scrap of paper Megan had written Ben's cell number on sat innocently beside her phone. Since Amber was out visiting teaching, now would be the ideal time to make the call. Megan's nerves were twisted into a knotted mess. She could not do it. Bowing her head, Megan prayed for courage. Maybe it wasn't so important. Maybe . . .

The phone rang, jarring every muscle in her body. Megan knocked the receiver off the charging pad and fumbled with it. Finally placing it to her ear, she managed a weak, "Hello."

"Hi, Megan. It's Ben."

Megan didn't know what to say. Her ability to create the perfect image was no longer so well defined. After being away from Scott for all these months, Megan's pretense had crumbled and left her vulnerable and defenseless.

"I . . . I was going to call you," she was stuttering. She couldn't believe it. In her most stressful arguments in court she never stuttered. She was smooth, logical, and articulate.

"You were?"

Did he sound pleased or merely surprised? Megan wasn't sure. "I wanted to thank you for the cookies. They were delicious."

"I'm glad you liked them." There was a short pause before Ben asked, "Which was your favorite kind?"

"Chocolate chip." Megan wanted to add, "Because they reminded me of the day I spent with you." She bit her wayward tongue and said, "I liked them all though."

There was another silence in which Megan had the distinct impression that Ben was as nervous as she was. The thought was comforting.

"I've been really busy lately," Ben finally stated.

Megan's comfort evaporated. Busy with what? Summer term was supposed to be a breeze. Was there some other girl he was dating? Some cute coed who had seen Ben's brown-sugar eyes and recognized his kind heart? He was only her friend, she repeated sternly to herself. Megan gulped, swallowed too quickly, and choked.

"Are you all right?'

"I just swallowed down the wrong pipe," Megan sputtered.

"I'm sorry."

"I'm fine."

"Well, I was wondering whether . . ." Benton hesitated and then switched in mid sentence. "I've been letting your history lessons lapse, and I think it's time for another field trip."

Once more, Ben paused while Megan could almost picture him fiddling nervously with something. She heard him take a deep, ragged breath, then he continued, "That is, if you haven't decided on a new teacher."

"No, I'm satisfied with the old teacher." Yes, Megan thought, she was very satisfied, especially if their field trips were going to become more frequent.

"On Saturday we could drive up to Concord and Lexington. It's beautiful this time of year, although fall is nice too. Shall we wait for fall?"

He was teasing. Megan liked it very much. Without considering her words Megan joked, "If I wait until fall, will I still have my private tutor?" The minute the words left her mouth she wished she could call them back. They were too bold, too flirtatious.

Ben didn't seem to mind. He laughed, "That's a good question. Fall semester is always heavy and I'll be teaching full time. May I make a recommendation?" He sounded like a waiter offering the daily special. After her "uh huh," he finished, "I suggest you take your private tutor up on his June extravagance."

"A June extravagance. The whole month?" Megan was enjoying their banter.

"But of course." Benton instantly followed up with a salesman-like pitch. "Naturally it would culminate with a fabulous Fourth of July in downtown Boston with the Boston Pops, the 1812 Overture, and the guns firing."

"Even if I didn't like my tutor, this would be very tempting."

"And if you liked your private tutor, it would be irresistible," Ben's voice vibrated with innuendo and a sudden infusion of confidence.

Megan didn't notice since she was having too much fun. With a mock prim and proper attitude, she prissily announced, "So it would be, but what is the bottom line? The cost, you know?"

"It won't be cheap."

"I never imagined it would be."

"Shall I pick you up on Saturday afternoon at one then?"

"You never said how much." Megan pointed out.

"I never discuss private matters over the phone," Ben's voice was thick with double entendre.

Megan was thinking of some witty comeback when the study door crashed open. Amber burst into the room. "I came walking up the stairs and your home teachers were on the landing. I thought you buzzed them in."

"No," Megan briefly answered not wanting her conversation to be interrupted.

"Who's on the phone?"

"Ben."

"Is he coming up this weekend?"

"Can you wait a minute? Amber just came home." Megan's attention shifted back to Amber. "He's coming on Saturday. We're going to Concord and Lexington."

"That's great," Amber enthused. "Jason just got a new sports car and he wants to try it out. Would you mind if we came along too?"

Amber cheerfully reached for the phone. "Hi, Ben. Did you hear me? Yeah, a new car . . . No, I don't know what kind, but it's red and very flashy," pause, "that sounds good to me. Bye." Amber clunked down the receiver and looked toward the living room. "Oh, I forgot your home teachers! I told them you'd be right out."

Benton pocketed his cell phone thinking that this was not exactly what he had anticipated. His master plan included a series of historical Saturdays alone with Megan. He resolved to follow through with his idea despite this minor setback, and was determined to be active instead of waiting on the sidelines like he had last time.

Maybe having Jason and Amber along wouldn't be that big of a hindrance. Their presence might ease the tension between him and Megan. Sometimes Benton could actually feel Megan withdrawing and placing a safe distance between them.

An image of a small, red car flashed in Benton's mind, causing him to freeze in his footsteps. Yes, this might be very good. He and Megan would be squeezed into the microscopic backseat. Benton Kilgallen's face creased with a wide, devious grin.

As they headed toward Lexington on Saturday, Benton thought that everything was as he had expected, only more pleasurable. Megan was squashed so delectably close to him that he could feel her leg pressed against his thigh. There was absolutely no place for his arm to go, so it was only natural to drape it around Megan's shoulders. She smelled of a delightful mix of fruity soap and some intoxicating perfume. When she spoke to him, he turned and their lips almost met. *Yes,* Benton thought, *he loved Jason's new car.*

Megan couldn't remember what she was about to say. She'd heard of people's minds going blank, but this was not that. Her brain was whirling with delicious sensations she hadn't felt for years. Her pulse throbbed in her throat while a tingling feeling electrified her. She took a deep breath and turned to stare out the window. This was not what she had expected. She knew that she cared for Ben, but this was different. It was pure attraction raging in her blood.

She remembered the night when Ben had fallen to the floor and faked being hurt; he had hugged her tightly and said, *"It's been a long time since a man's held you, and you've forgotten how wonderful it can be."* Megan realized he had been right. She leaned her head against the window and felt guilty and afraid.

She was dead, an unrefined pencil sketch of a person. If she gave up her hollow pretense, she had to feel, and that was terrifying. Scott had made it abundantly clear that she could never measure up. Was she somehow flawed and never able to make any man happy? Would the end result always be harsh words and rejection?

Along with the fear, guilt ate at her. Megan carried several varieties of guilt. She was at fault because she had never been able to make her marriage work. Another form of guilt insisted that she had betrayed Scott, because it felt wonderful to be in Ben's arms.

Megan stiffened her resolve and forced herself to remember the last time Scott had called. She had hung up on him. Afterward she had walked and walked while she had felt something changing inside her. "And maybe I've changed eternally too," Megan whispered to herself. The hours and years of praying, the act of forcing herself to get up in the morning when there was no hope, the wise counsel of her bishop that she couldn't quite comprehend, and the inspiration to move away from Utah all flowed together into a soothing sweep that washed over her.

Perhaps she wasn't totally healed, but there was a whisper of hope. Megan thought she might have crossed a crucial bridge, forged a major river, or climbed an important peak. The way would still be bumpy at times, but it would also be smoother. A sweet, bitter twist of gratitude fluttered in Megan's heart as she began to see things from a different perspective. At least she didn't have to deal with the pain of explaining divorce to her child or face the agony of fighting for legal custody. For the first time in years, Megan was glad Scott had never wanted children.

Ben shifted and tightened his arm around her, affectionately pressing her shoulder. Inadvertently a thought popped into Megan's head. She wanted to have children with a man like Ben, a man who had a gentle, spiritual nature. Shutting her eyes Megan determined that she was not going to think about any of that right now. Today she was going to enjoy herself and live life fully.

Resolutely she opened her eyes and forced a light teasing tone into her voice. "I'm not getting my money's worth. Where's my historical lecture?"

With a slow smile Ben said, "We haven't decided on a price yet."

Abandoning her fears, Megan turned to face Ben. "I'll worry about that later."

Her hair had swung around and brushed against Benton's face. It smelled like green apple shampoo. Benton sat stunned for a second, while pure delight rippled through him. Despite the intense physical attraction which their close proximity generated, Ben sensed a new element entering their relationship. It reminded him of how intensely he had wanted to love before, only instead of feeling dumb and insecure, he felt dashing, handsome, and irresistible.

Benton immediately began the most outrageously funny historical monologue. He laughed. She laughed. Amber giggled. Jason had difficulty staying on the road, because his sense of humor got out of control. Ben rode on a crest of euphoria where Megan's encouragement sent him soaring higher and higher.

It was a day like Megan had never experienced before. She knew she'd repeat everything that happened over and over again in her mind for weeks. Both today and the other Saturday she had spent with Benton ran together and combined into a whole new attitude. She loved history! Why had she never thought of majoring in history before going to law school? Political science suddenly seemed dull and boring. A tiny something whispered, *It's your private tutor.* Naturally, Megan refused to listen to such an insignificant voice. She was too elated, too excited, and too content to bother with random whisperings.

Saturday became Megan's favorite day of the week. It meant Louisa May Alcott's house, Walden's Pond, Bunker Hill, the Minute Man Museum, and much more. Megan had always looked forward to the Fourth of July; her sense of patriotism and appreciation for freedom and the law made it one of her favorite holidays. Now she hoped it would never come, because it signaled the end to her historical tour with Ben.

As Benton sanded the front door, he promised himself that Amber and Jason would not be allowed to tag along on his dates with Megan anymore. Dust and paint went flying with his aggressive sanding. If he stained the door now, there wouldn't be time for it to dry. He'd have to hang the door like it was so that he could lock the house and enjoy the Fourth of July in Boston.

For a brief moment, Benton stopped working and looked around the yard. A possessive sense of satisfaction eased the tense muscles of his neck and shoulders. The block sander hung listlessly from his fingers as his mind recalled the condition of the yard two weeks ago. He replaced the old image with how everything looked today. It was a marvelous contrast. The grass was cut. It was still weedy, but improving. The roses had bloomed and were curving gloriously around the front entrance. The window boxes had been repaired and were ready to receive colorful flowers.

Benton couldn't remember a time when he had ever worked so hard. Every free second was soaked up by the cottage that was beginning to fit his goal and dreams. The name "the cottage" fit Benton's goal and his dream. Wondering if everything he'd always wanted was finally coming together, Benton peered into the empty entrance of his house and tried to see the future. Would Megan someday be waiting in the doorway ready to greet him? Would the two little girls, one with masses of curls and the other with soft wispy hair, be standing on each side of Megan?

With a distasteful shock, Benton felt reality invade his dream. Megan was an attorney, had a big-time career, and loved Boston. Her condo, her car, her clothing, and all her possessions were expressions of the financial resources she could and would accumulate. Benton could never hope to duplicate such wealth. History professors made a pittance in comparison to lawyers like Megan. She'd been wooed by the firm to make the move to Boston. What perks and incentives would convince her to toss all that away for a mere teacher's salary and a run-down cottage? If she were truly in love with him she might, but it was a big maybe.

This was a repeat of the last time he had become too interested in a girl, the same feelings, the same hopelessness, except now Benton was determined to make it different. Previously, he had said nothing and remained in the background where he'd watched and hoped instead of taking an active role.

It was easy to recall how he had never gotten the courage to do anything. Even after all these years, he remembered standing in the shadows watching her teach the Gospel Doctrine Class. Her face had glowed with a spiritual knowledge, while at the same time her command of the English language had excited Benton. He loved big words and innovative ways of teaching that encouraged people to take gospel principles and apply them in their everyday lives. She reminded him of a perfect sister missionary who taught from the heart and let the Spirit enter in and change people's lives.

Sunday School class wasn't the only time Ben stayed hidden in the distance and watched. With amazing clarity, he recalled the Saturday afternoon their ward had gone to a retirement home to visit and assist the elderly. The ward had prepared a wonderful meal, as well as a program for the lonely men and women. While Ben had stood singing with the ward members, he watched the girl he admired silently slip away from the choir. She crossed the room and went directly to the second row of diners, where an elderly woman sat in the last chair pushed up against the table. The poor woman's hands were so gnarled with arthritis that her repeated efforts to pick up her utensils were fruitless. Her sad eyes lingered on the plate of home cooked food and then lifted to the choir.

The girl sat down in the chair beside the elderly woman. She smiled and said something that made the woman look at her with pure gratitude. They both laughed while the young woman took up the knife and fork and cut the meat into bite-size pieces. Throughout the program, Ben watched as the girl fed the elderly woman. The Gospel Doctrine teacher not only preached, but she also lived what she believed with her whole being. Benton watched and was never able to forget the beautiful light that surrounded the young woman and the elderly lady. It increased his desire to court her, to know her, and to talk with her. But somehow it was easier to stand back and watch.

Even when the opportunity came to work with her on a committee, Benton hadn't been able to take full advantage of the situation. Five ward members had been called to arrange the food for a ward parking lot party. Benton had decided the he was going to do something. As soon as the meeting was over, he stood near the door and waited to talk with her. With great difficulty he made himself ask, "How's school going?'

The moment the words were out of his mouth he felt like an idiot. How dumb could he get? She didn't seem to notice. She stopped next to him while he watched her long hair swaying over her shoulders. Her smile did things to his stomach.

"It's pretty good."

"What's your favorite class this semester?

He had to keep her here longer.

She smiled, "It's funny, but it's not even in my major; I love my Humanities class. We've been studying the art in Italy. You can't believe how wonderful it is."

They had spent a long time talking about art. Benton felt almost secure because his major had included one class in European history. He knew something about the period of history where Michelangelo and Bernini created their great works.

Long after their conversation was over Ben continued to think about what they had said. He seriously doubted that she would remember it like he did. But maybe he could find a way to talk to her again.

Somehow the opportunity never came. He'd waited, hoping someday he'd have the courage to speak to her about more important things, to tell her of his admiration. When Benton had finally reached within himself and discovered the fortitude to motivate himself, it was too late. The other man had used his charismatic personality to win her.

This time was going to be different. This time, Ben was determined to fight. As far as he knew, there was no other man, and he intended to keep it that way. He'd already devoted a month or more of Saturdays to courting. At times, he had even felt charming and debonair, but the courage to seriously hold her hand or attempt to kiss her had escaped him. The only physical closeness he'd ever achieved was when they'd been crammed into the backseat of Jason's flashy red car.

"If I were a swearing man, now would be a good time to swear!" Benton hadn't realized he'd spoken aloud until he heard Mitch laughing.

"The door's not turning out right?" Mitch came out of the house, and moved toward Ben.

"It's not the door," Benton confided. "It's a woman."

Mitch only smiled and shook his head.

"Aren't you going to offer me some advice?"

"Nope."

"Why not?"

"Too risky." Mitch's grin widened. "Can't understand the one I've had for forty-five years."

Together they heaved the door off the sawhorses and headed for the entrance. They hung the door and turned to look at their handy work.

"It'll be real pretty with a stain or a coat of paint." Mitch cocked his head and looked around. "You've done a good job. The house is starting to look good. It reminds me of better times."

"I couldn't have done it without your help."

"No, you would have. It just would have been a little slower, that's all." Mitch smoothed a length of thinning hair off his forehead.

Benton looked awkwardly around the room and finally broached the subject that had been bothering him. "When I was in the local hardware store, some men were talking about how Mitch Brown had been conned out of his sister's house. They said you weren't paid anything near what the house was worth."

It was Mitch's turn to look uneasy. "New Englanders don't take kindly to outsiders. It's just talk, that's all."

"Mitch, I'm a New Englander. I know how we are. But this was more than that." Benton fingered the smooth surface of the door. "I don't want to take advantage of you. If I didn't pay you enough—"

"They don't know the details of our agreement. I'll make plenty of money in interest since I'm carrying the loan," Mitch insisted. "Before you go on, how about we take a look at the washer hookup? One of the lines needs—"

"Mitch," Benton laid a hand on the older man's arm. "I don't think I paid enough for the house."

"It's all you could afford," Mitch flatly stated. "I'm okay with it."

"How do you know it's all I could afford?"

"You signed for a credit report. I looked at it. I'm not a fool. I had to make sure you could make good on the loan."

"Then you also know I have a little other money saved up."

Benton stared suspiciously at Mitch. "I could have paid you more."

"Nope! You needed the money to fix the house up."

"Mitch, I don't think this is right."

"It's more right than you know." Mitch hung his head and refused to make eye contact.

"I don't understand what you're talking about."

Mitch shrugged his shoulders and mumbled, "You wouldn't." He turned his back to Ben and quietly stated, "It was a long time ago, but it still hurts."

Benton wasn't sure what to say. He didn't understand what Mitch was trying to say. "You mean Ellie?"

Mitch's gnarled hand gripped the door jam. "I've thought about telling you a lot of times, but I couldn't. I was afraid it would change things. You might think I'm crazy." His head jerked around and he gave Benton a steely, intimidating look, "I'm not senile."

"No, you're not," Benton calmly assured him, "I've worked with you enough to be sure of that."

"You see that first day when I saw you standing in front of the house," Mitch's voice was gruff with emotion, "I thought for a moment you were my son."

"The one that doesn't come to visit much?"

"No the other one." A tear slipped down his leathery cheek. "I knew it wasn't possible, but I wanted it to be true." He left the tear where it was and unashamedly let another follow the same course. "You see, you look a lot like Jimmy. And I haven't seen him in a long time."

"I look like one of your sons?" Ben repeated still confused.

"I'm not explaining this very well." Mitch shifted and turned his body towards Ben. "He was only eighteen. Jim was a good boy, but I didn't like some of his friends. It was a wild crazy group, headed for trouble. One night we got into an argument about his friends. We both said things neither of us meant, but somehow we couldn't take them back. He was gone the next morning. Every once in a while he sends Myra a card, but other than that we haven't seen Jimmy for years, too many years to count. "

With a forceful swipe, Mitch brushed his tears away. "That day I saw you standing there, just for a second I thought you were Jimmy. You see, I wanted it to be Jimmy real bad. I leaned forward to get a closer look and I accidentally hooked the horn. Then I got out of the car and we talked. Up close you still looked like Jim, maybe the way he'd look at your age. I don't know.

It probably sounds stupid, but I felt like I could sell you the house, almost like you were family. And Myrna's been saying for years that we should sell, so I sold it to you. And then working with you was like working with my son. Building and doing things around this house were the kinds of things I always wanted to do with Jimmy."

Benton knew he had to say something, but words seemed simple and worthless. Mitch's loneliness and the loss of his son affected Ben deeply. Finally, he managed to say, "I'm glad you sold the house to me."

"I'm glad too." He straightened his stooped shoulders and suggested, "Well, we'd better get the doorknob on this door so you can lock it up and get off to Boston for the fireworks."

Chapter Seventeen

As Benton drove to Boston, his mind was filled with thoughts of Megan. He began praying, seeking for answers and help in understanding what he should do. Sometimes Benton prayed aloud and felt like an idiot when other drivers glanced over and saw him talking to an invisible passenger. After considering it, Benton decided he didn't care. He needed an answer. His feelings were not in question. Benton felt like he'd been in love with Megan since the first moment he saw her. The last few weeks had only intensified his emotions.

The questions that troubled Benton were complicated and intertwined. He was uncertain of Megan's feelings. Even if she were in love with him, was it right to pursue her? Did he have the Lord's approval? What if the Spirit assured him that marriage was possible and Megan only wanted to be friends? She could choose to reject him. God would always allow His children to exercise their agency.

As Benton thought and prayed, it continually came back to his innate shyness and fear of rejection. There had been a feeling growing steadily within him that his relationship with Megan was good and acceptable to the Lord. Fear was the menacing impediment that must be thrust aside. For once, he must stand up and actively seek what he wanted. Benton was ready. When he wavered, he thought of the cottage and the two little girls calling him daddy.

As the day progressed, Benton grew more and more confident. He had never seen Megan so happy. The parade with all the American flags and fanfare delighted her.

Over lunch and dinner, Megan had talked and laughed with an openness that contrasted dynamically with her earlier detachment. Now, as they settled on their blanket in the park, listening to the Boston Pops, Benton experienced a surge of hope. He leaned closer and gently clasped Megan's hand. She didn't balk or withdraw her hand. Benton was elated.

"What have you been doing?" Megan asked lightly, fingering the rough calluses on his hand.

"Fixing up a house." Benton wondered why he'd never told her about the cottage. Then he knew. Without realizing it, he had tucked away and hidden from himself the idea that he wanted to surprise Megan with the cottage when he asked her to marry him.

"It must be hard work."

"I'm enjoying it." Eager to change the subject and discover some of the answers to all the questions he had been asking himself, Benton asked, "What do you think about working mothers?"

Megan tilted her head and looked at him with a funny expression on her face. "What kind of question is that?"

"A real one," Benton seriously contended, watching the setting sun cast glowing shadows behind the towering buildings. "Our modern world is rather confusing for women. I simply wondered how you felt about juggling motherhood and careers."

Megan didn't answer. Instead she stared straight forward. Benton seemed prompted by some inner stirring. "Suppose you had two little girls. Would you want to stay in Boston and raise them so you could work at the firm?" Benton remembered that first day at the cottage and wished with all his heart that he could have seen the little girls' mother standing beside them. It would make things so much simpler.

Megan's hand slipped out of his as she bent her legs and rested her chin on her knees. "It would depend a lot on the circumstances." Megan's voice was slightly distant.

The wetness and the humidity were suddenly overwhelming. Benton wiped his brow and abandoned the subject. "What's your favorite thing about the Fourth of July?"

"I think it's you!" Megan's whole expression lightened. "You've made the Fourth of July more meaningful to me. All those historical sights you've taken me to have helped me understand more clearly the sacrifices our countrymen made in order to make America free. I've been meaning to thank you. It's been wonderful."

Her shining eyes and complimentary words embarrassed Benton. He dropped his head and turned away. Megan liked his shyness. It was cute and endearing. The next instant, Ben's eyes lifted and stared boldly back at her. She was disconcerted and dropped her hands from around her knees.

"The final exam is coming up."

Megan couldn't breathe. She was positive Ben wasn't talking about her education in history. "Yes?" she barely managed the single word.

"I think it's time for extra credit." The gold of the setting sun was reflected in his eyes.

He doesn't mean anything, Megan told herself, but she didn't believe it. "What kind of extra credit?"

"I'll let you know when the time comes."

Megan didn't dare ask for an explanation. She was terrified that he might give her one.

Benton moved around behind Megan. "You must be tired. Lean back and rest."

For a second, Megan hesitated and then gave in. As she relaxed against Ben, she thought of how long it had been since she'd felt this content. She thought of Scott, of her need to repair her relationship with her mother, of her old bishop, then of Ben. The comfort of Ben's closeness, the rhythm of the Boston Pop's music, and the humid heat combined against Megan, making her eyes droop.

He woke her just as the Boston Pops began playing the 1812 Overture, knowing she wouldn't want to miss it. For a brief moment, Megan was disorientated. Her eyes flashed with fear and embarrassment. Benton laced his fingers through hers and said, "Enjoy! This is the best part: the music, the cannons, and the fireworks."

Megan was grateful the darkness hid her red cheeks. Had she snored or slept with her mouth open? Ben squeezed her hand, helping Megan realize that he didn't care. In her mind she recalled Scott complaining, "You always sleep with your mouth open. You look like a drowning fish."

The gentle pressure of Ben's fingers told her that Ben was different. She wanted to take a chance again. If she didn't, she would spend the rest of her life alone, slaving over someone else's legal problems. Megan looked at Ben in the shadows and felt as if the cannons and fireworks were going off inside of her. As Megan threw her head back, she hit Ben in the chest, causing them both to laugh. There were cannons and fireworks, and they were real.

After the last splash of color had exploded in the sky, silence descended and fluttered lightly over Megan and Ben. As they folded the blanket, packed up their picnic dinner, and carried it back to the car, they didn't speak. It was as if they had done this a thousand times before, each one knowing their part. He opened the trunk. She put in the picnic basket. He unlocked her door. She got in. He drove. She rode.

As silences go, it would have been a peaceful, almost content quiet except for one thing. Underneath all the calm was a constant, steady throbbing. With each passing minute, the intensity of the beat accelerated. Anticipation lurked in the shadows, making their breaths shallow and their pulses erratic. Megan's hands shook. Ben's were sweaty.

He drove into the narrow alley behind Megan's condo and double parked behind her car. The sound of the motor died away. Ben's voice seemed loud and foreign as he said, "Let's go for a walk."

They got out of the car and sauntered over to the little courtyard that could be seen from Amber's bedroom. Benton languidly leaned his broad shoulders against the brick wall and watched Megan. Her hands flittered nervously at her sides. Smiling, Benton reached forward, clasped her hands, and pulled her close.

The kiss they had both known was coming took them by surprise. Ben had intended a soft kiss, but the instant his lips met Megan's, fireworks erupted. When he realized his passion was being returned, his nonchalant lean on the wall became necessary; his head was swimming and his knees were weak.

Megan tried to step back. Her lungs were on fire with the breath locked in them. She managed to gasp, "Ben."

He smiled and kissed her again.

It was wonderful, beautiful, and she had to tell him. Before she could speak, Ben whispered her name so tenderly that tears flooded her eyes. It took all her strength to place a hand on his chest and push him away. This was what she had always wanted. It wasn't just the glorious kiss; the depth of their relationship fueled and charged their physical exchange.

"Ben, you don't really know me," the words were wrenched out of Megan's soul.

"Oh, but I do."

Megan looked up at Ben and lost heart. He was looking at her in such a warm, loving way that she couldn't shatter the moment. She would tell him tomorrow. Just for tonight, she would pretend that she had no past. Megan made no protest as Ben laced his fingers through hers and guided her out of the alley. They were going for a walk, and that was all that mattered.

The next morning, Megan climbed out of bed feeling rested and refreshed. She couldn't remember the last time she had slept so well. As she breezed around the apartment getting ready for work, she couldn't help but smile. She collected her keys and locked the front door. Her pace down the stairs slowed as Megan remembered that she had to tell Ben everything tonight.

Opening the apartment's outer door and stepping out onto

the front porch, Megan prayed that Ben would understand. She looked up. Her breath burned and singed her lungs as she stared in shock. In a crazy, mindless way, Megan thought, *"He's the most handsome man I have ever seen."*

Scott rested his hand languidly on the taxi door and smiled up at her. "Let me pay the driver and I'll be right with you, sweetheart."

From his dark head down to his wrinkle-free slacks, he appeared to be every girl's favorite fantasy. While Megan stood mesmerized, Scott paid the fare and closed the taxi door. He turned his heavily lashed eyes on her and bound up the steps to stand beside her on the porch. "I know you always love surprises." His smile widened, showing his perfect teeth.

"You should have been a movie star," Megan irrelevantly said.

"And you would make any movie star proud. Megan you look fabulous. You know I've missed my little wife."

The word *wife* snapped Megan out of her trance. Stiffening, she remembered that Scott's fabulous looks hid his constant ridicule, his need to control and consume, and his determination to succeed at all costs. She was fairly certain that one of the reasons Scott continued to try to win her back was because he couldn't stand to lose anything. The other reason, she didn't even question. Too many times, he had proven to her that she was a possession, an object, a doll, but she was his.

Dolls didn't walk away. They stayed firmly on the shelf or in whatever place you casually tossed them. They were soft, stuffed toys that were there whenever you felt like taking them out and playing with them. You could do whatever you wanted with a doll, and it never complained or talked back. This doll had come to life and walked away. Megan knew that Scott couldn't handle her rejection of him. He had to get her back under his control, and then, without a thought, he would shove her back on the shelf and forget she even existed.

As Megan gazed up at Scott, his handsome looks faded and were replaced by everything that she knew he was. In a tired voice, she stated, "I'm on my way to work. I don't have time."

"It can't hurt to be late once. You were always such a hard worker. I'm sure nothing's changed. Your firm can give you a little time off to be with me." Somehow his hand found its way onto her bare arm. "I really need to talk to you. Call in sick."

Megan's stomach began to churn as she fumbled in her bag for her cell. It would be better to settle this now. Anyway, the shock of seeing Scott would make her worthless at work. After making the necessary arrangements, Megan dropped her phone back into her bag and said, "Okay, talk."

"Here?" Scott scoffed. "Let's go up to your apartment."

"No." With the denial, Megan seemed to grow stronger.

Scott looked at her out of the corners of his shimmering, dark eyes and smirked knowingly. "Afraid, huh?"

"No, merely wise," Megan brushed off his arm and came down the last few steps. Walking toward the Coop and Harvard, she said, "We can talk as we walk."

"So you're setting the terms?"

"Absolutely."

"I like it." Scott fell into step beside Megan and grinned. "You're afraid of me. That's why you're so cautious. This indicates—"

"Nothing. It indicates nothing, Scott. Why are you here?"

"Megan, can you slow down? You're walking way too fast."

Megan continued to walk without slacking her pace. Scott stopped, looked at her surprised for a moment, and then had to run to catch up. "Okay, okay, we're on your terms."

"Scott, there is no we."

"You know we're almost running."

Ignoring his comment, Megan pointed, "If we turn here, we'll end up on campus. It's very Ivy League; literally the walls are covered with ivy and other climbing plants."

"What is this, a tour?"

The word *tour* reminded Megan of Ben. Walking along in silence, Megan thought of all the places Ben had taken her. For a moment she even forgot Scott. He rudely called her back to his presence. "Megan, you've changed."

She nodded, not knowing how to answer. Really seeing the area around her, Megan realized they were in one of the older quads of Harvard. History permeated the air around them. The old red brick walls reeked of the past. Years of students had walked through these doors carrying their books, dealing with their problems, filling their own hopes, and experiencing their own personal joys. Megan smiled serenely. Ben had opened her eyes to so many wonderful things.

"Can we sit? I'm a little tired; jet lag." Scott moved toward a stone bench.

Returning to the present, Megan sat beside Scott and turned to face him. "There is no we. There is no us. You should never have come. It's a waste of your time and money."

"Will you please listen to me?" He smiled his most charming smile and took her hand. He was dripping with confidence. "You don't wear my ring anymore." He looked so wretched and so disappointed, that for a second, Megan was almost moved.

It occurred to Megan that they were playing an ugly game she had played a million times before. It went like this: he'd promise to reform and then would waste their money on inappropriate things. He'd say it would never happen again, but it always did. When she'd complain and try to help him stop, he'd verbally abuse her and sometimes resort to squeezing or pinching the flesh underneath her arm. Scott always inflicted bruises in places that were never visible to anyone else. The next day a dozen red roses would arrive with a sweet note dangling from the glossy blossoms. Then the insidious cycle would begin again. He'd be so repentant, so dependent upon her, and so conscious of fulfilling her every need that he would convince Megan that there was hope and everything was going to be okay. It would last for a brief time until Megan found out it was all a fake: one continuous lie.

She looked at Scott and her heart wept for what could have been. Taking her look as encouragement, Scott pulled her into his arms and kissed her passionately.

Chapter Eighteen

Ben felt stupid, but he had to see her this morning. Since he had spent the night sleeplessly tossing on Jason's couch, it was no big deal to get up early. He slipped on his jogging clothes and decided to run by Megan's condo and say hi before she left for work.

As he ran, he kept thinking he should be exhausted. Instead, he was on an energized high. Last night he had kissed Megan, and she had kissed him back. The road was licked up under his feet. Ben jogged in place, waiting for the traffic light to change. He didn't even mind the noise or the smell of exhaust. He dashed up the steps to Megan's condo and pressed the buzzer, and stretched while he waited. There was no answer. He'd missed her. It was disappointing, but he'd see her tonight.

Ben bounced down the steps and started running toward Harvard. He would hit his favorite places on campus and then jog back to Jason's. He loved the ivy-covered brick, the arches, and the design of the old architecture. Stopping on the edge of the old quad, Ben leaned over to catch his breath and then looked up to enjoy the rich history that always permeated the air around the university. It felt great to exercise. His euphoria died in his throat as he saw Megan sitting on a bench. She was embracing a man and kissing him. Ben turned and ran faster than he had ever run before.

Megan pulled away from Scott. Before she thought about it, her hands rose up and she shoved him away. Immediately, he gripped her upper arms and yanked her back toward him. She could feel the bruises forming where his fingers dug into her flesh. Panic invaded her mind, making her relive every time Scott had been abusive. She felt helpless, worthless, and blown about like discarded trash. The pain in her arms was becoming unbearable. It finally snapped something inside of her.

"Let go of me this instant!" her voice was so coldly infuriated that Scott dropped his hands and stared, shocked by her outburst.

"Don't ever touch me again!" Megan stood, her eyes burning with intensity.

"Sweetheart, it's been so long . . ."

Megan glared at him, and the words withered on his tongue.

After a few seconds of intense silence, Megan said, "I don't ever want to see you again."

"You don't really mean that," Scott smiled sweetly while his dark brown eyes glowed with confidence and a disturbing kind of determination. "I've bought two plane tickets to Salt Lake City for tomorrow morning. Let me take you home, back where you belong."

Megan stared at him, stunned. The anger drained out of her, leaving only a depressing sorrow. He thought he could win her back with a smile and a plane ticket, pluck her off the shelf and return her to his collection, like a possession bought and paid for. It was sad and so pathetic that all Megan could mumble was an emotional, "I'm sorry."

"I'm sorry too."

She almost believed him; the expression on his face was convincingly sincere. If it hadn't been for the glitter of something hard and excited in the depths of his dark eyes, Megan would have bought his performance as she had so many times before.

She knew that look and remembered it well. It reminded her of when Scott accepted a challenge and when he allowed his obsession with winning to overshadow everything else: his honor, his integrity, and his spiritual nature. She clearly saw him in the past bragging about his superior mind and his ultimate cleverness in handling the prosecution. He thrived on control and loved to battle for supremacy. The more difficult the conflict, the more heady the victory. Megan didn't want to become another one of his victories.

Cautiously, she took a step away from the bench. Scott immediately rose and gazed forlornly down at her. Despite his expression, Megan could tell he was enjoying the sensation of power rippling through his system. Scott thought he was going to win and come off the great conqueror. It showed in his arrogant smile, in the prideful twist of his lips, and in the assurance of his bold, physical stance. His entire posture made a mock of his fake repentance. He was so sure of himself that he had bought two plane tickets back to Salt Lake.

As Megan stood silently staring at Scott, inspiration enlightened her mind and soul. It spoke gently and broken-heartedly of Scott's indiscretions and his weakness and taught her that Scott's insights and beliefs had been limited by his sins and rationalizations. Her eyes instantly stung with gritty, hot tears. It was all so sad and such a pitiful waste of potential. Why did she have to watch how far he had fallen, how much he had changed? Why did she have to go through this over and over again, always hoping that this time it would be different? When would it ever be finished?

"We can't let go of what we had, can we?" Scott quietly said. "We've meant too much to each other to walk away forever."

"Scott, it's not going to work."

"Megan, I only want what's best for you, for us."

"Then you'll let me go and never try to see me again."

Nothing real showed in Scott's face as he dejectedly sank down on the stone bench. He artfully clasped his hands in his lap and looked pitifully up at Megan. "I want you to be happy."

His movements and his expression looked practiced as if he had rehearsed them a dozen times until he'd perfected them. Scott lowered his head, hiding his eyes under his thick, dark lashes. "If you really don't ever want to see me again, I can understand." Scott's pause was a little too long, giving it an exaggerated quality.

Megan waited, wishing he'd let this end now without anymore fighting, without anymore manipulative games. There had been enough fighting and enough manipulation over the years.

"I'll get up and walk away right now if that's what you want me to do." Scott raised his head and there were tears shimmering in his brilliant dark eyes. Quickly, he brushed the tears away and said, "I'm so sorry about all this. You see, I love you so much that's it's hard to let you go."

For once his words rang with sincerity. The truth of what he had just said hung in the air between them. The thought that Scott might have really changed swayed and worried Megan. Maybe this wasn't the old cycle. She closed her eyes for a second and whispered, "Scott, it's over. I don't think we can ever go back, even if we wanted to."

"I know," Scott's sigh came off like a work of art. "But I can't forget that day in the temple. As we knelt across the altar, I felt so much love for you. I thought that you were the most beautiful woman in the world."

It was the wrong thing to say. Megan's hope and sympathy vanished as quickly as it had come. She stiffened and stared at Scott through angry, pain-ridden eyes. "If I was that beautiful to you and you loved me so much, it sure didn't last long. Less than six months after we were married, you turned to a porn queen on the internet." Bitterness burned in Megan's throat and chest. "Have you forgotten how irritated you were with me every time I checked the computer log? How you screamed at me and told me I was a nagging witch, keeping you under surveillance all the time?"

Megan hated herself for the intensity of her emotions, for the fear she felt waiting for him to respond, for still caring even though she didn't want to. Confronting Scott never did any good. He always lost control and shouted hateful things. A tired, defeated feeling washed over Megan, leaving her limp and aching all over. She no longer wanted to deal with any of this.

Instead of the anger Megan expected, Scott didn't respond at all. A genuine expression of fear and uncertainty crept over his face. He seemed to be struggling with a mixture of emotions. Finally, he nodded and spoke softly. "I was horrible. I don't like to remember those days. But I want you to know that I've repented now. I truly have. I don't do those things anymore. It's been a long time."

Megan wasn't softening. Her doubt showed clearly in her eyes and in the firm, straight line of her lips. These were the same words she had heard repeated far too many times. They had no effect on her anymore. She saw them for what they were: hollow and manipulative.

"The moment you left," he whispered, his eyes filled with a pathetic sadness, "I realized what I had done. I've been a fool and lost everything that mattered most to me. For days after, I didn't know what to do." He reached up, took both her hands, and gently pulled her back down on the bench beside him. Scott lifted his thick lashes and stared at Megan. His eyes burned with a little too much intensity. "I knew this time I had to stop or I'd never get you back."

Scott still had her hands firmly clasped between his fingers. Megan tried to pull free. His grip tightened, but he managed to caress her fingers. Megan wiggled harder, attempting to get free. "Please," he pleaded, "wait just a second and hear me out. I need to say this so that I can make some kind of restitution for all the wrongs I've done. You're probably right. You shouldn't fly back to Utah with me. I don't deserve you."

She saw him look down and then peek up under his lashes to gage how things were going. Megan closed her eyes trying to draw strength before saying, "It's all in the past now. Let's leave it at that."

"I can't!" he cried. "I want you to understand just one more thing. I haven't looked at pornography since the day you left for Boston. You've changed me." This time his words and expression were nearly perfect. They had their effect on Megan.

As she sat quietly facing Scott, her heart grew cold and heavy. An instinct somewhere at the back of her mind triggered an uneasy response and a deeply troubled feeling. Confusion and uncertainty tugged unmercifully on her emotions. An urge to pray gently warmed Megan's heart. Silently, she asked Heavenly Father for help, for understanding, for discernment, and for peace. The Spirit began to whisper through her soul, soothing and opening her mind.

"Megan, I know that you don't want to hear this right now, but I'm ready to keep the promises I made at the temple that day. Give me another chance."

Megan stared at him while she slipped her hands out of his clasp. He was asking for another chance. It played upon her gentle disposition. In the beginning, there had been so many good times, so many sweet memories. But those days were followed by the crushing of her spirit and the smashing of her dreams. There was horrible pain, constant self-doubt, and so many lies. There were thousands of lies from him and almost as many lies from her when she tried to cover his secret life.

And where was trust? Lies came so easily to Scott. Megan needed security and someone she could believe in. Could she ever trust him again? Trust came from the quiet steadiness of people like Ben who had no secrets, no hidden agendas, and no practiced deceit. Megan wasn't sure if she could ever trust Scott again. To be absolutely honest, she wasn't sure she even wanted to try.

"Before you make a decision," Scott's voice sounded with arrogant confidence while his handsome face glowed with false sincerity, "you need to understand one more thing. I know I said I wasn't ready to have a family. But Megan, it's different now. I'd like to have a son. If we get back together, I'd like to start our family."

Megan was shocked, and tears burned under her eyelids. As she looked at Scott, something strange happened. It was as if

Scott's soul was laid bare before her and she could see into every hidden part of it. What she saw reflected there troubled her even more. Before her was his wall of deceit, his fortress of manipulation, and his tower of self-absorption. They were all major obstacles so massive and so well fortified that she had never been able to break through.

He was too sure of himself, spoiled by his extraordinary good looks and his charismatic personality. Megan remembered giving him so many chances to change, so many chances to step outside of his walls of selfishness. Each year she had died a little inside, withered by his unkindness, stabbed by his addiction, and humiliated by his petty pinching and verbal abuse. No, she did not want to go back.

She recalled the day the Spirit had let her know she no longer needed to remain in the marriage. That same Spirit came to her now, letting her know that she must free herself from Scott.

"Megan, did you hear me? I'm ready to have children."

Children. The word brought such sweet longing to Megan that she had to look away. She stared at the beautiful, old architecture and its curved arches and tried to think. The more she attempted to focus, the more her mind persisted in seeing Benton sitting on the couch reading to his nephews. She remembered how the youngest boy had been curled up on Ben's lap, fast asleep with his thumb hanging halfway out of his mouth. The two older boys had been snuggled up on each side of Ben. The oldest boy, Zack, had been protesting that Ben wasn't reading the story right. The boys' laughter, the expression of love on Ben's face, and the sweetness of that moment filled Megan's heart with beautiful peace.

Turning back to her ex-husband, Megan thought, *What kind of a father would Scott be?* There would be no magical reading of stories—only impatience and neglect. She remembered the times Scott had lost his temper; his hateful words; his blows to her self-esteem; and the humiliation of his petty, physical abuse. Scott would treat their child the same way.

For the first time, it was really over. No matter how many

times Megan had believed their marriage was finished before, this moment confirmed it. She realized that she had always saved and hidden away a tiny bit of hope, wishing that the perfect life that Scott was so good at creating would somehow become real. His fantasy world had only been a trap, a snare to keep her in an empty marriage and to ensure she did his bidding. The other times when she had thought she was finished with Scott had only been like small steps moving away from their dysfunctional relationship. At this point, there was enough distance and healing for Megan to see clearly where she had come from. The Spirit softly warned her that she must not be enticed by his sweet persuasion. The life he was offering her was a pit of pain and disillusionment. The reality of their relationship burned the fantasy world Scott had created until there was only a pile of ashes left. Not a single coal glowed. There was just cold, gray ash.

There was no anger in her, only an empty, weary comprehension that this portion of her life was concluded. This was her other life. From now on, she would segment it and keep the old life permanently in the past. Without realizing it, Megan spoke aloud. "It's finished."

"What are you talking about?"

"Everything I went through for the last years of our marriage." Megan took a deep breath. "Scott, I need to go to work. I'm already late. But before I go, I want you to know I mean it. I don't want to see you again."

"You'll change your mind."

"I won't."

"I'll sit on your doorstep until you do." Scott's voice began to rise while his face darkened and hardened. The image he always carefully constructed crashed as he vented his anger. "I'll make you come home with me. Do you hear me?"

She knew what was coming next. Because they were in a public place, he'd be more careful. Probably he'd grab her upper arm again and pinch the underside until he drew blood with his nails. How could she have ever considered going back to this?

Standing up and backing away, Megan calmly stated, "I'm

going to work now. And if you ever come near me again, I'll get a restraining order." Megan didn't wait for his reply. She turned on her heel and walked away.

Chapter Nineteen

At first, Megan wasn't even aware that Ben was quieter than usual. She was trying so hard to forget about Scott's visit this morning that she didn't notice Ben's increased reserve. Once she recognized Ben's change in behavior, it made her uncertain about her own behavior. It was difficult to know what to do or say.

As the evening progressed, Megan wondered if it was worth it to tell Ben everything. Maybe their kiss last night hadn't meant anything. Maybe Scott was right. She'd never had anything worth giving. Scott's unexpected visit seemed like it had been days ago rather than this morning. Tormented by her thoughts and fears, Megan remained silent as they drove into the alley behind her condo. She and Benton got out of the car and stood awkwardly by the little cobblestone courtyard.

Despite her mixed and confused emotions, Megan still needed to tell Ben about her past. This desire was potent, but she didn't know how to begin. She clenched her hands and finally whispered, "There are some things you should know." All the joy she'd felt in this same spot on the previous night had vanished somewhere in the last twenty-four hours.

Ben stiffened and straightened his shoulders. He looked as if he were preparing himself for something unpleasant. As Megan stared up at Ben, she wondered if he was attempting to distance himself. Fear briefly froze her heart, but the need to unburden herself was more powerful. "Last night you kissed me, and I should have told you then."

"You're in love with someone else," Ben unemotionally stated.

"No, it's a long story." Megan looked at the ground and shrugged her shoulders.

Despite his personal pain, Ben had compassion for her. He reached out and took one of her hands. Massaging the spot on her finger where Scott's ring had rested for so many years, he encouraged, "I'm willing to listen."

"I . . . I was . . ." She couldn't do it. Attempting to free her hand, she pleaded, "Oh, Ben, it's so hard."

"Then just say it."

Megan opened her mouth and shut it. Her confession would change everything.

"I already know."

The words were so quiet that it took Megan several seconds to assimilate what he had said. His gentle caress of her ring finger appeared to confirm his statement.

"You know?" Megan was dumbfounded. "You know I'm divorced, and you still kissed me?"

"Yes."

Megan pulled away from Ben and began to pace up and down the little stone square, "How did you know?"

Benton hesitated, unsure of how to answer. He didn't feel like explaining. It was too humiliating, yet he wanted to be honest. "I didn't know for sure, but I guessed."

"And it doesn't matter to you?"

"It matters a lot to me."

Megan had known it would. She was used, tarnished, and had failed in her marriage. He deserved someone who hadn't been foolish enough to marry the wrong man. "It's okay. I understand."

"I don't think you do," Benton said reading her despondent stance accurately. "It matters a lot to me, because you were hurt so badly."

Her head lifted so that she could stare disbelievingly into his eyes. She wished that it were lighter so she could see his face clearly. Instead, he stood like a silhouette with the light shining behind him.

For Ben, the glow of the street lamp illuminated her beautiful features. He wanted to reach out and touch her face. What he had seen in Harvard Square that morning stopped him. She needed to talk, to tell him, and then he'd have to walk away with as much dignity as he could salvage.

"I don't understand how you could know," Megan whispered, starting to hope and then praying silently that he would still care for her despite what she had to tell him.

"Remember when I asked you about your jeans?" Ben quietly reminded her. She shook her head, feeling tired and confused. Ben smiled sadly. "Well, I asked you why you ironed your jeans. I'd never seen anyone with a crease up their jeans before."

Megan nodded, trying to recall how she had answered.

Ben assisted her. "You said that it made them look nicer, and then you shrugged as if it wasn't a big deal. But I felt like it was important." Benton looked down at the little wrought iron table beside him. "Maybe I was wrong, but I still think it matters. You don't have an obsessive compulsive personality. So there had to be another reason why you ironed your jeans."

Megan plucked at the crease in her jeans until she realized what she was doing.

"Your marriage wasn't happy. You felt insignificant so you fought your insecurity by ironing your pants and making sure you always looked perfect. It helped you feel—"

"Better when he constantly told me that I was never good enough. I could never measure up to his expectations. I tried, Ben. I honestly did."

It cost him a lot, but he held his arms open to her. She came rushing in, desperately needing all the comfort he was offering. At first, she sobbed and then finally she spoke into his shoulder. Her voice was a feathery, light whisper, but Benton heard every word. Her pain pierced his heart and left him bleeding.

"In the beginning, Scott and I were so in love. We were getting married and going to law school. The temple was beautiful and the whole world was before of us."

Megan shuddered. "During our second year of law school, everything changed. Scott became moody and preferred to be alone. I thought it was the pressure from school, so I offered to study with him again. He said he had to do it by himself.

"Scott became more vocal in his dissatisfaction with me. He didn't like how I dressed. I was too unsophisticated. He began to make crude, cruel jokes about how I was little Miss Perfect."

Megan lifted her head from Ben's shoulder and moved wearily to one of the metal chairs. After sitting, she folded her hands pristinely on the table. "We became two people who lived in the same apartment, but who never shared anything."

Benton walked over and leaned against the brick building, intently listening to every word.

"Our finances suddenly become desperate. My checkbook disappeared. He said he'd closed the account. I was afraid to ask for any details because Scott had the tendency to become angry if I questioned him. Eventually, he started sleeping in the office.

"Ben, I didn't know what I was doing wrong, so I tried harder. I fixed his favorite meals, left little encouraging notes, and prayed things would improve when we graduated. Instead, things became worse.

"When our ranking was published, I was shocked to learn that Scott had finished at the bottom of our class. I forgot about his temper and asked him what had happened. Scott instantly became furious and accused me of horrible things.

"To make matters worse, I landed a job with a prestigious firm in Salt Lake while Scott couldn't find employment. He finally took a job with a legal aid society. I suggested that we budget and start paying off our student loans. I'm sorry, this is getting long."

"No," Benton quietly affirmed, "go on."

"Scott refused to budget. I didn't know what to do. I told him I was going to pay off my student loans. He started screaming that I could pay for everything. He never paid for anything ever again. And every Sunday we'd attend church and pretended that everything was fine."

"What was wrong?" Ben gently asked.

"I had no idea until one night I decided to ask him if we could go in for counseling. I knocked on the door to the office. I don't think Scott heard me. Anyway, I walked in and found him on the Internet viewing pornography. I didn't know it then, but he was addicted.

"He said it was just a pop-up and some other lies. The next day I got smart and checked the computer log. The history was clear. This was a lengthy repeat pattern. I confronted him when he got home, and of course he was angry. Eventually, he promised to stop. We went to see our bishop, and I had hope. Before pornography, Scott had been a good person."

Megan sighed and rested her head on her hands. "I'd think things were better, and then I'd find he'd been on a porn site again. We'd repeat the whole process, see the bishop, get a new internet filter, and talk about counseling, but Scott always refused to go. Then he'd use his money to buy new internet access and pay for his filthy habit.

"I've decided that no one can compete with a fantasy. A real person makes mistakes, says the wrong things, isn't sexy enough. So Scott lived the fantasy, and I never measured up to his porn queens."

Benton moved off the wall and sat heavily on the chair across from her. "What happened after that?"

"One day, I had a strong spiritual prompting that the Lord no longer required me to stay in the marriage. I had done all I could and was now free to leave." Megan looked at Ben. "I remember my bishop telling me repeatedly that it wasn't personal, but it's hard to believe when your husband doesn't want you, because he's having an affair with a fantasy on the internet." Megan shuddered. "It's been two years since I started the divorce process, and I'm still struggling with what happened, but I know it was the right time to leave. The Lord has given me that peace."

Megan shifted uneasily in her chair. "There's something more. Scott showed up on my doorstep this morning."

Benton clutched the sides of his metal chair with both hands.

"We went for a walk because I didn't want to be alone with him. He doesn't seem to understand that it is over. Ben, he kissed me!" Megan wiped her lips as if to remove the vile taste of Scott's mouth.

Benton's heart picked up and began to beat a hopeful rhythm.

"I threatened him with a restraining order. I never want to see him again."

They both sat at the wrought iron table, lost in their own thoughts. Benton had been so sure it was all over when he had seen her kissing Scott that he wanted to shout. At the same time, he couldn't enjoy his newfound hope because he was overwhelmed by how much she had suffered. His heart ached for her while he applauded her strength, her determination, and her reliance upon the Lord. He was not sure if he could have withstood and endured as well as she had.

Megan almost wished she hadn't told him. Once she had started, it had been like a severed artery spurting out her anguish in a pulsating gush. She had revealed too much and left herself exposed and vulnerable. Megan pulled her tattered self-esteem around her and decided to make it easy for him. "You don't have to see me anymore. I understand."

Benton glanced up, astonished. Reaching across the table, he covered her hand. "You think because you told me this that I won't want to see you again?"

Megan lowered her head and nodded. The lamp light caught the sheen of her dark hair. Benton thought of how beautiful she was and how spiritually strong she had been. "I see," he softly stated. Clearing his throat, Benton watched her bent head. "Well, I'm afraid it's not going to be that easy to get rid of me."

Megan looked up at him. She didn't say anything, but her eyes searched his shadowed face, looking for answers.

"Megan, I have the strongest respect and admiration for you."

"For what, being divorced, or thinking about becoming less active? For not praying hard enough to receive the right answer? For marrying the wrong man?" Megan scoffed.

"Where do you want me to start?" Ben's voice was warm and reassuring. "I have this theory. I think there are two kinds of mistakes. The first is when you have a clear answer or you know from the scriptures and gospel teachings that something is wrong and you choose to do it anyway. The Book of Mormon calls it willfully rebelling.

"The second mistake is more an error in judgment. You try to receive an answer, but your mind is clouded by your own fears, your own limited understanding, or your own weaknesses that you're trying to overcome. So you make the best decision you can, attempting to do what's right. Sometimes it's right and sometimes it's a mistake. I think the Lord looks on these two situations differently. Megan, the Lord knows your heart. You would never willfully rebel."

Megan couldn't speak. The tears slipped down her cheeks.

"I respect you because you found yourself in a difficult marriage, but you didn't give up. Despite Scott's ridiculing, you fought to do the Lord's will."

Megan couldn't let him paint such a perfect picture, "Ben, sometimes I couldn't handle it. I screamed at Scott and nagged him. I wish I'd never done that."

Benton wouldn't allow it. "We all do things we're not proud of. It's the growing and trying again that counts. The most important thing is that you couldn't let go of the gospel. You kept trying to do what was right instead of falling away."

Silence whispered softly between them until Megan quietly confessed, "I couldn't picture my life without the Savior and Heavenly Father. I needed that wonderful spirit you feel when you're trying to live right."

Benton rose, came around the iron table, and stood behind her. As he rubbed her tense shoulders, he said, "I'm glad you told me about Scott. It helps me to understand," he intentionally lightened his voice, "but now I think it's time for a walk."

Megan rose almost feeling as if she had left the old Megan sitting on the chair behind her. It was an odd, eerie sensation, but at the same time liberating.

"I'm not working for the next couple of days," Ben cheerfully announced, "and I intend to spend as much time with you as I possibly can."

Megan willingly imitated his carefree tone. "Ah, there's so much history to see."

"Actually there is. Let's see, there's, John Adams' estate in Braintree, the witch trials in Salem. Did you know that Nathaniel Hawthorne worked in the Custom House in Salem?"

"No."

"Oh, dear," Benton lamented with fake concern, "you're going to need a lot of extra credit to pass this class."

"What kind of extra credit?' Megan's heart was starting to flutter.

"Let me figure this out," Benton teased. "You've fallen behind, you know."

"I have?"

"Yes, according to my calculations," Benton pretended to count on his fingers, "it's pretty bad. I wouldn't be against a little bribery." He looked down at Megan, his eyes bold and mischievous. "In order to pass, at the conclusion of every field trip, you must kiss your instructor."

Megan couldn't believe she was laughing. The tears on her cheeks hadn't even dried. In a solemn voice, Megan proclaimed, "You could always try."

Benton stared at her astonished that she hadn't said no outright. It gave him hope and put a smile on his face.

Chapter Twenty

Under normal conditions, Megan's workday whizzed past, but today every little thing distracted her. She fidgeted with excitement and felt her stomach knot with fear. Conflicting emotions swirled inside of her: elation, trepidation, and then elation again. Everything had changed last night when she had confided in Ben. It was strange how her secret had come surging out after she had carefully hidden it for so many years.

Ben's reaction had surprised her. She had anticipated a change in their relationship and was pleased that Ben still wanted to see her despite knowing everything. Thoughts of Ben warmed her heart.

As Megan sat staring at her computer, the magnitude of her involvement with Ben hit her. A chill of panic shivered down her spine as she realized that she felt much more than friendship. Determinedly facing her feelings, she cried out loud, "You might as well admit it, Megan, since you're halfway in love with the guy."

"How delicious!" Jane cooed from the open doorway.

Megan jumped. She hadn't heard Esther and Jane enter the office.

Jane hustled across the room, leaned one hip on the desk and chuckled, "It's like Hepburn and Tracy all over again. You both didn't want to get involved, but there was chemistry. I saw it last April when you danced with him at the company party."

"I hardly knew Ben then," Megan protested.

"Well, it sparkled between you two like fireworks ready to explode, and the Fourth of July set them off."

In her usual manner, Esther stood back and observed. Despite her casual stance, Esther's dark eyes glowed with emotion, betraying her hopes and her concerns. Megan looked over and saw the expression on Esther's face. The sincere caring reflected there caused Megan's emotions to bubble up in her throat. It was difficult to squeeze out her words, "I think he might be the cottage-in-the-country type."

"I always said he was," Esther gruffly reminded, but her cross words couldn't cover the hope and excitement shining in her eyes.

"What are you talking about?" Jane tipped her head to one side like a bird searching for a worm. "It's an old movie, isn't it?"

Both Megan and Esther laughed and answered simultaneously, "No."

"It's time for lunch anyway. Shall we go?" Jane shifted her weight off the desk.

Megan shook her head. "I'm going to work through lunch so I can leave early."

Jane raised her eyebrows and "oohed." A delightful blush tinged Megan's cheeks. "That's pretty incriminating," Jane pounced forward. "You have a date with Ben, don't you? There's going to be a lot to tell when you come back to work after your long weekend."

"You go too fast," Esther chided Jane. "Give her time to work things out carefully and slowly. She needs to be sure."

"Not at a moment like this," Jane enthused. "He's the marrying kind, right?" Without waiting for anyone to respond, Jane gurgled cheerfully on. "There's chemistry. He's nice. Just take the ring and say yes, it's not that hard."

Esther shook her head in mild disapproval. "Pray," she advised.

"Of course she'll pray," Jane said completely misunderstanding. "Every young girl prays for a handsome husband."

"Yes, well, just pray." Esther's smile was surprisingly gentle.

Megan gazed into Esther's eyes and understood. She realized that Esther was not only referring to being sure, but was thinking about heavenly signs, such as Gideon and the Golden Fleece. It was extraordinary how close she and Esther had become. Of course, she loved Jane too, but Esther had uncanny depths hidden behind her gruff exterior. Both of these women had become so dear to Megan. Smiling, she looked from Jane to Esther and warmly promised, "I'll pray and be sure."

After Jane and Esther had gone, Megan found it even more difficult to concentrate. Finally she gave up and left the office. Her head was swirling with thoughts of Ben, his laugh, his thoughtfulness, and his passionate kiss. Still at the back of Megan's mind, fear slunk from shadow to shadow, unsettling her. She had to be positive this time. Suddenly a sign like Gideon's fleece sounded awfully good.

It wasn't until Megan sat across the table from Ben at his favorite restaurant that she felt her fears start to subside. Ben's presence had a calming effect on her. As the dinner progressed, Megan found herself studying Ben closely. Was there some way to determine what was really in a person's heart? Was there some outward indication that a man was not what he professed to be?

As the waiter came and went, they chatted and ate. Finally, as they sat over their empty plates, the only thing Megan felt was peace. She had been so at ease all evening that later as they stood outside her condo, she allowed Ben to kiss her. A thrill rippled through her as their lips touched. Maybe this was her answer: delicious, wonderful peace.

All that night, she dreamed of Ben and their life together. Her youthful hopes of a happy, eternal marriage were revived. She awoke refreshed and excited. As she pulled on a pair of jeans and a T-shirt, she was glad that she had taken the day off from work. Her obsession with creased pants, immaculate blouses, and perfect hairstyles seemed ridiculous. She padded into the living room, her flip-flops making soft thudding sounds on the carpet.

Amber sat on the floor, surrounded by dozens of photographs, stacks of colored paper, and an odd assortment of memorabilia.

"You're up early this morning," Megan commented, watching Amber rummaging through a cardboard box.

As Amber's head turned, her thick ponytail swung over her shoulder. "I am. I wanted to get started on this before I have to go to work." She gestured toward the mess on the floor and said, "My mom found this box after Ben moved all his stuff into his new house. So now I'm doing Ben's scrapbook."

Megan was halfway to the kitchen when Amber called her back. "Hey, come and look at this."

Amber was holding up a photograph. "He sure was a butterball after his mission."

Megan unsuspectingly walked back and took the offered snapshot. She sank down on the couch and looked at the picture. There was something oddly familiar about the photo. It was Ben, that was all. A chubbier, fatter Ben, but simply Ben.

"I think it took him a couple of years at the Y to slim down," Amber chuckled, pulling a yellowed copy of the *Daily Universe* out of the pile.

A slimy finger of apprehension touched Megan's heart. "Ben was at the Y?"

"Yep," Amber opened the *Daily Universe* and a picture stuck in the folds of the paper dropped to the floor. "Maybe I should entitle this page, 'Benton the butterball.' Or maybe it would mean more to him if I used the nickname his friends had for him at the Y. 'Kelly the butterball.' No, 'Benton the butterball' sounds better."

Kelly. The name triggered something in the distant corners of Megan's mind. A hazy memory of a chubby, gentle boy on her doorstep with flowers almost seemed to be a fantasy rather than a real experience. Before Megan could remember clearly, Amber thrust a second photograph at her. The picture flipped upside down as Megan's fingers clasped it. The names scrawled in black ink on the back, seared Megan's mind. "Brian Durand, the weatherman; Benton Kilgallen, alias Kelly; and Scott Spencer, the man."

Megan's hands shook, her mind malfunctioned, and her stomach rebelled all while Amber kept causally pulling things out of the box: the tassel to Ben's graduation cap, a tiny cougar flag, and a mass of unsorted photographs. Amber was chatting and making funny comments, oblivious to Megan's stunned silence.

Somehow Megan's stiff fingers turned over the snapshot. Staring numbly into the faces of Benton and Scott, Megan realized she had also forgotten Brian Durand, the other member of the elders quorum presidency. Odd bits and pieces, shapes and faces, crowded Megan's mind. She remembered dancing with Scott and looking across the room at Ben. "I'm here with Kelly." Dropping the picture, Megan leaped to her feet while Amber, still engrossed in organizing, noticed nothing.

In a nightmarish way, Megan saw her purse lying on the end table. She picked it up and headed for the front door. Finally Amber realized that Megan was leaving. "Where are you going?" she inquired, merely curious since she'd missed all the vital cues.

"Out!" Megan clutched her purse with shaking fingers. Softening, she turned and smiled. Through clenched teeth, she lied. "I forgot, I need something at the store." Despite her pain, she didn't want Amber to worry. Yet, she couldn't stay in the condo for another second. A towering wall of emotion was driving her.

Amber accepted Megan's explanation without much thought. In fact, she didn't consider Megan's abrupt departure until she began sorting through a pile of photographs. One snapshot suddenly riveted Amber to the floor. There was Benton in his worn out, best left-over-from-my-mission suit with a boutonnière stuck in his lapel, standing beside a beautiful girl.

In her lovely, formal dress the girl looked like Snow White, not just any Snow White, but a Snow White that Amber was particularly familiar with. Megan's creamy white skin and her shiny black hair left no doubt which princess she resembled.

Amber's interest in the box doubled, tripled, and quadrupled as she fervently searched through photos and objects. In the end she had an odd pile of articles, a dried boutonnière (boys didn't do this did they?), two pictures of Ben and Megan at the dance, and a wedding invitation torn in half. Stunned, Amber fingered the edges of the announcement as she repeated over and over again the names printed on it. Megan Marie Jones and Scott Erik Spencer.

Amber's vision blurred as the memory of the day Ben had helped her move into Megan's condo focused clearly in her mind. She remembered asking Ben if he had ever been in love. It was all too easy to recall Benton's answer. *"I don't know. I think I was once."*

Amber had pressed Ben for more details. Had he been in graduate school at the time? He'd replied, *"No, at the Y."* When Amber had finally managed to pry the story out of him what was it he had said? Suddenly Benton's words sounded in Amber's mind with a vibrant intensity. *"She was the fairy tale princess and I was the frog. I never turned into the handsome prince, so she ran off and married someone else."*

Amber stared at the pile she had collected and suddenly understood what she had inadvertently done. Her legs were stiff and she felt ancient as she made a dash for the phone. It took an eternity to punch in Jason's number and even longer for Jason to answer.

"Is Ben there?" Amber cried.

"No," Jason replied, "he just left with Megan."

Chapter Twenty-One

Megan's legs trembled as she climbed the stairs to Jason's apartment. For a second she paused and placed a shaky hand on the railing. Her emotions were engaged in a fierce battle, each fighting to show their superiority. Anger was winning out because fear had joined its forces and increased its numbers. Rational, reasonable thought was facing a losing battle. Megan sank down onto the steps and tried to regain control. Instead, her mind kept repeating over and over again these painful words, *He keeps secrets from me. He keeps secrets from me.* Her head spun, whirling the words around and around and then throwing them off in new more damaging tangents. Ben had never told her that they had met before. Why? Was he going to use it to manipulate her in the future? Was he saving it like Scott would to stab her with?

Why had this happened again? Megan stiffened herself mentally, as well as physically. Well, the only thing that really mattered now was the knowledge she had gained. It was clear that Benton had betrayed her faith in him. He wasn't honest. Of course he had known she had married Scott. Everyone in their singles ward had known. The night she had told Ben about Scott why hadn't he said, "I know, I was in your ward at BYU." Instead he had pretended that he knew by some mysterious means. And Megan had been foolish enough to believe him.

"I trusted you," Megan whispered. Her face was completely dry of tears and empty of emotion. The mask she had worn for so long was fitting back in place. She had shared her innermost secrets and in return Ben had lied to her by pretending he didn't already know. If Ben had kept this secret, what other things was he hiding? Was he just like Scott, concealing his own little private world while he pretended to be something he wasn't? She had thought Ben was different: honest and open, and now she knew that Ben was just like Scott. He hid things.

Megan leaned her head against the railing and stared vacantly forward. She couldn't trust him. She couldn't trust herself either. Where did that leave her? Alone, it left her all alone again. But wasn't that better than fighting a secret world and always losing?

Panic grabbed hold of Megan's heart and whispered fear through all the secret corners of her mind. Would she find herself losing it again when things went wrong with Ben? Would she start yelling and screaming like a banshee and only hate herself more for her failure to behave with dignity? It was all so ugly. Here she was again in the same old place. She had fallen in love with another man she couldn't trust.

Megan stood and began making her way upstairs. She knew what she needed to do.

Benton opened Jason's door and stood staring at Megan. She looked so good to him that he smiled before he saw the expression in Megan's eyes. It was hard and cold like fencing blades crossed in the wintry sunlight. Benton had always thought her eyes were more blue than gray, but now he wondered.

She gripped his arm and pulled him out into the hallway while Jason called out a "Hi" from across the room.

Megan's "Hi" was short and tense. She immediately modulated her voice and added, "We need to go. Bye."

Benton irrelevantly thought that he was glad he was dressed and had his shoes on. Confused, he tentatively asked, "What happened?"

Megan seemed to realize that she still had a hold of Ben's arm and dropped it as if he was contaminated. "You happened," she said, marching down the stairs.

"I don't understand." Benton hurried after her.

Megan paused a moment in the open doorway of the apartment complex and then pivoted to face him. "You lied to me."

Benton was astonished. He had never lied to her and immediately said so.

With a swirl of insulted fury, Megan stormed out the door, down the steps, and onto the sidewalk. At this time in the morning, the street was deserted. Megan leaned against the wrought iron railing and glared at him. He had known who she was all along. He had known Scott, known they'd divorced. Ben had deceived her. He was just like Scott: a liar.

"Tell me what's going on," Benton pleaded. "Say something."

"Kelly?" the name came out of her mouth twisted with pain.

Only seeing Megan's suffering, Ben reached for her. She slapped his hand away, "Don't touch me."

Benton's hand fell listlessly back to his side. "I don't understand. Everything was fine last night."

"That was before I knew you had lied to me." A single tear broke through Megan's cold control. She angrily wiped it away before accusing, "I trusted you," Megan looked at him as if she were seeing him for the first time, "just like I trusted Scott! He'd tell me he hadn't been to any inappropriate sites. But the computer log said differently. We'd buy a new filter and only I knew the password. I'd think things were better until I found out he'd bought a new laptop and hidden it." Megan looked at the ground and whispered, "He always lied, and now you've lied too."

"Megan, I never lied to you."

"Maybe not out-and-out lied, but you deceived me."

"How?" Benton sincerely wanted to know.

"It's me that should have been asking how," Megan bitterly cried. "I was stupid and naïve, even after all I've been through.

I blatantly swallowed the idea that you already knew by some miraculous means that I was divorced and I never thought to question how you knew!"

Benton's chest tightened and breathing became an agony as he realized what she was referring to. "I didn't mean to deceive you."

"But you did!" Megan sounded like the attorney she was, pressing home a weak point in the opposition's testimony. She looked him directly in the eye, challenging.

"It wasn't like that," Benton insisted, gulping air into his stagnant lungs.

"Then how was it?"

Benton shifted his weight anxiously, "When we met again, I expected you to recognize me."

"And when I didn't?" Megan's voice didn't give Benton any hope.

"I was embarrassed. I remembered you quite clearly and felt stupid saying something like, 'Don't you remember me? I was the fat guy who took you to a ward dance.' I decided that telling you would only embarrass us both. So I said nothing."

"You allowed me to believe a lie!" her eyes were cold and eerily steady.

"That's not how I see it."

"Why didn't you tell me when I told you about Scott?" An acid taste filled her mouth as the fear and anger she'd felt in the stairwell pressed in around her.

"Megan, I wanted too, but I was shocked by what you told me. It's worse than you think. While I was out jogging, I'd seen you kissing Scott in Harvard Square. That night when we talked about your divorce, I expected you to tell me you were going back to him. I had no idea that your marriage was so terrible." Benton gripped the wrought iron railing with both hands.

Megan softened slightly and then stiffened up, "You should have told me."

"I wish I had, but everything you were saying was so shocking that I was just trying to comprehend it all. I assumed that you and Scott had divorced because you didn't get along. I never imagined that things were so awful. I thought Scott was an honorable man. We were in the elders quorum presidency together. I was deceived too!"

"It was his dirty secret," Megan whispered, looking down the street. "And for years I helped him keep it. I won't do that again, never again."

"I'm not asking you to," Ben gently acknowledged. "I'd be offering a much different life."

"A life where you'd allow me to believe something that wasn't true?" Megan whispered, so sick of lies that she couldn't tolerate even the hint of deception.

"I didn't think it was that important," Benton defended. "I figured you'd either remember in time or I'd tell you."

"Well, it's important to me." Megan's eyes wearily looked off in the distance.

A car passed, making it impossible for Megan to hear all that Ben had said. She only heard the, "I'm sorry," and completely missed the, "I love you."

"What did you say?" Megan asked without looking at him.

"I'm sorry," Ben repeated the first part, insecurity and fear gripping him so tightly that he couldn't say the words again.

"I'm sorry too!" The tears started to fall in earnest now. "I was hoping this would be different." Megan's sigh shredded Benton's heart. "I've been praying for a sign. After what happened last time, I told the Lord I needed a sign from Him before I could commit myself. I think this is my answer."

"What do you mean?" Ben's voice had a desperate quality to it as if he knew something unfortunate was waiting to hit him hard.

"I needed to know if this was the right thing. I couldn't stand to be hurt like that again." Megan straightened and stood taller, tapping some inner strength. The tears stopped rolling down her cheeks and her face looked determined.

"Megan, I promise I've never been involved in pornography."

"I'm glad," her voice was devoid of emotion, "but I prayed for a sign and I think Heavenly Father has let me know."

"Megan," Benton pleaded, watching his dream shatter for the second time.

"Ben, I've enjoyed your company and the history lessons. Let's just leave it at that." She pushed herself off the wrought iron railings and looked sadly up at Ben. "Thanks for everything. This is good-bye."

With a regal toss of her silky black hair, Megan walked confidently away. If Ben could have seen her face, he would have gone after her. Instead he only saw the cool, indifferent manner in which she turned and left him and never knew what it cost her.

In a defeated trance, Megan wandered aimlessly, walking and thinking until she remembered she'd driven. Carefully retracing her steps, Megan located her car and got in. How long she sat staring vacantly over the steering wheel, she'd never know. Some instinct for survival warned her not to drive. So she simply sat, going over every detail of her relationship with Ben.

She could get through this. It was insignificant compared to what she had struggled through before. This reasoning did not bring much comfort, since Megan couldn't stop picturing Ben's face. She liked how he teased her, how he was content to be silent, and how he had a gentle assurance about him.

Her feelings for Ben made her weak and vulnerable. She had to remember that she couldn't trust him and that he had deceived her. Clients who withheld information were dangerous, and so were men who didn't tell everything. It was safer to forget Ben Kilgallen and never again allow him into her life. The difficulty was that she had already unwittingly given Ben access to her heart.

Megan pressed her eyes closed and leaned her head back against the seat. The chimes of her cell phone sounded. If it was Ben she was not going to answer. Flipping the cover open, Megan determined to shut off her phone. It wasn't Ben's number that appeared on the screen, it was her parents' number that was displayed there.

Megan answered with what she hoped was a normal sounding, "Hello."

"Hi, honey, this is Mom."

"How's everything going?" Megan took a deep breath.

"Good, but we'd all be doing better if you came back home."

"I like Boston."

"But Scott's here."

"We've been divorced for over a year."

"I know, but Scott came by last night. He came here straight from the airport. Megan, he was so upset. I've never seen him like that before. He pleaded with me to call and talk to you. He said he wanted to beg for your forgiveness and you wouldn't let him. That's why he flew all the way out there. I think it broke his heart when you wouldn't listen." Her mother sighed sadly. "He couldn't seem to calm down and kept repeating over and over again that he would do anything to get you back."

The heavy burden of lies and pretence descended around Megan like a black, suffocating vapor. She suddenly wondered why she was still covering for Scott, trying to preserve his perfect image. In that instant, Megan made a commitment to herself. Never again would she evade or lie for Scott. "I'm sad to hear that, but it's not true."

"What do you mean it's not true? He even cried," her mother quietly insisted.

"I'm sure he did." Megan's voice took on a calm rational tone. "He always cried when he promised me he wouldn't get on the internet and look at pornography again." Megan could hear strange sputtering sounds on the other end of the phone. "Mom, are you all right?"

"Yes," her mother still sounded breathless, "I didn't know."

"I'm sorry. It's my fault," Megan looked blindly out the windshield. "I should have told you a long time ago, but it was so humiliating and Scott was always promising to change. If he had repented it would have been better that no one knew about his problem." Megan took a deep breath. "I really owe you an apology for the last year and a half before I moved here. I know I was cold and distant, but I wasn't coping very well and it just seemed easier to stay away from everybody. I'm sorry." Megan didn't have the energy to continue.

"I'm the one that should be sorry," her mother quietly answered. "I should have known or seen something, especially when you became so quiet."

"How could you know when I never told you."

"And Scott seemed so kind and brokenhearted."

Megan sighed, "It's part of his act and he's very good at it."

"I wish I had known," her mother sounded worried and upset. "I just thought it was little things, since you never complained."

"Mom, it wasn't something I wanted to tell anyone. At this point, I'm tired of pretending our divorce was over something trivial. I did my best to work it out."

"I'm sure you did," her mother's tone had a mournful, quality to it.

"For years I tried to help him. For a time, he'd do better and I'd feel like we were making progress, and then I'd find out he was back into porn again. Sometimes I wonder if he ever stopped. His little so-called dry spells where probably just a way to manipulate me and keep me there. Mama, it's so ugly; I don't want to talk about it anymore."

"All right, but Megan, I'm so sorry. I didn't understand. I never would have encouraged you to go back to Scott if I had known."

"I realize that. It's okay."

Megan could almost see her mother determinedly shifting the phone to her other ear, "Well, then you're doing well out there?"

"I am. I love my job. My roommate is great, and the singles ward is fun."

They continued to talk for another ten minutes about the family, her parents' Fourth of July barbecue, the fireworks over Lagoon and Kaysville, and little insignificant things. As Megan began saying the things you say just before you hang up, her mother quietly interrupted, "I know you don't want to talk about it anymore, but I need to know one more thing. I already assume you know that I'll tell your father. I tell him everything. But I think Kristy should know too."

All her many conversations with Kristy came painfully back to Megan. Scott had Kristy and Dan living in his world of fantasy where selective amnesia was accepted. The burden of untangling all of his lies and setting the truth free was overwhelming. Megan sighed heavily. "I don't want to talk to Kristy."

"I understand. Do you want me to talk to her, or would you rather I didn't say anything?"

"You can tell her."

After saying good-bye, Megan switched off her phone. She knew that she couldn't handle any more interruptions. Before she could return to the apartment, she had to have everything under control again. It was going to take time, but she had to do it. Megan started up the car and drove. Focusing all her attention on driving was a relief. She headed for the turnpike, deciding that by simply driving she could escape.

The rest of the morning and afternoon was a blur to Megan. She had been right. Driving was like therapy. It consumed her mind and soothed her soul. By late afternoon, Megan found herself lost somewhere in Massachusetts. On second thought, she wasn't even sure she was still in the state. She pulled the car to the side of the narrow road and sat. The leafy trees and thick vegetation surrounded her with lush green tranquility. She soaked in the beauty of nature and sorted out her emotions.

Megan attempted to convince herself that a break from Ben would not be so bad. By the time she drove into a small village and asked for directions, she almost believed it. As she climbed the stairs to her condo, she felt positive she could deal with Ben on a friendly level. Since Amber was her roommate, she'd have no other choice.

Megan was confident that she could respond to Amber normally. There was no need to expose the fact that she had foolishly fallen in love with Amber's brother. What Megan was not prepared for was Amber sitting anxiously on the couch waiting for her.

The moment Megan walked thorough the door, Amber leaped off the couch and crossed the room. "Are you all right? I was so worried."

"I'm fine. I'm sorry I worried you." It was surprising how easy it was to fall back into her old pattern of concealment. The mask she had worn for years still fit perfectly. Smiling pleasantly as if nothing important had occurred that day, Megan reassured Amber, "I went for a drive and got lost in the woods."

"Megan, Ben came by."

Her voice was the ideal mix of cool and calm. "That was nice of him."

"I think we need to talk." Amber closed the door behind Megan. "There's something you should know."

"Not tonight," Megan quickly forestalled. "I'm really tired. I think I'm going right to bed."

Amber started to say something and then shut her mouth. She made no comment on how it was only eight o'clock on a Friday night. Instead, she watched Megan with compassionate eyes and said one last thing. "Ben left you something. I put it on your bed."

Megan nodded and then closed the bedroom door, shutting Amber out. Megan told herself once again that she could do this. At that precise moment, she saw the bag with its familiar and distinctive logo. It meant delicious cookies. That little sack of gourmet treats conjured up images of walking through Quincy Market. She saw herself teasing Ben and refusing to share her cookies.

The tears she had been holding back ever since she walked away from Ben poured out. Megan realized she couldn't do this alone. She fell to her knees and prayed. Her fears, her hurt, and her anger flowed out in a steady stream of soft pleading words.

Amber stood on the opposite side of the door and heard the sobs. Her heart ached with the desire to make things right. She couldn't help but feel responsible for ruining things between Megan and Ben. It was the photograph that she had given Megan that had started everything. If only she had sorted through the box before she'd started handing things out and making stupid comments. If only she'd understood the significance of the objects she'd scattered so haphazardly around her.

Tomorrow, Amber vowed, she'd do all she could to make things right.

CHAPTER TWENTY-TWO

AMBER SAT PATIENTLY WAITING at the kitchen table. She periodically glanced up from her bowl of Cheerios and checked to see if the bedroom door was still closed. It was a testament to Amber's serious intent that she had not even looked at the job chart this morning. The Cheerios in her bowl were soggy and milk logged, but she still spooned them idly around. Her head snapped up the minute she heard Megan's door click open.

Abandoning her last few Cheerios to their fate, Amber walked purposefully toward Megan and stated, "There is something you should see." Amber studied Megan and felt a shiver of fear. Megan looked absolutely perfect from her shiny black hair and silky blouse down to her stylish, leather sandals. It was the same classy sophistication that had unnerved Amber the first day they had met, only today Amber saw it for what it was: sterile perfection, or protection, against the pain of living life.

Amber took Megan's arm and gently guided her toward the living room couch. The scrapbooking paraphernalia was scattered all over the floor. Megan was surprised that Amber had not cleaned it up last night.

"We need to talk about Ben." Amber sat on the floor.

Megan sighed and seated herself on the edge of the couch before unemotionally stating, "We've decided it's not going to work out."

Amber looked up from the pile of photographs she was toying with. "Who's decided? You or Ben?"

Megan's lips tightened into a fine line, but she didn't answer.

Apparently Amber didn't expect an answer, because she immediately said, "You decided. And I don't mean to upset you, but I don't think you have all the facts. Until yesterday, I didn't understand, and he's my brother!" Amber looked directly at Megan. "Will you give me a second and just listen?"

Megan nodded mutely.

"Okay, I want you to look at these things," Amber handed Megan the photograph of Ben and Megan at the ward dance.

Megan unwillingly took the photo. She stared at it for a moment and whispered, "I remember them taking our picture. I never got a copy."

"That's because there are two here." Amber held up the twin photograph to the one Megan was holding. "I guess Ben never had the courage to give one to you."

Amber allowed Megan a few more seconds to study the snapshot before she placed the dried boutonnière in Megan's hands. "I believe these are the same flowers in the picture. The ribbon is faded, but it's still mint green, like the boutonnière on his suit."

Megan let the faded ribbons slip through her fingers as she stared at the photo she had laid on the couch. Her memories of Ben at BYU were distant and just as faded as the ribbons on the flowers. Before Megan could remember more specific details, Amber held up a familiar wedding announcement and said, "Why do you think Ben kept this? Perhaps he didn't tear it. Maybe it got stuck and he pulled on it and it ripped. Either way, I don't think how the invitation was torn is all that important. To me it's significant, because Ben kept it despite its damaged condition."

Amber watched Megan hoping for some kind of reaction. None was forthcoming. Megan stared at the wedding announcement in a vague, trance-like manner. After a few uncomfortable seconds, Amber picked up the duplicate photo of Ben and Megan at the dance. "You look pretty in this picture." Amber smiled sadly, thinking that there was an innocent softness and a peaceful contentment to the girl in the picture that the present day Megan lacked. At that moment Amber received a tiny insight into how damaging Megan's marriage had been. No wonder Megan was reluctant to take a chance again.

But Ben loved her. Amber knew it. Somehow she had to convince Megan. Not knowing what else to say, Amber quietly repeated, "Why do you think Ben kept all these things?"

Megan did not make eye contact. She was still holding the dried flowers, running the pale green ribbons through her fingers. When she answered, her voice was so soft that Amber almost couldn't hear. "I don't know. I didn't even know he had a picture of me."

"It seems odd to me that he kept both of these pictures of you and him at the dance. Most of his other pictures don't even have girls in them."

Megan looked up, startled. Taking advantage of Megan's attention, Amber indicated the large, messy heap of photographs mounded on the floor, "In that whole pile, there was only one picture of a girl he went to the prom with. I know he went to other formal dances because I remember that he called home and asked Mom and Dad for a little extra cash so he could buy a suit. His mission one was pretty bad. So why aren't there any more pictures of him and those other girls?" Amber paused and waited before she asked, "Why did he only save your picture?"

Megan lowered her head and a cascade of black silk swung over her eyes. It was as if she were seeking protection behind a screen of hair.

Amber did not expect her to answer. "I think I've figured the story out. On your side, Ben was someone you went out with once. Then along comes Scott Spencer. In romantic jargon, he swept you off your feet. You fell in love and married him. But something happened. It didn't work out, and you divorced."

It wasn't a question, but oddly enough Megan answered this one, "Yes."

"I think I've figured out Ben's side too," Amber took a deep breath. "All those years ago at the Y, Ben fell in love with you. Boys don't usually keep flowers. Girls do, but boys don't. Yet, here's the boutonnière you gave him. He also kept your wedding invitation. He's been in love with you for years. I think it's why he never found anyone else." Amber waited for Megan to comprehend what she was saying.

Megan sat silently behind her screen of hair recalling the night she had sat with Ben in the stairwell above Jason's apartment. What had Ben said? It was something like, *"I went away to school and for the first time, I got seriously interested in a girl."*

Megan remembered asking, *"She was really special wasn't she?"*

His eyes had been like glowing amber as he had agreed. Later he'd said something about how he'd never felt like that again.

"Megan," Amber's voice made Megan look up. "Whatever happened yesterday hurt you badly, but it hurt Ben too. When he dropped the cookies off, he wouldn't come in. He just handed me the bag and left. He looked miserable."

Megan closed her eyes and bit her lip.

"There's something else I haven't told you." Amber studied Megan and then continued. "Once I asked Ben if he'd ever been in love. He said 'I think I was once, but it was a long time ago when I was at the Y.' When I pressed him for more details, he said, 'She was the fairy tale princess and I was the frog. I never turned into the handsome prince, so she ran off and married someone else.'" Amber reached over and took the boutonnière out of Megan's mindless grip. "Megan, I'm sure Ben loves you. Give him a chance."

If Ben had been in love with her all those years ago, that would explain a lot of things. Most importantly, Megan thought it explained why he hadn't confessed that he already knew her. It was too embarrassing and too horribly humiliating to admit that the girl you once thought you loved didn't even remember you.

Megan looked at Amber, a tiny shimmer of hope growing in her eyes. Amber nodded encouragingly.

"You really think he loved me all this time?"

"I do."

"Oh, Amber, I don't know. I need to be sure this time."

"I can understand that, but you've got to talk to Ben."

Megan nodded. "I think you're right."

"Go over and see Ben and work this out. Call him. He's at Jason's."

But Ben wasn't there. Jason answered the phone and explained that Ben had gone back to Amherst.

Megan hung up and turned to Amber. "He's gone back to Amherst."

"Call his cell."

"I don't want to. I need to talk to him face to face. Do you know how to get to his house?"

"I've never been there. He just bought the house recently," Amber informed Megan with a glint in her eye. "This is against my better judgment," Amber confessed reaching for the phone. "My mom will have directions to Ben's house. But you know what's going to happen?" Amber looked down her nose at Megan and rolled her eyes. "I'm going to be looking for a new roommate again."

Megan wasn't sure what she felt. The drive was taking too long and was passing by too swiftly. She wanted a sign, but was it in accordance with the Lord's will to be seeking a sign? Megan started praying, "I need the reassurance that this is right. I was sure it was right last time and look what happened."

A thought floated quietly into her mind. *If Scott had kept the commandments, you would have been happy together. I allow men their agency.*

"But I need to be sure about Ben," Megan pleaded. Silence greeted her as she drove on. Intensity was burning inside of her, but fear was licking up the flames. For a moment, Megan wanted to be a child again: safe and protected by her family.

Another idea whispered through her mind. *If you don't risk again, then you'll never have the chance to provide a safe, secure haven for your own children.* Empty barren years stretched before her. She saw herself slaving over the tangled lawsuits of corporate giants and coming home each night to a lonely, dark house. In contrast, Megan saw Ben's gentle face radiating consistency, companionship, and love. She saw herself with Ben holding hands and walking through laughter and tears, sharing in life as equal but different partners.

Immediately, the battle began again. Fear and uncertainty as to whether this was her own emotion, or inspiration, raged on inside her, while a shimmer of hope consistently pierced the darkness. The conflict reigned until Megan arrived in Amherst.

There was a quaint, small-town atmosphere to Amherst that instantly charmed Megan. *I could live here,* she thought smiling. On a summer day like today it was quiet and lazy, but come September, Megan was positive Amherst would be full of energy. She imagined the returning students and pictured their youth and vitality reviving the sleepy town. The sidewalk cafés would be bursting with students chattering and laughing. Their bicycles would be leaned up against the brick buildings, their backpacks resting against their chairs, and their love of life warming the crisp, autumn air.

Forgetting her dilemma, Megan drove on, following the directions Amber had written down. The road was narrow and twisted between gentle woods and grassy meadows. The instant Megan came around the bend she braked hard and pulled into a wide spot on the side of the road to take a longer look. It was like one of the cottages in her books, only run-down. Despite its dilapidated condition, it appealed to Megan, almost more so because she was thinking of how she could renovate the cottage and restore the yard.

This was ridiculous. She was supposed to be looking for Ben's house. Picking up the directions she'd dropped on the console, Megan scanned the paper for the address: 42 Bedford Road. In front of her car, there was a mailbox with a number freshly painted in shiny black. Megan sat stunned, staring at the 42 on the mailbox. She wasn't precisely sure how long she might have sat there if an older man had not come out of the house and gotten into an old, weather-beaten truck sitting in the driveway.

Deciding she was on the wrong road, Megan reached for her keys dangling from the ignition. Disappointment surged through her. It was silly, but she wanted this house to belong to Ben.

Well, she had better let the man back out of his driveway and then try to find Ben's house. Maybe she could get the man's attention and ask him for directions to Bedford Road. She rotated her head, watching for oncoming traffic. When she turned back, she noticed another man standing on the opposite side of the truck talking to the driver. From this distance, his face was unclear. The second she heard his laugh, she recognized him. Her breath caught in her throat and tears misted her eyes. She fought for control of her emotions as she watched the older man drive away. Ben turned, oblivious to her presence, and walked back into his house.

Slowly, Megan started the car up, drove into the driveway, and got out. She stood flipping the little leather tab on her key chain. The house was so beautiful that Megan simply stared. The planter boxes needed flowers, but the roses at the front of the house were a perfect frame for the unstained door.

While Megan stood gazing at the cottage, Benton came around to the side of the house where his saw was set up. He was cutting baseboards to replace the old pock-marked ones in the living room. As he bent to plug the saw into his extension chord, his eye caught a flash of refracted sunlight off something silvery blue. Leaning further around the corner of the house, allowed Ben to see that there was a car parked in the driveway. He straightened and took several steps forward in order to get a clearer view. He recognized the car and the woman standing, staring at his house.

Benton wasn't sure if he was more shocked or delighted. That she had come meant a great deal to him. Instinctively, he knew that he must treat her appearance lightly and with humor. He could only imagine what it had cost her to come here, and couldn't risk scaring her away.

Walking slowly toward her, Benton called out, "If you're thinking of buying, it's not for sale."

Her head turned at the sound of his voice. She looked frightened, but recovered quickly. "How about renting it out?" she inquired without moving.

Benton kept steadily approaching. "No deal. Besides, it's too far to commute to Boston."

Megan knew immediately that his statement was really a question. She remembered the Fourth of July when they had sat listening to the Boston Pops. Ben had asked what she thought about working mothers. He had been asking if she would give up her career and live in the country. "I assume there must be some law firms in Amherst."

Ben stopped walking and stood about two feet away from her. "Maybe, but what if there aren't?"

"I could take up gardening."

Benton raised his eyebrows and looked skeptical.

Megan courageously continued, "Or scrapbooking."

"Scrapbooking?"

"Yes, you learn the most interesting things about people that way."

"Oh, really, I wouldn't know."

"Some people," Megan took a sketchy breath and rushed on, "keep cardboard boxes full of stuff from their college years. That's really helpful for scrapbooking."

Benton's eyes widened, but he didn't say anything.

"They keep things like college graduation tassels and pictures of girls, maybe even a dried boutonnière that some stupid girl gave them."

"She wasn't stupid," Ben quietly corrected.

"And a wedding announcement from the girl who married the wrong man?"

"Did she?" Benton asked, looking extremely serious.

"She did. She was young and naïve and didn't know quality when she saw it," Megan confessed, trying to control the knots in her stomach.

"And now?"

The knot grew bigger as her courage faltered. "I don't know." Megan's hands shook so badly that she dropped her keys into her purse and grasped the shoulder strap with both hands. Taking a quick breath, Megan whispered, "Maybe the man doesn't care anymore. It was a long time ago."

"And if he does?"

"Now would be a good time for him to say so." Megan watched Ben and wondered if she could walk away gracefully if Ben said he didn't care anymore.

"I told you on the street yesterday that I loved you."

"You did?" Megan asked startled. "I never heard you."

"I know," Ben smiled ruefully. "You weren't exactly in the most receptive mood."

"I really wasn't. I'm sorry."

He waited, hoping she would say something. She didn't speak, because she was waiting, hoping that he'd say the words again and commit himself. The moment was suspended awkwardly in the air between them.

Swallowing his disappointment, Benton forced a smile on his face. "How about a tour of my new home? Let me warn you though. There's still a lot that needs to be done."

"I'd love to see it."

As Megan stepped through the threshold and looked around, something happened inside of her. A rich, calm assurance melted away her fears. She had been praying for a sign and now standing in the living room she had her answer, firm and strong. She didn't see the piles of sawdust, the partially installed baseboards, the worn, wooden floors, or the lack of furnishings. Instead, Megan saw herself sitting in this room with Ben laughing, talking, and being together. For one brief moment, she almost thought she heard real laughter, like little children giggling.

She reached for Ben's sleeve and caught hold. "Ben," she whispered, her eyes pleading with him.

His gaze was warm and encouraging, but he didn't help her. He merely waited, patiently.

"I . . . I . . ." she floundered, "I love this house."

Ben laughed. Megan immediately let go of his sleeve. "What's so funny?"

"You!" he chuckled trying to choke off another laugh. "Megan, of course you love this house. It's exactly like all the ones in your cottage books." He took her hands in his and suddenly became very earnest. "That's one of the reasons I bought this house. I hoped . . . and then there was . . ." Benton shrugged feeling embarrassed and wondering whether he should tell her about the little girls. His glance rose from their clasped hands and he saw the tears. They dripped off her cheeks and splattered onto her blouse.

"Megan," he groaned, pulling her into his arms.

She laid her cheek on his shoulder and whispered, "I love you."

He heard her. His heart soared and did acrobatics. Lifting her chin so that he could look into her eyes, he smiled. "I don't know how you got a box full of my old things, but I think you know that I've loved you for a long time." He touched a lock of her dark hair, smoothing it off of her face. "Remember that night on the stairs outside of Jason's apartment?"

Megan whispered, "Yes."

"When I said I'd gone away to school and for the first time became seriously interested in a girl, you said that she must have been very special. Well, that girl was you."

Megan smiled and the tears flowed harder.

"And now," Ben's voice cracked, "I've grown to love you even more. I'm so proud of how you've reacted to everything that has happened to you. I love and respect you more than I ever dreamed possible."

He bent his head and kissed her tear wet lips. A surge of happiness and peace pulsed through Megan. It stopped the flow of her tears and left her feeling warm and beautifully content.

Megan stepped back, looked into his eyes, and smiled.

"Will you marry me and live in this cottage?" He solemnly proposed.

"I will."

"You need to know, I'll never make as much money as an attorney. College professor just don't."

Megan smiled and reached up to wipe away her last tear. "The money doesn't matter."

"There's one other thing. About this house . . ."

"It's haunted," Megan cheerfully supplied.

"Why do you say that?"

"Because I heard children laughing."

"You did?" Benton smiled his slow, warm smile. "What if I told you I had seen two little girls? And they called me Daddy?"

"I'm okay with that as long as both girls are the perfect mix of me and you." Megan teased.

"I think they are." Benton marveled, wondering why he hadn't seen it before. Shrugging his shoulders, Ben smiled even broader. The glint in his eye deepened as he pulled his future wife into his arms and kissed her soundly.

Megan and Benton were so occupied with the discovery of their shared love that neither one of them heard the delighted giggles nor saw the chubby little hands clapping joyfully together.

Discussion Questions

1. Do you think it is possible for a woman who has been in an abusive relationship to trust another man enough to enter into a new relationship?

2. How did the singles ward help Megan to heal and begin to live life fully again?

3. Are there really men like Ben who bury their feelings deep inside and have difficulties sharing or acting on their feelings?

4. What strengths do you see in Megan that helped her overcome her trials?

5. Do righteous men often have spiritual experiences, like Ben did in seeing his future children?

6. How did Scott's addiction to pornography affect and influence Megan?

7. Would you choose to isolate yourself or withdraw from others, in order to handle life and survive? What methods of coping would you use?

8. Is it possible that someone close to you is struggling with a private trial that you are unaware of? (Think of how Megan's mom and sister didn't fully understand what Megan was going through.)

9. Was it wise of Ben to hide the fact that he knew and remembered Megan from his BYU years?

10. How does Ben's spirituality and love of the gospel help Megan to grow and heal? How does Megan's ability to stay close to the Lord influence Ben?

Katherine Adams

Katherine Adams was born and raised in the San Francisco Bay Area. Writing is something she has always enjoyed. In high school, she received special permission to write historical fiction rather than history term papers. She graduated from Brigham Young University with a degree in English. She married her college sweetheart, and they moved back to the San Francisco Bay Area. Since then, she has lived in Utah, Sacramento, and Boston. Besides writing, Katherine's other great loves are her family, good friends, teaching, reading, and dancing. Of course, her favorite read is a good romance!

0 26575 51746 0